PULSE

Tricia Rayburn is the author of *Ruby's Slippers*, the *Maggie Bean* trilogy and *Siren*. Despite fearing all creatures of the deep, she's still drawn to the water and makes her home in a seaside town on eastern Long Island in America.

You can visit her online at www.triciarayburn.com

by the same author
Siren

PULSE

A Siren Book

TRICIA RAYBURN

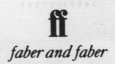

faber and faber

First published in the USA by Egmont in 2011

First published in this edition in 2012
by Faber and Faber Limited
Bloomsbury House
74–77 Great Russell Street
London WC1B 3DA

Printed and bound by CPI Group (UK) Ltd, Croydon, CR0 4YY

The right of Tricia Rayburn to be identified as author
of this work has been asserted in accordance with Section 77
of the Copyright, Designs and Patents Act 1988

This book is sold subject to the condition that it shall not,
by way of trade or otherwise, be lent, resold, hired out
or otherwise circulated without the publisher's prior consent
in any form of binding or cover other than that in which
it is published and without a similar condition including
this condition being imposed on the subsequent purchaser

A CIP record for this book
is available from the British Library

ISBN 978-0-571-27396-6

CHAPTER I

It was September first. The day my older sister Justine should have been starting classes. Buying textbooks. Thinking about her future. The day she should have been doing all the things freshmen do but wasn't, because her future had been decided the second she jumped off a cliff in the middle of the night three months earlier.

On this day, I walked a college campus instead.

'That's Parker Hall,' my tour guide said. 'And there's Hathorn Hall and the chapel.'

I smiled politely and followed him through the main quad. The pretty, park-like square was surrounded by redbrick buildings and filled with kids talking, laughing, and comparing schedules.

'That's Coram Library,' he continued, pointing. 'And right behind it is Ladd Library, the one-hundred-twelve-thousand-square-foot Mecca of learning.'

'Impressive,' I said, thinking the same thing about him. His brown eyes were warm, his dark hair slightly messy, like he'd fallen asleep on an open textbook before meeting me. His toned arms shone bronze against the sharp white of his crew team T-shirt. If Bates strived to appeal to teenage girls' romantic aspirations in addition to their academic ones, they'd picked a good representative.

'And comfortable. Trust me, I should know.' He stopped, took my sweatshirt sleeve in one hand, and tugged. As I stepped towards him, a Frisbee sliced through the empty air space my head had just occupied.

'I do,' I said.

We stood so close I could hear his quick intake of breath. His fingers tightened on my sweatshirt, and his arm tensed. After a few seconds, he released me and grabbed the backpack straps near his shoulders.

'What's that?' I asked.

He followed my nod to a tall building next to the libraries. '*That* is the deciding factor,' he said, starting down the pavement. When he reached the building's front steps, he turned towards me and grinned. 'Behold Carnegie Science Hall.'

I covered my chest with one hand. '*The* Carnegie Science Hall? Where some of the world's most brilliant, forward-thinking scientists conduct groundbreaking research that continues to shape the landscape of modern science as we know it today?'

He paused. 'Yes?'

'Hang on. I have to get a picture.'

'If you're familiar with the building,' he said as I rummaged through my purse for my digital camera, 'then you know the work it houses sets this college apart from the rest. Even if you're not a science major, I think that alone warrants the hefty two-hundred-thousand-dollar price tag.'

Vox clamantis in deserto.

I stared at the digital camera screen and my mind filled with images of green keyrings. Coffee mugs. A sweatshirt and an umbrella. All bearing the familiar Dartmouth shield.

'Vanessa?'

'Sorry.' I shook my head once and held up the camera. 'Say lobster.'

He started to speak but then stopped. His eyes lifted and landed somewhere behind me. Before I could look to see what had caught his attention, there was a tap on my shoulder.

'That's all wrong,' a guy said when I turned around. He looked about my age, maybe a year or two older, and was flanked by two other guys who smiled when I glanced at them. He wore cargo pants, a fleece, and hiking boots, like he planned to hit the trails as soon as he was done with classes.

'What do you mean?'

'I mean, it's a fine shot . . . but it'd be better if you were in it.' He held out one hand, palm up. 'May I?'

'Oh.' My eyes fell to the camera. 'Thanks, but –'

'Mitosis,' my tour guide said.

The hiker looked up, towards the steps behind me.

'I just remembered that there's an excellent photography exhibit of cellular mitosis inside. It's best seen right about now, in the late morning. We should get going before the light changes.'

'Right.' The hiker nodded. 'You know, you'd probably recruit thousands more students each year if you included her in the school's promotional materials.'

'I'll be sure to pass that along to Admissions.'

The hiker gave me one more appreciative look before leaving. I waited for him and his friends to walk away and round the corner, out of sight, before turning back. My tour guide stood on the same step, hands in his pockets, his face tight with . . . what? Nervousness? Jealousy?

'Is there really an excellent photography exhibit of cellular mitosis inside?' I asked.

'If there is, it wouldn't be on the tour. We don't want to bore kids into not applying.'

I held up the camera.

'Lobster,' he said.

I took his picture and put the camera back in my

purse. 'So, I realise the Carnegie Science Building sets your college worlds apart from others, but there's still one other thing I'd like to see before making any decisions.'

'The gym? Theatre? Art museum?'

'The dorms.'

My pulse quickened as he looked down. Thinking I'd made him uncomfortable, I prepared to offer an alternative – like someplace off campus, where there were fewer people, fewer distractions. But then he started down the steps and turned right, back the way we came.

'Just wait till you see the concrete walls and linoleum floors,' he said. 'You might never go home again.'

We didn't talk as we walked through the quad. Every now and then he greeted friends or classmates, but I stayed quiet. My head spun with thoughts of Justine, last summer, this fall, and I didn't know which thought would come out if I tried to speak. The spinning continued all the way across campus, into a tall brick building, and up four flights of stairs.

Fortunately, the silence wasn't awkward. It never was.

'I should warn you,' he said when we stopped in front of a closed door. 'The decor leaves something to be desired. That's what happens when you throw two bio majors together in one small space. Or any space, for that matter.'

'Is your roommate . . . ?'

'Out. At a four-hour seminar that won't end for another three and a half hours.'

My heart lifted, and my stomach turned. The mixed feelings must've been clear on my face because he stepped towards me, instantly concerned.

'Well,' I said, relieved when my voice was calm, even, 'if that's the case, we should probably get on with the tour.'

This seemed to reassure him. He smiled as he took his keys from the pocket of the jeans and unlocked the door. Once inside, he leaned against the closed door with his arms folded behind his back and surveyed the room. 'Interesting,' he said.

'What is?' I asked.

'The decor.'

I looked around. It was a typical dorm room with two beds, desks, dressers, and bookshelves. One side was messier than the other, and I assumed that side belonged to his roommate, who probably wasn't expecting company. The only accessories were a blue area rug, the college banner . . . and a framed photo of a girl in a red rowing boat.

'I knew something was missing,' he continued gently, 'and I'd had a pretty good idea of what that something was. But now I know for sure.'

My eyes found his and stayed there. He didn't move as I came closer. He was waiting to make sure that whatever happened next happened because I wanted it to. It had been two months and that hadn't changed. In two years – in two decades – it still wouldn't.

I stood as close as I could without our bodies touching. I smelled the soap on his skin and saw his chest rise and immediately fall. His jaw clenched, and his broad shoulders squared as he leaned harder against the door, locking his arms in place.

'Vanessa . . .'

'It's okay,' I whispered, tilting forward. 'I'm okay.'

My lips had barely grazed his cheek when his hands were on my hips. He pulled me to him, closing the remaining distance between us. His hands moved from my waist to my neck and then lingered there, cradling my face like it was made of glass. His eyes held mine once more, just long enough for me to feel their warmth, before lowering his mouth to mine.

The spinning stopped. My head cleared. There was just this, us, him.

Simon. My Simon.

The kiss started slowly, sweetly, as if our lips were getting to know each other again after a long separation. But soon they pressed harder, moved faster. I grabbed the front of his sweatshirt with both hands and held on as his mouth moved across my cheek, over my ear, down my neck. He paused only once, when he ran out of bare skin. Not wanting him to stop, I released his sweatshirt and pulled mine up and over my head. By the time I dropped it to the floor, his was already there.

He rested his forehead on my shoulder and his palms moved slowly down my back and over my jeans. We kissed all the way to the bed, until he was lying down with me on top of him, my legs hugging the sides of his waist.

'We can stop,' Simon said softly when I pulled back. 'If you're at all nervous or unsure . . .'

I smiled. If I was ever nervous or unsure around Simon, it wasn't because I was afraid of being too close to him.

It was because I was afraid of not being close enough.

'I missed you,' I said.

'Vanessa . . . you have no idea.'

Except that I did. I knew it every time he looked at me, every time he said my name, every time he held my hand or kissed me. He'd said it only once, but reminders weren't necessary.

I knew Simon loved me.

Unfortunately, I also knew why.

He opened his mouth to say something else, but I kissed him first. I kissed him until he seemed to forget whatever he was going to say, and until I pushed the familiar nagging thought far enough aside that I could focus on him, on us, together in this moment.

Because this moment would end. It would have to. Sometimes I was so caught up, so happy, I let myself pretend it didn't . . . but reminders were never far off.

Like when we lay together later, our legs entwined, my head on his chest. While Simon's fingers twirled absently through my hair, I stared at the picture of the girl in the rowing boat on the dresser next to the bed and counted the steady, relaxed beats of his heart.

'Be right back,' I whispered.

I gathered the sheet around me, stood, and forced my feet to walk to the closet. After switching the sheet for Simon's robe and taking a towel from the shelf, I retrieved my purse from the floor and left the room.

In the hallway, I ran. I'd noted the bathroom on our way up and found it easily. Ignoring the curious looks of kids passing by, I flung open the door and flew inside.

Each shower had two parts: the actual stall and a small area to change and dry off. I dashed into the last shower and yanked the vinyl curtain closed. I dropped my purse three times before my shaking hands got a good enough grip to hold it open and grab the container inside. Once they did, I dropped the purse and Simon's robe to the tile floor and stepped into the stall.

My chest and skin were on fire. I couldn't feel my legs. It took every bit of strength I had left to turn on the water and prise the lid off the plastic container.

I tilted my head towards the shower nozzle so water streamed down my face. I opened my mouth and brought the container to my lips, coughing as the water and powder shot down my throat.

But then, finally, relief. It came little by little, with every swallow. Slowly, the invisible flames on my skin extinguished and the burning in my chest subsided. Feeling stronger, I took handfuls of salt and spread them across my body. The tiny granules scratched then soothed as they mixed with the water.

It's just body wash, I told myself, *that exfoliates, like at a spa.*

As soon as I could feel my legs again, they folded beneath me. I sank to the floor and brought my knees to my chest. Cold water flowed from my head to my toes, washing away the warmer liquid that seeped from my closed eyes.

Justine had always said the best way to deal with your fear of the dark was to pretend it was really light. It was a theory she'd applied to countless situations when we were growing up – and for better or worse, it was one I still relied on whenever I found myself too scared to think straight.

Which was why in a few minutes, I'd stand up, dry off, and walk down the hall. I'd climb back into bed and curl up next to Simon. And when he kissed me and asked if I was okay, I'd assure him I'd never been better.

Because when it came to telling Simon the truth, I'd never been more scared in my life.

CHAPTER 2

Since our return to Boston from Maine two weeks ago, my parents had been surprisingly good about not hovering. As a literature professor, Dad had always respected the importance of alone time, but he'd been even more respectful. (Though whether that was for his sake or mine, I wasn't sure.) And Mom, who'd once monitored my comings and goings like they were her clients' Wall Street stocks, now settled for once-a-day, dinnertime updates. I thought this was their way of making the transition back home, without Justine, as easy as possible, and assumed they'd keep it up until I made it clear they didn't have to.

I was wrong.

'Six forty-five!' Mom sang on the first day of school.

Underwater, I didn't move.

'Six-fifty!'

I inhaled deeply, the lukewarm liquid sliding down my throat to my chest.

'Um, Vanessa?' This voice was lower, softer. It seemed to come after a longer stretch of time. 'I made

breakfast . . . and I thought if you had a few minutes
. . . that maybe we could all sit down and –'

I sat up. 'Be right there.'

There was a pause and then the slow, heavy footsteps
moved down the hallway. I stood, lifted the tub's stop-
per, and turned on the shower. I washed with extra soap
to make sure I didn't smell like I'd spent the morning at
the beach, then sprayed the tub's sides with the hand-
held nozzle. When the lingering white film was gone, I
turned off the water, dried quickly, and replaced the blue
salt container behind stacks of toilet paper rolls in the
linen closet.

New bathing routine aside, if last summer had never
happened, this was exactly how the morning would've
gone. I still would've gotten up extra early. Mom still
would've knocked on the bathroom door to hurry me
along. Dad still would've made breakfast. Justine still
would be gone.

That's what I told myself as I headed down the hall
towards my room – or, more accurately, to Paige's room.

She stood in front of the full-length mirror with her
back to me, wearing the Hawthorne Prep uniform: a
short, navy-blue skirt; fitted white shirt; and crimson
sweater vest. On the floor next to her feet was a leather
messenger bag, its flap opened to reveal new notebooks
and pens.

'Vanessa,' she said, turning around. 'Thank goodness! I was two seconds away from wearing this tie as a belt.'

As I walked towards her to help, I saw that she held her cell phone to her ear.

'Here. Grandma B wants to say hi.'

Holding the phone between my ear and shoulder, I looped and knotted Paige's blue silk tie. 'Morning, Betty.'

'Vanessa, my dear, all set for the big day?'

I smiled at the familiar warmth in her voice. 'As ready as I'll ever be. And thanks to your lovely, studious grand-daughter, I have more new pens and Post-its than the biggest office supply store in Boston.'

'Always better to be overprepared than the alternative,' Betty and Paige said at the same time.

'Guess that means I should probably get dressed,' I said.

'I won't keep you,' Betty said. 'Have a wonderful day. And thank you again for taking such good care of my girl.'

We said goodbye and I gave the phone back to Paige, who said her own goodbye and hung up.

'You'll get an official lesson later.' I tightened Paige's tie and straightened it. 'Learn once and you'll never forget.'

'I hope that's true about the rest of today.' She turned to the mirror. 'Hawthorne's, what? Your third school?'

'Fourth. Before that there was John Adams Pre-School, Ralph Waldo Emerson Elementary, and John F. Kennedy Junior High.'

'My last schools were named after towns, not past presidents and famous intellectuals. Impressive, right?'

'It is impressive.' I headed for the middle of the room. 'You live where rich Bostonians drop tons of money to vacation. If they were as smart as you, they'd sell their fancy Newbury Street brownstones and move to Maine for good.'

'Lived.'

I stopped and turned around.

'I *lived* where rich Bostonians drop tons of money to vacation.'

My chest tightened. I wasn't the only one who'd suffered a loss last summer. In fact, if it was possible to put a number on such a thing, Paige had lost four times as much. That was why she was here instead of home in Winter Harbor.

'This isn't for ever,' I said. 'It's not even a week if you don't want it to be.'

She sniffed once, and I started back, prepared to hold her for as long as she wanted to cry. But then she fanned her watery eyes with both hands and smiled her famous smile. It was the same one that had put me instantly at ease when I first met her at her family's restaurant three months ago.

'Why don't you head down to breakfast?' I gave her a quick hug. 'I'll be there as soon as I'm dressed.'

Paige agreed and we headed down the hall together. At the last door on the left, I turned and she continued towards the stairs.

Inside my new bedroom, I faced my red suitcase. It still sat where I'd left it on our first night back in Boston, when I'd moved into Justine's room so Paige could have mine. I'd removed my shorts and T-shirts, refilled the suitcase with fall clothes, and been living out of it ever since. Jeans, sweaters, and bras littered the surrounding carpet like trash around an overflowing garbage can. Normally, the mess would've been picked up on Tuesday, when the cleaning lady came . . . but the cleaning lady didn't touch this room any more.

I found all the pieces of my uniform, dressed quickly, and threw my wet hair in a ponytail. I was searching for socks when my cell phone buzzed.

It was on the nightstand next to a half-filled gallon of water. I drank from the bottle as I opened the phone and read the text message.

INTERESTING ADMISSIONS FACTOID #48: THE

AVERAGE GPA OF INCOMING BATES FRESHMEN IS 3.6.

I smiled as I texted back.

INTERESTING PROSPECTIVE FACTOID #62: I HAVE A 4.0 GPA. MAYBE I SHOULD QUIT WHILE AHEAD & HEAD NORTH NOW? CAN'T WAIT FOR LATER.

I reread the message and then hesitated. What I needed to quit was this . . . this flirting, this relationship that would only end worse the longer it lasted. But wouldn't he worry something was wrong if I didn't write back? Deciding that, yes, he definitely would, I hit Send and went downstairs.

'There she is!' Mom declared without looking at me as I entered the kitchen. She was slicing strawberries at the table. 'Can you believe our baby is about to start her last year of high school?'

She aimed this question at Dad, who was at the counter pouring chocolate chips into a bowl of batter. Before he could answer, she glanced – and then stood – up.

'Vanessa, sweetie . . . what happened?'

She reached for my arm, but I ducked out of the way and veered around her. I swung by the counter for a handful of chocolate chips and then dropped into a chair. Dad looked up as I passed; I knew he noticed what had gotten Mom's attention, but he didn't comment.

'You've got to try these.' Paige slid a plate of cinnamon croissants towards me. 'Louis would freak.'

Louis was the chef at Betty's Chowder House, the Winter Harbor restaurant Paige's family owned. She said his name easily, like we were being served this breakfast at a restaurant down the road instead of three hundred miles away.

'Vanessa.' Mom stood before me. 'You look like you've been sleeping in those clothes for weeks.'

'No one irons senior year. It's like a rite of passage.'

'No, it's not. Justine always –'

She looked down. Said aloud, Justine's name could end a conversation so fast it was like it never started at all.

'Are you excited for work today?' I asked, reaching for a platter of scrambled eggs. 'It's been a while.'

'Paige, honey, what else can I get you?' Mom asked. 'Coffee? Cereal?'

Paige looked at me. I watched Mom dart around the room. She poured a cup of coffee and left it on the counter. Washed a plate and dropped it back in the dirty sink water. Took a box of Corn Flakes from the cabinet and traded it for a carton of orange juice in the refrigerator.

'Your mother's taking a little more time off,' Dad said. He stood next to me holding a tray of pancakes.

'It's already been two months.'

'She said she wanted to be here when you got home from school.'

'But that hasn't happened since –'

I cut myself off. I was going to say that that hadn't happened since Justine and I were in elementary school . . . but we never said her name more than once per meal. If Mom was this worked up now, I had no idea what she'd do after a second mention.

'But back to the original question.' Dad's voice was brighter, louder, as he speared two pancakes with a fork and dropped them onto my plate. 'No, I can't believe our baby's about to start her very last year of high school.'

I stared at my food, feeling a hot heat spread across my face. *Our baby.* How could he say that? And even more perplexing, how could she? After seventeen years of practice, did lying just come that naturally?

'May I have the salt, please?' I asked.

Paige handed me the shaker. I waited for Dad to return to the stove and Mom's head to disappear into the open refrigerator before seasoning my food – including the pancakes, which were so sweet they could double as dessert.

The rest of breakfast passed without incident. Dad

stopped cooking and Mom stopped running around long enough to sit and eat. Paige asked Dad about the classes he was teaching this semester, setting him off on a twenty-minute monologue. And I ate without speaking, thinking of the thousands of meals I'd had at this very table, eating the same pancakes, having the same sorts of conversations . . . never guessing how much I didn't know about my own family.

I was glad when it was time to leave. I wasn't exactly looking forward to school, but I welcomed the excuse to be out of the house for a few hours.

'Do you have everything?' Mom hurried behind us as Paige and I headed through the living room. 'Notebooks? T-Passes? Lunch money?'

'Yes, yes, and yes.' I opened the front door and started down the steps. Fall wouldn't cool the smouldering city for several weeks, and the air was still warm and thick with humidity. I could almost feel my pores pop and my face moisten with perspiration, and I hoped that I'd packed enough salt water to stay hydrated throughout the day.

'Are you sure you don't want a ride?' Mom continued from the open doorway.

Dad stood next to her and put one arm around her waist. 'They're fine.'

Mom didn't say anything else, but her eyebrows

lowered and the tip of her nose shone pink, the way it always did when she was worried or stressed. She looked like she had last June, on the morning I'd left to return to Winter Harbor – all alone, and about to drive ten times further than I'd ever driven before.

I'd felt bad for her then, but I felt even worse now. So much so that I jogged back up the steps and kissed her cheek. 'See you soon.'

I turned to head down again just as Dad leaned forward, his free arm extended. There was an odd pause as he waited for some sort of affectionate goodbye, and I debated whether to give him one. Finally, I squeezed his hand and hurried down the steps.

'Let's cut through the Common,' I said to Paige. 'It's faster.'

Walking through the city's main park actually added fifteen minutes to the trip, but the most direct route was the one Justine and I had always taken together, and I wasn't ready to go down that road – literally or figuratively. Plus, now that we were out of the house, the dread that had been simmering low in my belly for days was starting to boil.

Fortunately, Paige was good for distraction. She had questions about every landmark we passed, from the Duck Tours to the Public Garden to the Boylston Street Station, and somehow, I had answers. We hadn't been friends very long, but we'd been through enough together for each to know when the other wasn't in the mood to talk about whatever was bothering her. Which meant that in the past few weeks I'd learned more than I ever wanted to know about lobster chowder and restaurant management, and she'd learned more than any guidebook could tell her about Boston. The only problem with our little game was that every now and then I thought about how proud it would have made Justine ... which kind of defeated the purpose.

'Vanessa?' a soft voice called out.

Out of the corner of my eye, I saw Paige slow slightly and glance behind her.

'Vanessa!'

I kept walking, away from the voice and the footsteps that were growing closer, faster, but soon there was the light pressure of a hand on my back.

'Natalie,' I said, turning around to find one of Justine's best friends. Her head dropped to one side the second our eyes met. 'Hi. I thought you'd be at Stanford by now.'

'I'm going to MIT instead. My dad made some calls to get me in after I'd turned them down. After Justine ... after what happened ...'

I looked down as she tried to find the words. I hadn't even made it to school yet, and it was already starting.

'Life's just so short, you know? And I couldn't move three thousand miles away from my parents.' She sniffed and stepped towards me, her eyes travelling curiously across my wrinkled uniform. 'How are *you*, you poor thing? You must be a wreck.'

'Who's that guy?' Paige asked.

My stomach turned as I followed her finger, but it was only pointing to a tall grey statue. 'Robert Gould Shaw. Born in Boston to a prominent abolitionist family and served as colonel of the Civil War's Fifty-fourth Regiment.'

'Fascinating,' Paige said as Natalie frowned.

'We should get going,' I said. 'It's my friend's first day at Hawthorne, and we don't want to be late. But it was great to see you. Really.'

I turned – and walked right into Maureen Flannigan. She was in my class, though I didn't know her very well. That, however, didn't stop her from hugging me.

'Vanessa,' she said, her arms like a straitjacket around my torso. 'I'm so sorry about your sister. I can't imagine what I'd do if my brother got himself killed doing something stupid – and I don't even like him that much.'

'Thanks.' I shot Paige a look, but she was already on it.

'So sorry to rush,' she said, taking my elbow, 'but I have that new-student orientation before homeroom.'

I offered Maureen a small smile as she released me. 'We should go. But thanks. It was good to see you.'

By the time we reached the tall iron arch marking Hawthorne Prep's entrance, we'd collected a dozen similar greetings like they were sympathy cards. Apparently, my classmates were very concerned about whether I was okay and if I needed anything. A few even gasped when they saw me, as if I was the one who'd died and was returning to haunt some of Boston's most privileged teens.

'You're so popular,' Paige said as we stopped just outside the gate. 'I mean, I'm not surprised – *I* know how great you are. But you just never talked about your other friends.'

'Those girls aren't my friends. They're rumour-mill cogs. I'm the grease.'

'Actually,' she said, 'I wasn't talking about the girls.' I looked at her. Her eyes shifted to a group of kids standing a few feet down the pavement, to another across the street, and to another in the school's front courtyard. In each group the girls watched me until they realised I saw them, and then they gave me quick, apologetic smiles and turned away.

But the guys, many of whom were the girls' boyfriends, watched me, their eyes wide and lips parted, like their girlfriends weren't standing right next to them. Like they didn't even have girlfriends.

Like I was the only girl who existed.

My feet started moving backwards. I'd thought that going to school would be the best distraction I was going to get, and that it was one I was ready for . . . but maybe it was too soon. I suddenly wanted to go home, crawl into bed, and pull the blankets over my head until it was easier. Until people could look at me not like I was the side effect of some terrible disease, but like I was just a normal girl living a normal life.

'Vanessa?'

I stopped. Paige stood several feet away, where I'd left her. The bell must have rung during my retreat, because kids were filtering slowly through the iron arch – and Paige looked up at the imposing brick building like it was a prison filled with murderers instead of a school filled with teachers.

'I can't do this,' she said when I stood next to her again. 'I thought I could. I thought that if I came here, if I started over in a completely new place . . . that it would be easier to . . . that maybe I could forget . . .'

'Paige.' I took her hand and turned her towards me. 'You won't forget. It doesn't matter where you are or how much time passes.' I took a deep breath, emboldened by my own words. 'But you'll go into that building. You'll go to class, meet new people, and get from one day to the next. So will I.'

She gave me a small smile. 'And here I was thinking you were afraid of your own shadow.'

I *was* afraid of my own shadow – probably now more than ever. I was also afraid of the dark, of flying, and of scary movies. But right then, I was most afraid of not doing everything I could to help my friend, who felt more like a sister every day we spent together.

I hooked one arm through Paige's and led her under the iron arch. I walked her to the main office, stayed with her as she filled out the paperwork, showed her where her locker was, and took her to her homeroom. And as I ran to my own locker on the other side of the building, I felt calmer and more confident than I ever had on a first day of school.

Which was why the next time I was asked if I was okay, I answered honestly.

'No,' I said, not bothering to see who'd posed the question on the other side of my open locker door. 'Last year, people couldn't put a face to my name without consulting the Hawthorne yearbook first. This year, they're staring and whispering and feigning concern like their Ivy League admissions depend on it. Yes, my sister died. But no, that doesn't make you and me friends.'

I swung my locker door; it closed with a clang.

'Your sister died?'

My mouth fell open. Nothing came out.

'I'm so sorry. Really. I had no idea.'

Parker King stood before me, looking like a preppy Ralph Lauren ad and smelling like one, too.

Parker King had never stood before me. He'd never talked to me. He'd probably never even seen me; when he wasn't warding off water polo players in the school pool, he was surrounded by herds of pretty girls clamouring for his attention. Yet here he was, asking if I was okay and sounding sincere.

I believed Parker when he said he didn't know about Justine. This should have been comforting, since it meant he wasn't making conversation in false sympathy.

But it also meant he was making conversation for another reason. And that one was much, much worse.

CHAPTER 3

Five long days later, Paige and I sat in Ladd Library at Bates, waiting for Simon.

'How many books did your tour guide say this so-called Mecca of learning had?' she whispered, dropping into the armchair next to mine.

'Six hundred thousand,' I whispered back.

'All those books, and only two itty-bitty volumes about sirens.'

A sharp, sudden pain pierced my chest. I hadn't told Paige about the change I'd undergone last summer – which was the same one she would have experienced had her mother and sister had their way – and the unexpected reference hit too close to home.

'I thought you were looking for the secret trashy novel collection,' I said.

'Voilà.' She held up one of the books.

'*The Siren's Call: When She Rings, Should You Answer?*' I frowned at the voluptuous mermaid hugging a man's headless torso on the cover.

'It might be more entertaining than this.' She held up

the second book, which had a plain brown cover and no jacket.

'*The Odyssey*?'

'Total yawn, I know, but I've never read it. My last school wasn't so keen on the classics. Or maybe it used to be, before certain books were banned by a certain over-bearing community member.'

I studied her expression as she flipped through pages. There was only one overbearing community member she could be referring to: Raina Marchand. But Paige hadn't talked about her mother – or Zara, her sister, or Jonathan, her boyfriend – in months. Not when she was in the hospital, recovering from losing the baby her body hadn't been equipped to carry. Or when she was released and resting at home. Or even when I'd invited her to spend the school year in Boston. That didn't mean she never thought about them; her face went blank and her eyes grew teary often enough to know that she probably thought about them more than she didn't. But this was the closest she'd come to mentioning any of them out loud, and since she did so casually, I was more concerned than I'd be if she broke down in tears right there in the library.

'Paige . . . are you sure this is a good idea?'

'I'm going to have to find out more eventually. Why not now?'

Before I could answer, Simon came around from behind the chair and sat on the coffee table in front of us.

'Hey,' he said. 'Sorry I'm late. Once my orgo professor gets going, it's hard for him to stop.'

'Orgo?' Paige asked.

'Organic chemistry.' He smiled. 'It's good to see you, Paige. I'm glad you came.'

'I tried not to, I swear.' She raised one hand, as if under oath. 'But Vanessa said that if I didn't come, she wouldn't either, and that simply wasn't an option.'

Simon turned his smile to me, and the pain in my chest was instantly replaced with warmth. If we weren't in such a public place, I would've launched myself into his lap and thrown my arms around him.

'Seventy-one.'

I looked up, surprised to see another guy standing behind Simon. He was tall with curly blond hair that was brushed out into a soft frizz. He wore baggy jeans and a Bates crew team T-shirt and held a laptop open in front of him.

'It's seventy-one degrees and only two o'clock. If we leave now, we'll have plenty of time.'

'For what?' Paige asked.

The guy peered over the top of his computer screen. I held my breath and braced for the look I'd been trying to avoid at school all week, but he didn't even seem to notice me. As soon as his eyes found Paige's face, they stayed there, transfixed.

'The beach,' Simon said. 'Riley, my Southern California-born-and-bred roommate, was just saying that we should take advantage of the nice weather and head off campus for a while.'

'I'm Riley,' Riley said to Paige, apparently missing Simon's introduction. 'And you're . . . ?'

'Paige,' she said as her cheeks shone pink. 'Vanessa's friend.'

Riley shifted his laptop so it rested on his left arm and reached out with his right hand. 'The famous Vanessa. It's great to finally meet you. You'll be happy to know that whenever Simon's feeling lovesick – which is pretty much every second of every day that he doesn't see you – I do my best to help those seconds pass as fast as possible.'

'We watch a lot of movies,' Simon said.

I smiled and shook Riley's hand. 'Thanks. It's great to finally meet you, too.'

'So how about it? A little fun in the sun? A quick dip in the ocean? Before the brutal assault that you Right Coasters call winter takes over?'

'Aren't we pretty far from the beach?' I asked.

'Forty minutes,' Simon said.

'Thirty,' Riley said. 'I'll drive.'

Simon looked at me. Behind his glasses, his brown eyes were concerned. I knew he was thinking of the last time I'd gone swimming in Winter Harbor. I almost didn't make it out of the water then; the fact that I did was still an inexplicable miracle to him, because he didn't know the whole truth.

But he would during this visit. As soon as the moment was right, I'd tell him everything. That was one of the reasons I'd insisted that Paige come to Bates this weekend. I didn't want to leave her alone in Boston, but I also wanted her with me after I did what I had to do. I wasn't sure how Simon would react, but I was certain there was no way we could still be a couple once he knew the real reason we were together in the first place. And after we broke up, I'd need Paige's distracting chatter more than ever.

But maybe going to the ocean first was a good idea. I hadn't been swimming since that night three months ago. I'd taken countless showers and baths, but water from a faucet, no matter how much table salt I added, never made me feel the way natural salt water did. Swimming now might relax me enough to get through what was bound to be the hardest conversation I'd ever had.

'A quick dip sounds good to me,' I said.

*

Twenty minutes later, we were in Riley's Jeep Cherokee, heading for the coast. Paige had claimed shotgun – presumably so Simon and I could sit together in the back seat – and was quizzing Riley about California.

'Get out,' she said. 'You have palm trees in your front yard?'

'And orange trees. You haven't had OJ until you've had it freshly squeezed from Haverford's homegrown orchard.'

'You've obviously never been to Betty's Chowder House.'

'Nope. Please enlighten me.'

Paige paused. I tried to catch her eye in the side-view mirror, but before I could decide whether she needed me to interject, she ignored his question and asked if San Diego was really sunny three hundred and fifty days of the year. Riley, clearly already smitten, was happy to play along.

'She seems okay,' Simon said near my ear. He had one arm around my shoulders, and his face was so close to mine I could feel the warmth of his breath. 'Much better than I thought she'd be.'

'Paige isn't one to curl up in a ball and cry. I think she's determined to move forward.'

'Sounds like someone else I know,' he said, pressing his lips to my temple.

I knew I shouldn't, but I leaned against him. He slid down the seat until his back was against the window, and I followed until my back was against his chest and my legs were outstretched. He put his arms around me and lowered his chin to my shoulder, and we stayed that way, not speaking.

As we drove, I couldn't help but think about how this outing resembled another one Simon and I had taken not long ago. Although then we were in Simon's old Subaru with us in the front seat and Justine and Caleb, Simon's younger brother and Justine's secret boyfriend, in the back. That was how our tight-knit foursome had always travelled – to Eddie's Ice Cream, mini-golf, Chione Cliffs – once Simon got his driver's licence. Until the day we didn't any more.

'Oh, man. Check out those waves.'

Beneath me, Simon tensed. I moved so he could sit up, and we both scooted forward and peered between the front seats and through the windscreen. Simon watched the dark blue Atlantic roll on to a deserted stretch of sand several times before releasing his breath.

'They're big . . . but not unusually so.'

'Still wish I'd brought my board.' If Riley heard the relief in Simon's voice, he didn't let on. He hopped out of the Jeep and ran around the front of the car.

'Don't worry about me,' Paige said over her shoulder

as Riley grabbed the passenger's-side door handle. 'You just worry about each other.'

We did as we were told. While Paige and Riley headed towards the water, Simon and I walked down the beach. Reaching a long jetty about half a mile down, he helped me up and across the rocks.

He'd just jumped to the sand on the other side and held out both hands to assist me down when I froze.

Raina and Zara Marchand. They were about twenty feet away, wearing long skirts and sweaters, walking with their backs to us. As I watched, heart hammering and palms sweating, Zara started to turn around.

My eyes widened. I tried to say Simon's name but couldn't.

'Vanessa?'

I leaped back when fingers wrapped around my ankle.

'You okay?' Simon asked.

I looked from my ankle, to his hand resting on the rock's edge, to the women down the beach. They'd stopped at a wicker basket and were talking and laughing as they packed up remnants of their lunch. I had a clear view of their faces now and saw that they actually looked nothing like Raina and Zara.

'Sorry. I'm fine.' I quickly closed the distance between us and jumped. By the time my feet hit sand, the women had disappeared down a trail leading away from the shore.

'Your very own private beach only a short drive away from campus,' Simon said as we walked. 'That's a pretty good selling point.'

He reached for my hand. I let him pull me close. We stood there, my arms around his waist and head against his chest, his arms around my shoulders and chin on top of my head. It was the safest – and happiest – I'd felt since the last time we were together two weeks ago.

'I talked to Caleb this morning,' he said a few minutes later.

I pulled back enough to look up into his eyes. 'How is he?'

'Hanging in there. He's working a lot at the marina, helping to close up for the season.'

'I'm still surprised he went back. I know he loves Captain Monty . . . but you'd think he'd be happy to stay on land for a while.'

'I think he feels closer to her when he's out on the water. Or ice, as the case may be.'

I didn't say anything. This made some sense – Caleb had been with Justine when she jumped off the cliffs and into the thrashing pool below for the last time – but it still struck me as sad. I'd gotten to know Caleb in a different way when Simon and I had talked to his friends as we searched for him after the accident, and then after we'd found him, when the three of us tried to figure out what was causing a series of drownings in Winter Harbor. He was a good guy – nothing like the lazy slacker my mom had always assumed he was. And it turned out that he'd loved Justine, *really* loved her, and that she'd loved him back. She wouldn't have wanted him to keep missing her, to become stuck in the past he couldn't change. She would have wanted him to move on.

It was what I wanted for Simon, too. At least that's what I told myself.

'He said it's finally starting to warm up. Yesterday it reached sixty – only a few degrees below normal for this time of year.'

'What about thunderstorms?'

'There hasn't been a cloud in the sky in weeks.'

I relaxed in his arms and pressed my cheek to his chest. 'That's a relief.'

'There's something else, though.'

I stared at the rippling horizon, hoped he couldn't feel my heart accelerate.

'Vanessa?'

'It's thawing.' It wasn't a question.

He pulled away and lifted my chin. 'It was frozen for three months.'

I nodded.

'Frozen solid, from top to bottom. Whatever was alive is dead now – and has been for a long time.'

I wanted so desperately to believe him, but too many previously unthinkable, scientifically implausible things had happened. The frequent, fleeting storms that had pummelled Winter Harbor – and only Winter Harbor. The tides that had risen and retreated four times an hour. The men who'd washed ashore, looking happier in death than they'd probably ever been in life.

And the women. The women who breathed salt water like oxygen. Who controlled the heavens. Who enchanted men and then dragged them deep below the water's surface until their lungs exploded, their lives extinguished.

Women like me.

'I shouldn't have told you.'

I started to protest, but he continued before I could.

'I kept going back and forth. My first instinct was to protect you from knowing and worrying for no reason . . . but then I couldn't not tell you. You deserved to know.' He paused to gently brush my hair away from my face. 'Not to mention, you . . . this . . . I want to do it right. I know it's not always going to be easy, but no matter how hard it gets, I want us to always be able to talk to each other. About everything. Just like we always have.'

And there it was. The right moment. The perfect moment to tell him what *he* deserved to know.

The waves crashed on shore. My heartbeat drummed in my ears. Simon looked at me, his eyes concerned yet happy, so happy, as I opened my mouth and started to speak.

'Will you swim with me?'

He kissed me then. It was long, and sweet, and almost made me forget that it shouldn't be happening.

Almost.

CHAPTER 4

Paul Carsons. Charles Spinnaker. Aaron Newberg.

I read the names as I scrolled down the page, past photos of handsome men dancing with their wives, holding children, steering sailboats. My eyes lingered on certain words in the accompanying blocks of text: 'was found', 'cause of death', 'asphyxiation'. The *Winter Harbor Herald*, the small town's only newspaper, which mainly served as a guide for tourists, had gone all out in its coverage of 'High-Seas Tragedies', and continued to update the special section with images and information about the victims' families. Before a few days ago I hadn't visited the website in weeks, but after learning that the ice was melting, I was now checking it whenever I could steal a few minutes on a school library computer.

So far, the good news was that no new bodies had washed ashore. The bad news was that it was getting warmer every day. According to the site's cartoon sun, it was currently sixty-three degrees in Winter Harbor. Temperatures would eventually drop again with the arrival of fall, but by then the harbour might be completely thawed – and it likely wouldn't freeze again. Until this summer, it had never frozen before, not even in the dead of winter.

Before I could reach Justine's entry, I returned to the home page. The main photo had been taken yesterday and showed two people on the harbour. One person ice-skated on a still-frozen patch; the other bobbed in an inflatable tyre in one of the small melted pools.

Shivering, I closed the Internet and logged onto Hawthorne's e-mail system. After each *Herald* visit I usually couldn't stomach being on the computer another second, so I hadn't checked my messages in a few days.

I watched the new e-mails fill my inbox, scanning over the usual ones about the weekly lunch menus, theatre auditions, and sports tryouts. Of the new messages, only two were addressed to me personally.

The first had been sent last week.

To: Sands, Vanessa
From: Mulligan, Kathryn
Subject: College Applications

Dear Vanessa,

Congratulations! After working so hard for so long, you've finally made it to senior year. The upcoming months are crucial to the next phase in your educational career and will be filled with exciting opportunities and challenges. I'm meeting with each senior to discuss his or her college plans, and I'd like to schedule an appointment with you during your free period on WEDNESDAY, SEPTEMBER 25, at 11:30 A.M. Please confirm upon receipt of this e-mail.

Here's to your future!

Regards,

K. Mulligan
Guidance Counsellor

I reread the note, which obviously had been sent to all seniors. The only personalisation besides my name was the meeting date and time.

The second e-mail, however, was for me only. It had been sent early this morning.

To: Sands, Vanessa
From: Mulligan, Kathryn
Subject: Today's Meeting

Hi Vanessa,

I haven't heard from you regarding today's appointment and wanted to confirm that we'll be meeting in my office at 11:30.

I know things probably seem quite uncertain right
now. I hope you'll let me help you sort them out.

All my best,

K.M.

I moved the mouse to delete the e-mail just as a head
appeared over the top of the computer cubicle. I looked
up to see Jordan Lanford, senior soccer star.

'Tragic,' he said.

'What's that?' I asked reluctantly, returning my gaze
to the computer screen.

'You there. Me here. So close yet so very far.'

My cheeks warmed. Hearing whispering, I glanced
behind me. A few girls sat at a nearby table. They
must've been lowerclassmen because I didn't recognise
them, but they seemed to know who I was. They talked
quietly behind their hair and hands and looked at me
like I'd once seen countless girls look at Justine: frown-
ing, with their brows lowered and eyes narrowed.

Like they were jealous.

I turned back to the computer, signed out of e-mail,
and gathered my stuff.

'Where are you going?' Jordan asked. 'Can I walk
with you?'

'I don't think so. But thanks.'

I hurried away from the computer terminals. When I neared the main entrance, I checked behind me to make sure he wasn't still watching, and then veered left. I darted through the reference section and into a dark alcove nobody liked to use because of its lack of windows and wi-fi.

Unless, of course, they couldn't wait for the end of the day to make out with their significant others. Which was what Parker King was doing with Amelia Hathaway on an old plaid couch.

I turned quickly, quietly, and rushed back down the aisle.

'Stop,' Amelia said.

Assuming she was talking to me, I did.

'What's wrong?' Parker asked.

My face burned as I waited for her to point me out. They kissed again, and I was about to throw an apology over my shoulder and flee the reference section when she continued talking.

'This,' she said as clothes rustled and couch springs squeaked. 'I can't do this.'

'Actually,' Parker said, 'you can. And quite well.'

This was followed by more squeaking. Taking advantage of their movement, I ducked between the ends of two bookcases and slid down one until I was crouching. I peeked out once to see Parker lean towards Amelia, who pushed him away.

'I'm serious,' she said. 'It was fun . . . but I'm kind of over the constant, meaningless hooking-up.' She straightened her sweater vest, patted his knee. 'We had a good time, right? Let's leave it at that.'

'But we're not just . . . *I'm* not just –'

He was cut off as she stood up. I pulled back behind the shelf and waited until she passed before peeking out again. Parker was slouched down, his head resting on the back of the couch. He pressed his thumb and index finger into the corners of his closed eyes, as if to keep them from leaking.

'Wow,' I whispered. Parker King was usually the one doing the breaking up, not the other way around.

'Vanessa?' he asked, sounding confused.

I flew back behind the shelf. Hearing the couch screech again as he got up, I half stood and disappeared into the next aisle. I kept my head lowered and didn't stand up straight until I reached the circulation desk. Then, not daring to look behind me to see if he followed, I ran the remaining distance to the library entrance.

It was the middle of the period, so the hallway was empty except for a few teachers talking outside the main office. I tried to walk normally, but when I heard the library door open behind me, I quickened my pace and darted into the first non-classroom doorway I came to.

'Vanessa!'

45

My back was to her, but I recognised her voice.

Ms Mulligan. I'd fled to the one place I didn't want to be more than the library: the guidance office. Checking the wall clock as I turned around, I saw that it was 11:45.

'Sorry I'm late,' I said.

'Don't give it another thought. I'm just so happy to see you.'

In her office, Ms Mulligan waited until I was sitting to close the door, like I might make a break for it. I looked around as she retrieved my file from a nearby cabinet. The main reason parents enrolled their kids in prep school was to increase their chances of being accepted into the Ivy League, and Hawthorne was no exception. Ms Mulligan and I had spent quite a bit of time together over the past three years; in some ways, her office, with its fancy degrees and college posters, felt more familiar than anywhere else at school.

In other ways, it felt as if I'd never been there before.

'So,' she said, sitting across the desk from me. 'Dartmouth.'

'Excuse me?'

'The last time we met, you said Dartmouth was your first choice.' She removed a piece of paper and held it up so I could see her notes.

'Oh. Right.' Now I remembered. Last spring, Ms Mulligan had been determined to get a first choice out of me so that we had a clearly defined goal. I'd said Dartmouth because that's where I'd thought Justine would be. And what had been even more important than a college's academics or internship opportunities was its proximity to my sister.

'Have you changed your mind?' Ms Mulligan asked.

'I haven't really given it much thought.'

She closed my file and crossed her arms on the desk. 'Of course you haven't.'

Here it came: She was so sorry for my family's loss. Poor Justine. Poor me. What did I need? What could she do to help?

'My father passed away when I was seventeen.'

Or, even worse: she could relate.

'He was sick for a long time, so we knew when the end was probably near. We prepared as best we could, but it was still such a shock when it finally happened. I cried for weeks.'

'I'm sorry to hear that,' I said.

She leaned towards me. 'Do you know what helped get me through it?'

'School?'

'College. Planning, organising, thinking about where I'd be in six months, a year, five years.' She sat back and studied me. 'Justine was an excellent student. She applied to thirteen schools and was accepted to every one.'

I swallowed my response. Ms Mulligan didn't need to know that Justine had lied. She hadn't been accepted anywhere because she hadn't even applied. That wasn't something Justine had wanted to share. I'd discovered the truth only on the day of her funeral, when I found a blank common application hidden underneath pictures on her bulletin board.

'Your sister knew the importance of higher education, Vanessa. She wouldn't want you to risk yours . . . especially not because of her.'

'You're right,' I said. 'I'll definitely think about it. Soon. And hard.'

Her lips turned in as her eyes turned down. After a moment she reached for her mouse and squinted at her computer screen. 'How's this time next Wednesday?'

'For what?'

She started typing. 'I think we should meet once a week. Even if we don't make any big decisions right away, it will help to have time to talk things through.'

'That's okay,' I said quickly. 'I mean, thanks, but I'm sure I'll come to a decision soon enough. My dad's a professor at Newton Community College, so I can ask him any questions I might have about the application process.'

The printer hummed behind her. She took the paper it rolled out and handed it to me.

'A copy of the e-mail I just sent you,' she said. 'Next week, same time, same place.'

I barely felt my legs as I stood, took the paper, and started for the door.

'Oh, and Vanessa?'

I paused, one hand on the doorknob.

'It does get easier. That hurts to hear . . . but it's true.'

I tried to thank her, but my lips wouldn't move. I opened the door and left without answering.

In the hallway, I swung my backpack around so that it sat against my side. As I rummaged through its contents, my lips felt like they were shrivelling, shrinking. I tried licking them, but my tongue was as dry and heavy as a brick. My hands shook more every second, so it took several seconds to find the plastic bottle and yank it from my bag.

I drank as I walked. The salt water was lukewarm but felt like an icicle sliding down my throat. I emptied the bottle in five gulps and then stopped in front of a display case as the liquid did its job. Whenever a student or teacher passed by, I leaned closer to the glass and pretended to read the trophy engravings so they wouldn't ask questions.

The third time I did this, my eyes landed on a familiar name.

Justine Sands.

Her name was in a dozen different places inside the display case – on field hockey trophies, soccer plaques, softball certificates. All of her life Justine had been the best at whatever she did, including sports, which she'd played every season at Hawthorne.

I don't know ... but neither do you.

The sentence, handwritten on a lined piece of paper, flashed before my eyes. I blinked and shook my head to clear it.

Justine's face took its place. Her lips were parted in a smile, and her blue eyes were wide with excitement as she kicked the winning goal against Thoreau High. She looked so beautiful, so happy. Judging by the picture, you'd never know that she played the game not because it was fun ... but because she'd thought she had to.

A classroom door opened nearby. I turned and hurried down the hall. By the time I reached the girl's restroom, my entire body felt like it had been baking on tarmac in the blazing hot sun for days. Somehow I managed to check the stalls and, when I saw they were empty, lock the door.

'Come on,' I whispered, turning on the faucet and holding the bottle underneath. The water couldn't come fast enough; the bottle was only half filled when I pulled it away and poured in salt from the container in my backpack. I gave it a hard, single shake, tilted my head back, and drank. I turned on the water in the next sink, plugged the drain, and added salt. I spent the next five minutes alternating between drinking and splashing my face. Eventually, my thirst abated.

Exhausted, I leaned against the wall across from the sinks and slid down until I was sitting on the floor.

This was my future. Hiding in bathrooms. Guzzling salt water. Trying to keep from dehydrating to death. Ms Mulligan and I could talk college every day of the week, but it wouldn't matter. Even if I made it there – classes, schoolwork, my major, my potential career – none of it would change the fact that I was going to be only one thing when I grew up.

A monster.

A few minutes later, I reached for my backpack. I opened the front pocket, took out my cell phone, and turned it on. As tears slid down my cheeks, I dialled the number that I'd erased from speed dial in an act of good intention, but that I still knew by heart.

Simon's voicemail picked up on the second ring.

'Hi.' I winced when my voice trembled. 'It's me. I know you're in class right now . . . but I just wanted to hear your voice. Call me later? Please?'

CHAPTER 5

'Text messages or beeswax.'

I looked up from my AP calculus homework. Paige sat on the bed, a book open in front of her.

'Those are Simon's choices,' she said.

My heart skipped. 'For what?'

'For regaining control when you distract him to the point that he loses sleep, friends, and life as he knew it. According to these books, breaking up by text or plugging his ears with beeswax are the only ways he can escape his siren.'

I stared at her. She smiled, but when I didn't smile back, her face fell.

'I'm sorry,' she said. 'That wasn't funny. It's just, of course you're not, you could never be a –'

'It's okay. And *I'm* sorry. I guess I'm still getting used to that word.'

'You and me both. That's why I want to learn more. If I understood who they were, why they do what they do, what they did . . . maybe it all wouldn't seem so strange.'

'Paige, if you really want to learn more, why don't you ask Betty?'

'After she tried so hard for so long to keep the truth from Raina and Zara? Who not only defied her wishes but used what they learned against her?' She shook her head as she turned a page. 'Talking about it will only hurt her, and I can't do that. She's been through enough already.'

'It's not an ideal situation,' I admitted, 'but she's still your grandmother. She'd still do anything for you.'

Of this I was certain. After all, Betty had let Paige spend the school year here, depriving Betty of her only surviving family member. She loved Paige so much that she wanted her to be able to start over in a new place, one without constant painful reminders.

'Want to hear something crazy?' Paige asked a moment later. She'd closed the book and now looked at me, her blue eyes wide, like she was about to share a secret she couldn't believe was hers.

'Sure.' I thought of the last secret she'd told me several months earlier, when her cheeks were flushed and her belly round. That one had almost killed her.

'I saw them.'

A silver streak flashed before my eyes. I blinked it away.

'Raina and Zara, in the park. My English class met

53

there today. We were reading *The Winter's Tale*, and the story was so dull, I closed my eyes for a few seconds. When I opened them again . . . I saw them. On a bench. Looking right at me.'

Simon's reassurances flew through my head. *It was frozen . . . whatever was alive is dead now . . .*

'Crazy,' Paige said when I didn't say anything. 'I know.'

'It's not crazy.'

'But it is impossible.' She climbed off the bed and sat on the floor across from me. 'You know how you could hear Justine? After she was gone?'

I nodded.

'Maybe it was something like that? Maybe I made them up? Not because I miss them, but because I'm so traumatised – or whatever – by what happened?'

I hadn't just imagined Justine's voice then, but it was good that Paige still believed that. For now, anyway.

'It's okay to miss them,' I said. 'Raina was your mother and Zara was your sister for a long time before they . . . changed. It's okay to miss the people you thought they were.'

Her blue eyes hardened. 'They killed dozens of people and would have killed countless more if we hadn't stopped them. They killed Jonathan. They locked Grandma Betty in her bedroom for two years and then left her to die.' She shook her head. 'I don't miss them. I *won't* miss them. Not ever.'

This was the harshest I'd ever heard Paige speak about anyone. I was tempted to change the subject for both our sakes, but there was one thing I had to know before I did.

'What did they do when you saw them?' I barely heard the question over my pounding heart.

She shrugged, her face softening slightly. 'I blinked, and they were gone. Because they were never really there.'

Of course they hadn't really been there. Despite what they were, they still had hearts. They still needed oxygen. Like Simon said, there was simply no way a siren could survive two months locked in ice.

'Anyway, it was nice of Riley to check these books out for me, even if they were completely useless.' She reached up and took *The Odyssey* from the bed. 'He seems like a good guy.'

'Simon wouldn't be friends with him if he wasn't.' I reached forward with my pencil and tapped the toe of her slipper. 'And he thought you were pretty okay, too.'

That triggered the small smile I was hoping for. 'Yes, well. He's not . . .'

Her voice faded, but she didn't have to finish the sentence for me to know what she'd started to say. Riley, as nice as he was, wasn't Jonathan.

Thinking she might want a few minutes alone, I closed my notebook and stood up. 'Mom's attempting brownies tonight. Interested?'

'Extremely,' she said, covering her stomach with both hands.

In the hallway with the bedroom door closed behind me, I leaned against the wall and put my own hands to my stomach. I braced for movement inside, for something zipping around like a fish in a tank. That was what Paige's baby had felt like the one time I'd pressed my palm to her belly. It had been sick, and restless, and physically draining, because her body hadn't been ready to care for a baby.

But thanks to the accidental transformation over the summer, when my cellular water was replaced with ocean water, *my* body was. I thought of the last time Simon and I had been together. We'd been careful. We were always careful. But I still told myself that each time was going to be the last time, no matter what else happened between us. I always believed it, too . . . until he touched me again.

My stomach remained still now. Temporarily relieved, I continued down the hall.

'You're just in time,' Mom said when I entered the

kitchen. She stood at the counter, pouring batter into a pan. 'The first batch is still in the oven. But here.' She took the electric mixer from the counter, popped out the dripping whisks, and handed me one. 'A sneak peek.'

I tasted the batter, then turned to rinse off the whisk. 'Delicious. Only a few weeks in and you're already Julia Child.'

She laughed. 'You have to say that because you're my daughter.'

I looked up. In the reflection in the window above the sink, I watched her pat her hands on the frilly green apron she wore. 'I tried to make grilled cheese after school today,' I said. 'I burned the sandwich so badly, the cheddar evaporated between the bread.'

'Why didn't you ask me? I would've been happy to make you another one.'

'That was actually an improvement over the last time I tried. I just can't cook to save my life.' The whisk was clean, but I let the water keep running. 'I wonder who I get that from. You and Dad are both so good in the kitchen.'

She'd just removed the brownie pan and now stopped, her face in front of the open oven. She was still for only a second – if I hadn't been watching for a reaction, I wouldn't have noticed it – but my words definitely caught her off guard.

'Speaking of your father,' she said, her voice light, as she closed the oven and placed the pan on the counter. 'He's working outside. Will you please go see if he'd like his brownie à la mode?'

I turned off the water and looked out the window, past Mom's reflection. My chest tightened when I saw Dad sitting on the small back stoop, typing on his laptop. 'Sure. I'll bring him a sweater, too.'

It was eight o'clock at night and still seventy degrees out, but Mom didn't seem to think the sweater idea strange. That, or she hadn't heard me over her own thoughts. Either way, it gave me an excuse to duck out of the kitchen instead of heading directly for the back door.

Dad's office was a tiny room at the other end of the first floor. I hadn't been inside in months, and inching the door open now, it didn't look like much had changed. Dozens of books sat in tall, crooked stacks around the room. Papers spilled out of filing cabinets. Old coffee cups were abandoned on bookshelves, on the fat arm of Dad's favourite leather chair, and on the floor. The only place that wasn't completely cluttered was his desk, which was tucked under an eave that made standing upright impossible.

I closed the door and wove through the maze of book towers. Guilt burned like a hot coal in the bottom of my stomach, but I kept going, telling myself I wouldn't be there unless I had no other choice. Piles of student essays surrounded the desk like a protective moat, but I scaled them quickly and then sank into the chair.

The desk was immaculate; it held only Dad's computer and two picture frames. My eyes lingered on the photos. One was of Mom sticking her tongue out at the camera in a moment of playful protest, and the other was of Justine and me when we were little girls, sitting on the brownstone's front steps, blowing soapy bubbles through plastic wands.

I opened the desk's top drawer and sifted through pens, paper clips, and breath mints before moving on to the next drawer, and then the next. My heart sank when each opened easily. Didn't people guarding huge secrets usually hide clues in locked desk drawers?

I jumped up and climbed back over the piles of essays. I yanked open filing cabinets, but they offered the same thing the desk drawers did.

Nothing.

I turned slowly in the middle of the room, looking for . . . what? A hidden door? A secret passage? A treasure trove of information disguised as a flowerpot? I was about to lift the area rug to rule out a floorboard trapdoor when my eyes landed on the desk again. Or more specifically, on the computer.

Dad had two computers – the desktop and a laptop –

and he was always on one or the other. Their combined memory could probably offer more details about his life than his real memory.

As I headed for the desktop, I felt like I had on the day of Justine's funeral, when I first realised the pictures on her bulletin board hid something underneath and had debated whether to find out what that something was. I'd felt worse with each pushpin I removed, like I was about to read her diary.

But this was different. I already knew what Dad's secret was. And it didn't just affect him; it affected our entire family.

I returned to the desk and took the mouse in one hand. The screen brightened as the sleeping computer awoke.

A blue password box popped up. My heart dropped, then lifted. I had no idea what Dad's password was, but the fact that he had one might mean there was something on the computer worth protecting.

I typed the first thing that popped into my head: Jacqueline. I held my breath as the tiny digital hourglass turned upside down and right side up. A few seconds later, the box reappeared.

Invalid password.

It wasn't Mom's name. I tried mine next, then Justine's. I expected the program to tell me I'd reached its limit of password attempts, but it didn't. So I tried

Newton College, where Dad taught. Hemingway and Fitzgerald, his two favourite writers. Rad Dad and Big Poppa, two of countless nicknames Justine and I had given him.

Invalid, invalid, invalid.

My fingers hovered over the keyboard as I stared at the blinking cursor. There was one other name I could try. I didn't want to – I could barely think it, let alone type it – but passwords, despite all warnings, were often people or places important to the user. And besides our immediate family, there was one other person Dad might find just important enough. One person whose name no one but him would know.

Or so he thought.

I typed slowly, watching each letter appear on the screen. When I was done, I looked at the name and re-called the very first time I'd seen it, in Betty's bedroom in Winter Harbor. It should've been just another name, no different from all the others in Raina's scrapbook of sirens and their conquests. But it *had* been different. Because right above it was a faded picture of a beautiful woman in the arms of a young man with frizzy hair and warm eyes who looked so happy he could have died right then with no regrets. And according to the text next to the picture, the happy couple had had a child together.

The woman was Charlotte Bleu.

The man was Big Poppa.

The child was me.

A door slammed somewhere inside the house. I jumped at the sudden noise, and my thumb, which had been poised above the return key, shot down.

The hourglass turned. Each rotation seemed to take minutes. I stared at the screen, waited for the password box to clear and ask me to try again.

Instead, the box disappeared. In its place was Dad's electronic desktop, covered in dozens of cryptically labelled documents. There were so many they overlapped, reminding me of lines of playing cards in Solitaire.

My hand seemed to move on its own, and the mouse guided the cursor to a document in the middle of the screen. It was labelled 'Wo198'.

Beneath me, the chair vibrated. I assumed my nerves were making me shake, but then I realised the screen vibrated, too. So did the picture frames. And a coffee cup on a bookshelf across the room. Not continuously, but every other second.

And then I heard them. Footsteps. Slow, heavy, like whoever was walking was big, tired.

Dad. He was inside the house ... and coming closer.

I leaped out of the chair, knocking my head against the low, slanted ceiling. I bit my lip to keep from crying out and snatched the red cardigan from the back of the chair as I climbed over the essays. The tip of my sneaker hit the top of a stack, sending a flurry of pages drifting to the floor. As I fell to my knees and gathered them, the footsteps grew louder.

I threw the essays on top of a pile, scrambled to my feet, and grabbed a coffee cup from behind a stack of books.

The footsteps slowed, then stopped. The light beneath the door darkened. As it did, the light in the office seemed to grow brighter – especially the light coming from behind me.

The computer. It was supposed to be asleep, its screen dark.

The old brass knob creaked. The door started to open.

I lunged across the room, grabbed a handful of wires and cords, and pulled. The computer whined before falling silent.

'Vanessa?'

'Hey, Dad.'

He stood in the doorway, his laptop under one arm, a brownie sundae in one hand.

'I was just about to bring you coffee and a sweater.' I held up the coffee cup and cardigan, the latter of which was his favourite and a perfectly believable reason to be in his office. 'Would you like cream?'

He looked at the cup as I held it up. 'You were really going to bring me coffee and a sweater?'

I paused. 'Yes?'

'Well.' He smiled and stepped into the room. 'Thank you, Vanessa. You just made my day.'

Of course I did. I'd been distant since seeing him in Raina's scrapbook, and I knew he felt that, even if he didn't understand its cause. Were this gesture sincere, it would've been the closest we'd come to our old relationship in months.

'You're welcome.' I let him kiss my cheek as he passed, knowing the more I gave, the easier it'd be to leave.

'That's strange.'

I had one foot through the open doorway when he spoke. I turned slowly, feeling my face turn the same shade as his favorite sweater. 'Is something wrong?'

He was behind his desk, leaning over the keyboard. He typed, waited, and typed again. He tapped the top of the monitor and then took it with both hands and gently shook it back and forth. 'I know I left this on. Did we have a power surge while I was outside?'

He stood up straight and scratched his head. In that moment he looked so perplexed, so like my beloved Big Poppa whenever he was confused by new slang his students were using or technology he was trying to learn, that I suddenly felt terrible for snooping.

64

'That's what that was.' I hurried back into the room and picked up the cords. 'I tripped over these when I was getting your sweater. I must've disconnected the computer. Sorry.'

His face relaxed. 'That's okay.'

I plugged the cords back in and darted towards the door.

'Vanessa?'

I froze. He knew. I had thought unplugging the computer would shut everything down so that he'd never know that I'd been on the computer, let alone that I'd figured out his password and reached his desktop. But it hadn't. And now he knew. He knew that I knew about Charlotte, and –

'If you wanted to join me for coffee and dessert . . . I'd like that.'

'Sure, Dad,' I managed without turning around. 'I'll be right back.'

I closed the door behind me and headed for the kitchen, which was now empty. I put the dirty cup in the dishwasher and filled two clean cups with coffee and cream. I cut a huge piece of brownie, wrapped it in a paper towel, and grabbed two forks from the utensil drawer.

And then I took the coffee and dessert and went upstairs, where Paige was waiting for me.

CHAPTER 6

I woke up the next morning with a headache. I took three aspirin, drank a gallon of water, and soaked in the tub for an hour. Nothing helped. The pain continued into the weekend, when Paige and I returned to Bates, and I guessed it was caused by stress – related to Dad, school, and lying to Simon. Unfortunately, the physical relief I'd surely feel after coming clean during this visit was a small consolation.

'So tell me more about this famous party,' Paige said. She and Riley stayed a few feet in front of Simon and me as we walked across campus. 'Will there be games?'

'And prizes,' Riley said. 'And some of Adroscoggin County's finest livestock.'

I looked at Simon. 'As in cows?'

'Technically, it's a harvest festival,' he explained. 'Bates has one every year.'

Up ahead, Riley said something that made Paige laugh. She rocked to the right, bumping his shoulder with hers.

'He doesn't know about last summer?' I asked, lowering my voice.

Simon shook his head. 'He saw some of the news coverage on TV – along with the rest of the country – but he has no idea she was involved. He thinks she's your great summer buddy who moved to Boston to be there for you.'

'Good. If she wants him to know anything else, she'll tell him when she's ready.'

He lifted our clasped hands and pressed his lips to the top of mine. 'I'm glad you're here,' he said, his lips grazing my skin.

I hesitated, then kissed his cheek. 'Me, too.'

It was a warm fall day, and the campus was filled with people studying, sunning, and heading to and from the festival. As we walked, I listened to their conversations and laughter, thinking they all sounded so happy, so normal. I tried to imagine doing the same things on a college campus this time next year . . . but couldn't.

'So what do we think?' Riley asked when we caught up with him and Paige at the festival entrance. 'Scarecrow contest then tractor race? Tractor race then scarecrow contest? Or should we just skip ahead to the caramel apples and pumpkin-flavoured beer?'

'I could go for a hayride,' I said, spotting a long, horse-drawn wagon on the far side of the field. 'If that's okay with everyone else.'

It was. We took our time getting there, stopping along the way to cast our votes for the best pumpkin carving, watch a cider-making demonstration, and sample different varieties of locally made maple syrup. After we finally joined the end of the long hayride line, it took another thirty minutes to reach the front; by the time it was our turn, the wagon was packed and the next one wasn't due back for several more minutes.

'We can totally fit,' Riley said, surveying the narrow gaps between riders. 'We'll just double up.'

'You don't mind sitting on my lap?' Paige joked.

'In the interest of time and entertainment, no. I'd make that extreme sacrifice.'

Paige laughed. Simon looked at me.

'Let's do it,' I said.

We climbed a short ladder and over the slatted back of the wagon. Riley followed Paige as she navigated through legs, feet, and bales of hay, and, true to his word, sat on her knees when she found a small seat near the driver and horses. Simon squeezed in the back left corner of the wagon, then pulled me gently into his lap.

'I think I like the Bates Harvest Festival,' I said as he put his arms around me.

Roughly thirty people were crammed into the small

space – many of whom, judging by the occasional shrieks and loud laughter, had enjoyed some pre-hayride pumpkin-flavoured cocktails – but sitting in the back with Simon was so cosy, we might as well have been alone.

'How was your lab?' I asked as the wagon started moving. We talked so often I knew his schedule by heart.

'Long. Gruelling. Visually taxing.'

'I thought you loved science's little winged friends.'

'I do . . . when I'm not expecting very important company.'

I smiled. 'Important company? What kind?'

'Oh, the kind that makes me forget the atomic number of carbon, and how to convert Celsius to Fahrenheit, and the taxonomy of living things.'

'Kingdom, phylum, class, order, family, genus, species,' I recited, patting his chest lightly with each one. 'She must be something special to make you forget the little science even I know.'

His arms tightened around me. I rested my head on his shoulder.

It felt so good, so comfortable.

If only it didn't have to end.

'Caleb's birthday's next weekend,' Simon said a moment later.

'Right,' I said, grateful for the new topic. 'The big one-seven. Is he excited?'

'Against his will. He was just going to have a few friends over for pizza and a movie, but Monty had other ideas. And whatever Monty wants –'

'Caleb wants.'

'Hence the town-wide boat bash next Saturday night. Monty's decking out the *Barbara Ann*, Caleb's friends are rigging their fishing boats with lights and DJ equipment, and people are supposedly going to be jumping one ship for the next all night long.'

'Jumping ship?' I lifted my head and looked at him. I hadn't checked the *Winter Harbor Herald* website since yesterday morning. 'Does that mean . . . ?'

'No.' He lifted a strand of hair away from my face. 'It doesn't. Rowing boats might be able to sit in spots, but the water's still too frozen to launch anything bigger. Caleb just loves boats so much Monty wanted to make sure they were part of the party.'

I laid my head back down. Simon's heart beat faster against my palm.

'So, I know it's short notice . . . but would you want to come? With me? To Caleb's party?'

I opened my mouth to say yes. He sounded nervous, and I wanted to reassure him – and I also wanted to be wherever he was. But the word wouldn't come out.

'I know he'd love to see you,' Simon continued. 'So would my parents. But if it's too soon, I totally understand. It was just an idea.'

'No.'

'No? As in it's not too soon?'

Hot tears sprang to my eyes. Blinking them away, I sat up so his arms released me. I tried to look at him but couldn't.

'No . . . I can't go.'

'Can't. Okay. Do you already have plans?'

This was it. I had to do it. It was bad enough lying to him – I couldn't drag down his whole family, too.

'Simon.' Fresh tears welled as I said his name. 'I have to tell you something.'

He put one hand on my knee. 'Anything, Vanessa. Always.'

Anything. Always. Did he mean it?

I wasn't ready to find out but took a deep, shaky breath anyway. 'Do you remember –'

I was cut off as the wagon jerked forward. Simon's arms were back around my waist instantly. The air filled with shrieks and screams as the horses quickly sped up from a slow stroll to a full gallop.

'The Sleepy Hollow Stampede?' I practically shouted to be heard over the excited din and thundering hooves.

The long black banner, suspended between trees, disappeared as we charged beneath it and into a dark forest.

'I think we've been hijacked!' Simon yelled back with a smile.

Holding on to him to keep from tumbling out, I followed his nod. The wagon driver, an elderly man who'd been wearing overalls and a flannel shirt when we boarded, had either changed into a costume without our noticing . . . or been taken out by the Headless Horseman.

'Vanessa!' Paige shrieked.

Our eyes met across the wagon, and we both cracked up. Riley bounced in her lap, his eyes closed, his arms tight around her shoulders. Hers were around his waist. As the wagon flew over bumps and rocks, festival volunteers dressed as witches and zombies lunged from the trees. Passengers screamed, ducked, and gripped whatever they could – hay bales, the sides of the wagon, each other – to avoid being caught and falling off.

It was the first time I'd been scared by something unrelated to the events of last summer *since* the events of last summer. And because Simon was right there, holding me tighter than he ever had before, I enjoyed every second.

When it was over and the wagon slowed to a stop at the ride entrance, Simon, still smiling, brushed my windblown hair away from my face. He went to kiss my forehead, but I lifted my chin so his lips landed on mine.

We kissed for several seconds, ignoring the looks and giggles of other passengers moving past us as they climbed out. We might have continued – perhaps even taking another ride just so we didn't have to pull apart – but Riley had apparently been terrified into extreme thirst.

'Cider,' he gasped, standing just outside the wagon. 'Lemonade, witch's brew, I don't care. As long as it's liquid and can be swallowed.'

Simon's lips stilled against mine. He lowered his head to my shoulder and shook it.

'I could use a drink myself,' I said. After the excitement of both the hayride and kissing Simon, my body needed fuelling. I gave him a quick peck and climbed off his lap.

'But you wanted to talk. Maybe we should meet up with them later.'

It was stupid. And childish. And would probably only end up making things worse.

But I lied anyway.

'It's no big deal. It can wait.'

If he wasn't convinced, he didn't say so. He was quiet for a while, though, as we walked to a big white tent where dozens of students and teachers were square-

dancing. I worried he was upset that I'd put off the topic, but he seemed to relax after we spent some time at
the tent's refreshment table.

I relaxed, too. The refreshments consisted of bottled
water, pretzels, and mixed nuts, and chasing the salty
snacks with the regular water was surprisingly satisfying.
The music, played by a live country band, was good.
Paige, fuelled by Riley's jokes and attention, couldn't
stop smiling. Simon let go of my hand only to put his
arm around my waist.

I was having such a nice time I didn't even hesitate
when Simon asked me to dance.

Along with Paige and Riley, we formed a square with
two other couples. The large white tent was crowded,
and the portable dance floor shook from the dancers'
stomping and skipping. It took a few spins – and a lot
of knocking into each other – to get the hang of it, but
once we did, we do-si-doed like pros.

'College rocks!' Paige yelled as we hooked arms during one turn.

I laughed. I hadn't seen her so happy in a long time.

Which made me happy. So much so that I kissed Simon the next time we were paired together.

One country song led to the next. The caller encouraged the crowd to sing along, and eventually, catching
on to a simple chorus, I joined in.

Maybe it was the music. Or the white lights twinkling overhead. Or the way Simon caught my eye and grinned no matter where we were in the square. Whatever the reason, I didn't notice no one else was dancing until I went to hook my arm through Riley's . . . and it wasn't there.

It's okay . . . I told myself, turning slowly. *They're not looking at you . . .*

Except they were. All of them – students, teachers, the caller, Riley, Simon. Everyone but Paige. They'd formed a big, still circle. They didn't clap, dance, or sing along. They simply stood there, watching me.

The girls were pouting.

The guys were smiling.

CHAPTER 7

'Are you cold?' Ms Mulligan asked when we sat in her office Monday morning. 'Should I close the window?'

'I'm fine.' I pulled on the sweatshirt hood so it covered more of my face. 'Bad-hair day.'

Amore ac studio.' She said this expectantly. When I didn't respond, she nodded to my chest. 'With ardour and devotion. The Bates motto.'

'Oh.' I looked down at the logo, which was similar to Dartmouth's. The protective shield of higher education featured a book, a tree, and the fancy Latin slogan. 'I didn't realise.'

'Bates is an excellent school. It's consistently ranked one of the top twenty-five liberal arts colleges in the country.'

'It's my friend's sweatshirt.'

'You know a current student? Wonderful.' She turned to her computer. 'Many parents encourage their children to make clean breaks so that they're not distracted, but college can be overwhelming. I think having someone there you already know and trust would help ensure a smooth transition.'

I wanted to tell her that I wasn't interested in Bates – especially not after last weekend, when I'd accidentally introduced myself to the entire school – but I was too tired to protest.

'My local Hawthorne and Bates alumnus is available for an interview next Tuesday at seven o'clock,' she said. 'Does that work for you?'

'An interview? Thanks, but I don't think –'

'How about Beantown Beanery? Their mocha lattes are the best in the city.'

There was no point in arguing. Ms Mulligan would only try to convince me it was a good idea and wouldn't want to hear me say otherwise. Instead, I took my backpack from the floor and stood up.

She stopped typing and looked at me. 'Is something wrong?'

'I have an English test,' I said, shuffling backward. 'Next period. I just remembered.'

'There are still twenty minutes left of this period. This will only take a –'

'I have to review my notes.' I reached the door, grabbed the knob. 'But thanks.'

I knew she wanted to stop me, but she didn't. Just like she – or anyone else – hadn't said a word about my sweatshirt and wrinkled skirt. Deviating from the strict Hawthorne uniform was an offence punishable by detention, and though I'd gotten many looks from teachers and staff members since school started, no one had said anything.

They didn't want to upset me. They didn't want to push me any closer to the edge than I already was.

I used this to my advantage now. I passed several staff members as I hurried down the hall; they all opened their mouths to ask what I was doing in the hall in the middle of the period, but they didn't say anything. They didn't try to stop me. Mrs Hanley, my maths teacher, was right there when I reached the front doors and lunged against them, but she let me go without a word.

Outside, I ran down the steps and across the street. It was early October and the air had finally cooled, the leaves changed colour. People walked by in wool coats, chins tucked inside their collars and hands in their pockets. But I didn't feel the chill. In fact, I was so warm, if I hadn't needed the protection of Simon's sweatshirt, I would have taken it off.

I headed for the park. I'd never cut class before and wasn't sure where to go, but that seemed as good a place as any. It'd be crowded, and as long as I stayed hidden, no one would notice me.

I found an empty bench in a leafy alcove and sat

down. I pulled my water and a bottle of aspirin from my backpack and took two more pills. That brought today's total up to six – the recommended daily dose – and it was only noon.

But the headache wouldn't go away. It hadn't returned while we were at Bates, but it'd hit like a sledgehammer the second we crossed the Boston city line three days ago. Its strength had fluctuated since then, but even when I felt only mild pressure, it was still a reminder of everything I didn't know and everything I still had to do.

Which included talking to Simon. He hadn't seemed particularly surprised by my unexpected square dance solo, claiming it was understandable since I was the most striking girl in the room, but I'd never fully recovered. I'd been too nervous, too paranoid, and we'd spent the rest of the weekend watching movies and eating takeout in the dorm with Paige and Riley. He'd tried to bring up what I'd wanted to talk about only once, over the phone the night we got back to Boston, but I'd assured him it was nothing. And because he never pushed me to do anything I wasn't 100 per cent okay with, it'd been business as usual since.

Except for the headache. And the thirst. And the warmth and fatigue, which were new symptoms of whatever was making me sick.

I slid down onto the bench and closed my eyes.

I focused on the soothing sounds of leaves rustling, birds singing . . . people kissing.

I opened my eyes. I wasn't imagining it. People were making out, in the middle of the day, in the middle of the park. I couldn't see them from where I sat, but I could hear every breath and murmur, which meant they were too close for comfort.

As I grabbed my backpack and jumped up, I caught a glimpse of navy blue, a flash of maroon. The Hawthorne Prep colours popped out from behind a nearby tree as the happy couple shifted their embrace.

'Vanessa?' a familiar male voice called out.

I was only a few feet down the path when he spotted me. Without turning around, I tightened the hood around my face and quickened my pace.

'Vanessa, wait up!'

I walked even faster. Behind me, footsteps hurried to catch up.

'Hey, speed racer,' the voice said, suddenly next to me. 'You know school's in the other direction, right?'

He touched my elbow. I pulled away and veered left. Glancing over my shoulder, I saw Marisol Solomon, a fellow senior who modelled for J. Crew. She still stood by the tree where she'd just been abandoned, apparently too confused to tuck in her blouse or fix her hair. When our eyes met, she crossed her arms over her chest and frowned.

I took every turn I came to, passing through gardens and around monuments. I thought I lost my pursuer once, when I ducked behind a public restroom, but he was following me again seconds after I emerged from the other side. I was so worried about staying away I didn't pay attention to where I was going, and soon I reached the edge of an open field. I stopped short and scanned my surroundings. The only shelter was the Parkman Bandstand; it stood thirty feet away, in the middle of the field.

The footsteps sounded further back now. I looked behind me but didn't see anyone.

I was so tired I could've collapsed to the ground and taken a long nap right there, but instead I summoned what little strength I had left. If I couldn't see him, he couldn't see me, so all I had to do was make it to the bandstand. It resembled a gazebo so wouldn't provide total protection, but its short walls were still tall enough to hide someone who didn't want to be found.

I took a deep breath and ran.

My legs grew weaker with every step. My heart clenched and wouldn't release. I gasped for air faster than my lungs could expand and contract. I was about to give up and brace for the awkward encounter that followed, but then I glanced behind me once to see how far away he was ... and saw Raina and Zara instead.

They walked slowly, side by side, wearing long dresses that had once been white but that were now grey, and torn, and clinging to their shrivelled limbs. Their skin was blue, their dark hair matted. Their silver eyes were narrowed ... and aimed at me.

I lunged the remaining distance to the bandstand and tripped inside, landing hard on my knees. The impact left thin rips in my tights and scrapes on my skin. Ignoring the pain, I crawled across the floor and out of sight of the entrance.

'Please,' I whispered, closing my eyes and hugging my knees to my chest. 'I'm sorry. Please don't –'

'Please don't what?'

My breath caught.

'Suggest that you've been wasting your time at Hawthorne when you could've been an Olympian gold medallist by now?'

I opened my eyes to see Parker leaning against a stone pillar and breathing heavily. He loosened the neck of his crimson tie and then used its length to wipe the sweat from his forehead. He watched me climb to my feet and look out over the low walls of the bandstand.

'Where's the fire?' he asked. 'I didn't see flames, but

the way you hauled across the park I figured there had to be one somewhere.'

There wasn't a fire. There was also, thankfully, no one else in sight.

I shrugged off my backpack and leaned against the pillar across from his. 'Shouldn't you get back to your girlfriend?'

'What girlfriend?'

'The one you were simultaneously suffocating and resuscitating behind a tree,' I said, sifting through my backpack.

'Marisol's not my girlfriend. Or a friend. In fact, she's so tightly wound, sometimes she's barely a girl.'

Barely a girl. I could relate.

My fingers finally landed on familiar plastic ridges. I yanked out the water bottle – and felt like crying when I saw that it was empty. I was so physically and emotionally drained, the tears would've streamed down my face if I'd had any salt water left to cry.

'Hey.'

I looked up. The cockiness was gone from Parker's face. In its place was something I never would've expected to see unless I'd actually witnessed it first hand.

Concern.

He reached into his messenger bag and removed a Nalgene bottle. He started to step towards me, but then seemed to think better of it and stopped. 'Here,' he said, holding out the water.

My throat tightened. I didn't want anything from Parker King. Not only because his conceit bordered on obnoxiousness, but because I didn't want to encourage him. After all, he'd just chased me through Boston Common. Who knew what he'd do if I was anything except cold to him?

But I'd have to deal with that later. I was so thirsty I wouldn't make it out of the park if I refused.

'Thanks.' I took the bottle, turned, and walked to the other side of the bandstand so he wouldn't see my face crumple in relief. It was regular water, of course, but it still helped slow my aching lungs and racing heart.

'Hold still.'

The mouthful I'd just swallowed shot back up. He knelt by my feet, his fingers on my shin. The water burned as I forced it down. 'What are you –'

'You're bleeding.' He adjusted his hands quickly so that one was firm behind my calf, keeping me from moving backward.

And then I saw it. Dark red liquid, leaking from my knee, trailing down my leg, staining my white tights.

Images flashed across my vision. Justine, in the woods, in Caleb's arms. Blood trickling from an open wound.

It's just dirt, or seaweed . . .

'I need to . . . I think I'm going to . . .'

He jumped up as my legs gave. I sank to the floor, vaguely aware of his arm tight around my shoulders.

'It's okay.' He took off his blazer, poured some water on a sleeve, and used it like a washcloth on my face. 'You're okay.'

Too weak to argue, I tilted my head back and closed my eyes. Every now and then warm plastic pressed to my lips, and I opened my mouth. Between drinking and the makeshift cold compress, my skin started to cool, my internal temperature to drop. Eventually, I felt well enough to open my eyes again.

'Strawberry Shortcake?' The printed Band-Aid was the first thing I saw.

'My little sister doesn't let me go anywhere unprepared.' Parker held up a plastic baggie filled with more Strawberry Shortcake Band-Aids, Cinderella tissues, and Jolly Ranchers.

I looked at him, almost seeing, for just a second, what every other girl at Hawthorne must see in him. His dark blond hair was brushed back away from his face and grazed the top of his shirt collar; his blue eyes occasionally glinted green (like now, in the early-afternoon sun); and he had smooth, golden skin. But even more disarming than his physical characteristics was the easy, fearless attitude behind them. Parker knew he was attractive, but looking at him now, something told me he didn't care. His confidence was fuelled by more than that, which somehow made his appearance the least interesting thing about him.

'I'm sorry,' he said. 'For chasing you when you obviously wanted to be alone. But I wanted to give you something, and I've had trouble finding you.'

He'd been looking for me? Was my draw, my unintended – and unwanted – appeal to the opposite sex already worse than I'd thought?

'We don't have any classes together, you're never at your locker, and I haven't seen you in the library again. It was either this or wait until our paths crossed in Winter Harbor next summer.'

Before I could ask what he meant, he reached into his blazer pocket and took out a photo . . . of Justine. Eating an ice-cream cone on Winter Harbor's crowded Main Street. She wasn't looking at the camera, which meant she hadn't known it was aimed at her.

'I wasn't sure who your sister was,' he said apologetically. 'When I asked one of my friends, he told me and showed me that. He had a thing for her and sneaked the picture when we were up there two summers ago.'

'I don't remember ever seeing you around,' I said, gently taking the picture.

'That's because I wasn't around much. That summer

was the first time we visited, and we were only there a week. My parents bought a place last summer, but Dad was busy and we never made it up.' He hesitated before continuing. 'Anyway, I asked if you were okay the other day because you looked really hot, like you might have a fever. But I was an idiot for not knowing what happened. And I just thought that giving you the photo was one small thing I could do to make up for it.'

'You didn't have to do anything,' I said. 'To be honest, someone not knowing was actually refreshing.' Or it would've been, if I hadn't been too taken aback by his sudden attention.

'Just like an escorted visit to Nurse Benson will be? I did what I could with what I had, but you were in pretty bad shape a few minutes ago.'

'Thanks, but I'm fine. I always get sick at the sight of blood.'

'Okay,' he said, not convinced, 'but I insist on walking you back to school.'

'You don't have to.' I stood quickly, my head spinning. He grabbed my arm when I started to sway to one side. I closed my eyes and waited for the spinning to subside. When I opened them again, Parker's eyes were waiting.

'I'm carrying my backpack,' I said.

'Fair enough.'

We didn't talk as we started across the field. I was grateful for the silence; it gave me a chance to try to sort out everything that had happened. Parker had seemed sincere and interested only in making up for not knowing about Justine. He'd been genuinely concerned and had taken care of me when I almost passed out. But was all that because he felt badly for not knowing about Justine and wanted to make it up to me? Or was it because I'd already affected him?

We were halfway through the park when my cell phone buzzed. I took it from my skirt pocket and opened the new text message.

MISS YOU. THOUGHT YOU SHOULD KNOW. – S

I glanced at Parker. He was looking straight ahead and didn't seem to even notice me check my phone . . . but this was a good opportunity.

'Just got a text,' I said. 'From Simon. My boyfriend.'

I watched his face for a frown, tension in his jaw, lowering eyebrows – some sign of disappointment or jealousy. But there wasn't any. Not only that, it took him a second to respond, like he was distracted. Like he wasn't thinking of me at all.

'Cool.' He flashed me a quick smile, then looked straight ahead again.

I stared at the cell phone screen without seeing

Simon's words. This was good news. Whatever was going on with Parker, his feelings for me were still platonic at best.

But that meant I knew even less about my condition than I thought I did.

CHAPTER 8

The only thing I wanted to do when I got home from school later that day was soak in a cold bath. I'd visited the water fountain and refilled my bottle between each period, and though my thirst and headache had abated, my skin still felt tight, like it was too small for my body.

But as soon as we opened the front door of our house, I knew a bath would have to wait a few minutes more.

'Did I unpack too soon?' Paige asked.

'Don't worry.' I closed the door and stepped over a large cardboard box. 'We're not moving. We're having a meltdown.'

'Oh, good – you're home!' Mom called up the basement stairwell. 'Vanessa, sweetie, do you remember what I did with the talking witch?' The question faded as she walked away from the stairs without waiting for an answer.

'She turns to stuff when stressed,' I explained as a loud crash sounded downstairs.

'I think I'll give Grandma B a buzz,' Paige said. 'Unless you want me to . . . ?'

'No,' I said, eyeing the basement door. 'But thanks.'

As she headed for the kitchen, I took another look around the living room. Dozens of cardboard boxes were scattered across the floor and furniture. Long plastic storage bins sat in stacks taller than me. Black trash bags filled doorways. Dust floated through the air.

Mom liked her house one way – pristine – so whatever had set her off this time must have been serious.

'A talking witch?' I asked when I reached the stairwell landing.

She stopped pulling my old stuffed animals from a shelf and spun around. 'What are you doing down here?'

'I thought you needed help.'

'And I thought you'd just yell down the stairs.' She stepped towards me, holding the ratty stuffed crab Dad had bought me at the New England Aquarium years ago. 'You hate the basement.'

She had a point: I *used* to the hate the basement. But things were different now. Mostly because I'd learned that the scariest monsters didn't hide in shadows, waiting for you to find them. If they wanted you, they came and got you.

'Halloween's in three weeks.' She turned back to the shelf and started replacing the stuffed animals. Her

91

other drawers were also dead ends, offering only yellowing English notes and course syllabuses. By the time I closed the last drawer, Mom had moved on to another stack of boxes; I waited for her to turn her back to me, then ducked behind a steel utility shelf.

She obviously hadn't made it to this corner of the basement yet because the shelves were still filled, their contents grey with dust. My eyes travelled over old books and vinyl records, searching for anything that might suggest a secret life outside this brownstone.

The light dimmed as I walked down the aisle and away from the overhead lamp. It was so dark when I reached the concrete wall I almost walked right into it. The sudden nearness surprised me and ignited familiar feelings I normally experienced as soon as I passed through the basement door. Heart thudding and limbs tingling, I spun around and hurried back down the aisle.

I was halfway down when the toe of my left foot caught on a roller skate. I grabbed the shelf to keep from falling, and the force sent a cardboard box tumbling down to the floor.

My eyes locked on the handwritten label.

JUSTINE, 0–2 YEARS

The top had opened in the fall, and as I turned the box right side up, tiny pink dresses and purple layettes spilled out. I immediately recognised some of the baby outfits from old pictures displayed throughout the house and pictured Justine smiling in her stroller and giggling in her high chair.

I picked up the fallen clothes, running my fingers along ivory lace edges and pearl buttons. Blinking back tears, I refolded them and placed them gently in the box. As I stood up and put the box back on its shelf, I noticed several more like it: JUSTINE, 3–5 YEARS; JUSTINE, 5–7 YEARS; JUSTINE, 8–10 YEARS.

I stepped back and looked up. Because Mom wasn't one to reuse what you could easily buy new, I'd never inherited Justine's hand-me-downs. That meant I should have my own collection of boxes.

I found them on the highest shelf, their labels barely visible in the dim light. But while Justine's clothes were divided into two-year batches starting at 0 years old, or when she was a newborn, my clothes were divided into two-year batches starting at 1 year old.

I reached up and inched out VANESSA, 1–3 YEARS.

I recognised these clothes, too; I'd seen them all in countless pictures and photo albums over the years. But the smallest size was 12–18 months.

I suddenly recalled what my parents had always told me about the missing photos from my first year of life. While Justine's first smile and steps were chronicled in a thick embroidered album, my recorded memories didn't

95

start until I was a year old. Mom claimed that was because Dad had chosen those twelve months, of all the months ever, to play professional photographer, and that *my* first smiles and steps had been lost in a series of unfortunate darkroom experiments. They even had a box of blurred images to prove it.

But anything could be blurry if developed incorrectly, couldn't it?

My palms sweated and my throat dried as I started down the aisle again, but the physical discomfort was nothing compared to what was going on inside my head.

'Look what I found.'

Mom glanced up from a plastic bin of ornaments.

'Baby clothes,' I said brightly.

She stood and brought both hands to her face. 'Is your favourite yellow jumper in there? The one with the butterflies?'

I pulled out the jumper and held it up so she could see, then placed the box on a metal folding chair between us.

'Paige came home from the hospital in the middle of a blizzard,' I said as she rummaged. 'Except it was May, so her mom, thinking the weather would be warm, only packed a sundress and light sweater for her.'

'That far north, it can flurry through July.'

'Right.' I watched her pick up a denim skirt, turquoise

tights. 'Anyway, the pictures are really cute. Paige wearing her sundress and wrapped in a blanket the hospital gave them, surrounded by swirling snowflakes.'

'I'm sure she was adorable.'

So far, so good. I'd never seen pictures of Paige coming home from the hospital; I didn't even know if she had any. But Mom believed me, and that was what mattered.

'I forget what I wore home from the hospital.'

Her hand froze.

'I know you must've told me a million times . . . but I just can't remember.' I stepped towards the box. 'Is the outfit in here?'

Her mouth opened. 'I gave it away,' she said several seconds later. 'To a woman in my office. She had a baby a few months after you were born, and when we had a shower for her, she insisted on hand-me-downs only.'

I had to give her credit: She was good. A year ago, I might have believed her.

'What did it look like?' I asked.

'What did what look like?' she asked, already moved on.

'The outfit I wore from the hospital.'

She dropped the clothes she held into the box and faced me. Her lips were even, her forehead smooth. I thought she might actually come clean and braced myself for the truth ... but then she smiled.

'Pink gingham. Ralph Lauren.' She held out one hand. 'The nurses said they'd never seen a prettier baby.'

I put my hand in hers. She lifted and kissed it. Then she returned to the Christmas decorations.

'Will you grab a few garbage bags from upstairs? I might as well tidy up while I'm down here.' She opened a new box and pulled out a strand of glittery garland.

Pretty silver ... magical silver ... the silver of Christmas tinsel ...

Which was how the waitress had described Zara's eyes when Simon and I went to the Bad Moose Café to look for Caleb. The memory made me bolt across the room and upstairs.

In the living room, I hurdled boxes and darted between bags. My mouth and throat stung like I'd just downed a bottle of sand, but instead of sprinting to the kitchen to replenish, I headed in the opposite direction.

To Dad's office.

It was three o'clock. He wouldn't be home from his afternoon lecture for two hours.

Reaching the room, I threw open the door and charged inside – or at least I tried to charge. My body weakened more with each passing second, like I was running on a dying battery. As I crossed the small space, my legs quivered and my feet stumbled. Instead of stepping over the moat of papers surrounding the desk, I summoned any remaining energy and lunged for the chair. My legs hit the stacks and stayed there.

I grabbed the mouse and woke the computer. I watched the keyboard as I typed, not trusting my trembling fingers to find the right letters unsupervised. Once finished, I hit Enter and looked up at the screen.

I held my breath as the tiny hourglass turned once. Twice. Three times.

Invalid password.

I retyped the thirteen letters. When they were rejected, I tried again. And again. Until my fingertips numbed and I could no longer see the keys.

My body wasn't totally out of water after all. When I finally sat back, exhausted and defeated, there was enough to fill my eyes and slide down my cheeks.

CHAPTER 9

Raina's scrapbook was wrong. Charlotte Bleu didn't die during childbirth. She had me, and for the first year of my life, she took care of me. I was as sure of this as I was of the fact that Dad had changed his computer password to keep me from finding things he didn't want me to see.

What I didn't know was why. Why did she give me up? Why after a year and not sooner – or later? What happened? Did she die around my first birthday? Did Raina just have the timing confused?

These were the questions I'd been silently asking since finding the boxes of baby clothes. And as Paige and I pulled up to the Winter Harbor Marina for Caleb's birthday party almost a week later, I still didn't have any answers.

'I don't think I can do this.'

Instantly jolted out of my own thoughts, I glanced at Paige, who reached into the shopping bag at her feet and held up a CD.

'You can't listen to old grunge rock?' I asked, parking the car.

'I can't give it to Caleb.' She rolled down the window and tilted her head towards the party.

'Sounds like Pearl Jam.'

'It is Pearl Jam.' She waved the CD. 'So is this.'

'And?'

'And they're Caleb's favourite band – I learned that in school last year, when you could hear the music coming from his earphones a mile away. He must own every song they've ever recorded.'

'Which is why you bought the limited-edition live CD from when they played a tiny club in Boston ten years ago. The CD you can only *get* at the tiny club in Boston.'

I followed her gaze as she looked out the windscreen. The party was already in full swing. Dozens of people filled the marina parking lot and docks – talking, laughing, and dancing. Beyond them, boats bobbed on the harbour.

'The water surrounding the marina is fairly shallow,' I said quietly, guessing that the real problem had nothing to do with Caleb's gift. 'That's why the ice is beginning to thaw here. But Simon said the deeper parts are still frozen solid.'

She lifted her eyes to mine. 'Like at the base of Chione Cliffs?'

My head throbbed once, then stopped. 'Yes. Like at the base of Chione Cliffs.'

'Ahoy there, pretty ladies.'

We both jumped as Riley spoke near Paige's open window.

'Sorry,' he said. 'Didn't mean to startle. But I've been ordered to walk the plank and wanted to make sure I said hello before taking the plunge.'

'Right,' Simon said, coming up next to him. 'Ordered, offered. Same difference.'

'You offered to walk the plank?' Paige asked.

'And challenged other guests to do the same. It's kind of like musical chairs or pin the tail on the donkey, seaside-style.' He opened Paige's door. 'You look exquisite, by the way.'

I smiled as she blushed. Regardless of whether she wanted to like Riley, he clearly had a positive effect on her. She dropped the CD in its bag and climbed out of the car.

'I'd say the same about you,' Simon said, resting one arm on top of the open door and ducking his head to look into the car, 'but "exquisite" falls a bit short.'

My heart lifted. 'Hi.'

'Hey.' He smiled. 'Hungry?'

'For some of Winter Harbor's finest gourmet fare?'

'Also known as some of my dad's finest charred cheeseburgers?'

'Absolutely.'

He was on my side of the car before I'd unbuckled my seat belt. Opening the door, he held out his hand to help me out. Our fingers had barely touched when I jumped up and hugged him.

In between thoughts of Charlotte Bleu during the drive up, I'd decided to take the day off from trying to decide how to tell Simon the truth. It was a celebration, after all, and I didn't want to ruin the day for him, Caleb, or anyone else.

Plus, like Paige, I wasn't thrilled to be near the harbour as it melted. What I'd told her about the deeper water still being frozen was true, but not completely reassuring. Between that, what I'd just discovered about the first year of my life, and making sure I stayed hydrated so that I didn't collapse in front of the whole town, my head was too overwhelmed to reason with my heart.

So when Simon put his arm around my shoulders, I put mine around his waist.

'You feel warm,' he said as he steered me towards the party. 'Do you want me to carry your jacket?'

'I'm fine,' I said quickly. 'But thanks.'

I'd had trouble getting dressed that morning. Lately,

when I wasn't wearing my school uniform and a baggy hooded sweatshirt I was wearing jeans and a baggy hooded sweatshirt, but I'd wanted to look nice for Simon. And I hadn't been sure how to do that without attracting the attention of every other guy who happened to glance my way. Eventually, I'd decided on jeans, a tan V-neck, and a brown corduroy jacket. I couldn't hide in the clothes, but I hoped the neutral colours helped me blend into the crowd.

My outfit was a stark contrast to Paige's. She'd taken advantage of the opportunity to dress up and wore a burnt-orange miniskirt, a denim jacket, and cowgirl boots. Her legs were bare, as was her neck, since she'd gathered her hair in a high ponytail.

Riley was right; she looked exquisite. And as they walked ahead of us, she should have turned the head of every boy she passed.

But she didn't. A few looked at her and smiled, but then their gazes shifted behind her . . . to me.

'Don't worry,' Simon said, noticing me noticing them. 'The more they drink, the less they'll pay attention to anyone but themselves. We should be practically invisible in another ten minutes.'

Simon had said on the phone last night that if things got too weird today, we could always duck out for a while, maybe go for a drive. He thought people might be surprised to see me back in town in the off-season – and us hanging out as more than friends. I didn't necessarily agree, since along with Justine and Caleb, we were together so much we could've been mistaken for a couple long before last summer, but I kept this to myself. I'd rather Simon assume that was the reason people were looking at me.

'There she is!' a familiar voice exclaimed as we neared the cooking stations.

'Hi, Mrs Carmichael,' I said with a smile.

She opened her arms, and I reluctantly let go of Simon to hug her.

'How are you, sweetie?' she said into my hair. 'How are your parents?'

'We're fine. Hanging in there.'

'You'll give them our best? And tell them we're taking good care of the house?'

I opened my mouth to answer, but then spotted Caleb coming towards us with a tray of hot dogs.

'Don't tell me you're reneging on your birthday promise already,' he said.

Mrs Carmichael squeezed me once more, then let go. 'Of course not,' she said with a sniff.

Caleb swapped the tray for a spatula on a nearby table. Joining us, he aimed the spatula like a flashlight at his mother's watery eyes. 'She's been weepy for days because, as she puts it, her baby boy's all grown up . . . but I told her she could keep the new car if she just curbed the hysterics tonight.'

'No one likes rain on a parade,' Mr Carmichael called out from behind a grill.

'You got him a new car?' Simon asked.

Mrs Carmichael brushed her eyes and laughed. 'He could blow out a million candles and that wish still wouldn't come true.'

'A guy can dream,' Caleb said, turning to me. 'Can't he?'

This time, I initiated the embrace. For several seconds I held him tightly, hoping he could somehow feel Justine's arms in mine. He tensed at first, and I wondered if it was too much, if I should let him go, but then he relaxed and hugged me back.

'Happy birthday,' I whispered.

'Thanks for coming, Vanessa.'

It had been only a few weeks since we'd left Winter Harbor, but it felt like for ever since I'd last seen Caleb. He'd lain low after the night the harbour froze, and throughout the rest of the summer I'd talked to him only when I was outside and happened to catch him leaving for or returning from work. I'd figured pulling back was just his way of healing and hadn't pressed . . .

but he almost sounded like his old self now. And that made me as happy as I knew it would've made Justine.

'Incoming!'

We pulled apart just as a red inflatable tyre landed at our feet.

'I think I'm being summoned.' Caleb picked up the tyre and tilted his chin towards the water, where a group of guys waved and yelled for him to join them.

'Have fun,' I said. 'We'll catch up later.'

As he headed for his friends and Mrs Carmichael joined Mr Carmichael at the grill, Simon reached for my hand. We found Paige and Riley, who were rounding up other plank-walking competitors, told them we were taking a walk, and then wandered around the marina. The music and noise softened as we followed the water's edge to the property's outskirts, where lines of boats sat waiting to be wrapped for the winter.

'It looks different,' I said.

'You're usually not here now,' Simon said. 'When leaves are falling and the harbour's almost empty.'

'It's not just that.' I stopped at a dock and looked towards the party's glittering lights. 'It's the ice. The way it's melting in some spots and not others. It's like the whole town's stuck in place, waiting to be freed.'

He stood behind me and slid his arms around my waist. 'It's getting there. We're getting there.'

I leaned against him and slowly scanned the water's surface. I didn't know what I expected to see. Beams of light shooting up into the sky? Beautiful women dressed in flowing white dresses? Caleb's friends walking towards them, eyes blank and smiles wide?

I knew one thing I didn't expect to see: Justine's and my boat, here on the harbour instead of at our lake house backyard.

'Simon.' I stepped forward, out of his arms. 'Is that...? Did Caleb...?'

He hesitated, apparently trying to figure out what I was talking about since I couldn't find the words. 'The red rowing boat?' he asked finally. 'No way. If Caleb had wanted to borrow it, he would've asked.'

'But there's a patch of green in the back, where the paint's peeling. And the front's rounded instead of sharp, just like –'

'The fronts of all rowing boats get after years of use?' I looked at him.

His face softened. 'I'm sorry. It does resemble your boat ... but we're standing a hundred feet away. And it's getting dark. It'd be hard to tell a rowing boat from a canoe in these conditions.'

I turned back and walked to the end of the dock for a better look.

'It's stuck in the ice,' Simon said gently, standing next to me. 'It was in the water when the harbour froze.'

'Then why wasn't it brought in? All of the other boats that were in the water that night were chopped out and hauled in.'

'Monty's removal services aren't cheap. Maybe it wasn't that important to its owners. Maybe they didn't mind waiting for the ice to melt.'

I knew he meant only to reassure me, and what he said made sense, but I wasn't convinced.

'Can we make sure?' I asked.

'How?'

'By going out there.' I gave him a small smile. 'It could be like walking the plank – another seaside party game.'

He looked out at the boat, then around the rest of the harbour, clearly calculating ice thickness and determining the potential safety issues of the area in question. I felt bad for putting him in this position; I knew he'd do everything possible to avoid saying no to me – but I also knew I wouldn't relax until I was sure that wasn't our boat.

'Further north the ice hasn't thawed at all,' he said. 'It should hold my weight.'

'I'm lighter,' I said quickly.

'I'm stronger. If it gives, I can pull myself out.'

If the ice gave while I was on it, I could breathe underwater until rescued. But Simon didn't know that. Before I could come up with another reason why I should go instead of him, he stepped towards me and brushed my cheek with his thumb.

'If it's important to you, it's more important to me,' he said. 'I'll be there and back in no time.'

'Wait –'

But he was already jogging down the dock. I watched him jump onto the tarmac and then run through the brush along the water's edge. He was slowing down, surveying the ice for the best spot, when an image flew through my mind like a bullet from a gun.

A parking lot. The dim light of a streetlamp. Simon, his face blank, his arms limp. Defenceless against the powerful force pulling him closer.

Zara.

I shook my head sharply and sprinted down the dock. 'Simon!' I yelled. 'Don't!'

But he didn't hear me. That, or I'd actually whispered the warning instead of shouting it – it was hard to tell over my pounding heart. I tried again, but he didn't even glance my way before starting out onto the ice.

I ran faster, ignoring my drying throat and weakening legs. I rubbed my eyes when white spots popped before them, hating to lose sight of him for even a second. He moved easily, purposefully, like he was in complete control . . .

But what if we were wrong after all?

Reaching the rowing boat wasn't worth the risk of finding out. I tried yelling once more, but the effort seemed to sever my shrivelling vocal cords. Grabbing my throat against the pain, I veered right, out of the brush – and onto the ice.

The sudden chill beneath my feet stopped me short. The air above the water was colder than the air around it, and my quick breaths formed small, fleeting clouds. I wanted to look down, to see if anyone – or anything – looked up at me from beneath the ice, but I couldn't. I was too terrified of what I might see.

Instead, I kept my eyes on Simon. He was halfway to the rowing boat now, but racing diagonally from here, I could still catch up with him. In desperate need of fuel, I kept my head level and bent my knees until I crouched above the ice. I lowered both hands to the frozen surface; it softened under the heat of my skin, and the salt water shot into my palms like an electric charge.

It was enough to get my feet moving again. I started out slowly, but in seconds I was flying across the ice like my shoes were attached to thin metal blades.

The distance between Simon and me closed. Apparently hearing my approach as I neared, he stopped and turned towards me. I was so relieved that I'd reach him before anything could happen, when he raised his arms, I thought it was so I could run into them.

But then my eyes met his. And I saw their fear.

'Vanessa,' he called out, his voice steady but loud. 'Don't move.'

I slid to a stop.

'It's cracking,' he continued. 'Behind you.'

And then I heard it. Creaking and snapping, like snow-laden branches breaking off trees.

'Stay perfectly still.' He lowered his hands and started backing up, away from me.

He continued towards the rowing boat. Instinctively, I took a step forward to follow him – and froze when the ice groaned beneath me. As I stood there, not breathing, I had a clear picture of Simon reaching the boat and pausing briefly before taking something from inside.

An oar. With a trail of shiny red anchors running down the handle.

It was the last thing I saw before the ice split between my feet, and I dropped into the chilled harbour below.

CHAPTER 10

'Are you sure you don't want to sneak out to your house?' Paige asked later that night. 'Ours is so draughty, we'd probably be warmer in a tent.'

'I'm sure.' I wasn't worried about draughts. I *was* worried about what else I might find at the lake house, in addition to a missing rowing boat. I'd been whisked off the ice too quickly for a close inspection, but Simon had admitted the boat looked more like ours than not – and ours was supposed to be locked up in the lake house shed for the winter. 'But if you're too uncomfortable, we can always go back to Boston.'

'Now?' She peered out at me from the small opening in the down comforter she was wrapped in. 'It's almost midnight.'

'I can drive. I feel fine.'

'You just stopped shaking, like, ten minutes ago.'

She was right – but that had nothing to do with being cold.

'By the way,' she continued, stretching out on the couch across from mine, 'how crazy was it that Grandma

Betty and Oliver just happened to be driving by the marina, their car fully loaded with blankets and dry clothes, five minutes after you fell in the water?'

'Not very, considering she's Winter Harbor's favourite super senior citizen.'

Paige smiled. 'Good point. She probably heard the ice cracking before Simon did.'

Ever since Paige's grandmother went swimming in the middle of a lightning storm two years ago, she'd had supersensory powers – excluding her vision, which she'd lost. She could apparently hear flowers blooming, whales singing, and hearts beating from miles away. When she'd arrived at the marina, she'd told the crowd gathered around us that she and Oliver (her favourite male companion, as she called him) had been on their way to make a donation to the thrift shop when they noticed the commotion . . . but the blankets were hot, as if pulled from a dryer only moments before, and the clothes were exactly my size. Thanks to her, I warmed up fast enough to convince Simon I didn't need to go to the emergency room.

'Did you see anything?' Paige asked quietly a moment later.

I focused on the flames flickering in the fireplace. 'What do you mean?'

'I mean, I know where you fell was miles away from

Chione Cliffs . . . but what lives underwater swims underwater, right?'

I looked at her and forced a smile. 'I was under for a matter of seconds. I saw ice, darkness, and Simon. That's it.'

She exhaled. 'Thank goodness. Maybe I'll actually sleep tonight.'

We fell into a comfortable silence. To keep distracted from my own thoughts, I focused on the sounds of snapping wood and howling wind, which were soon joined by the soft sound of Paige's deep breathing.

I closed my eyes and waited for sleep. When my cell phone buzzed in my sweatshirt pocket ten minutes later, I was staring at the ceiling and happy to have something to do.

ARE YOU AWAKE? – S

OF COURSE, I wrote back.

ARE YOU OKAY?

He'd asked this earlier, but I hadn't had a chance to give him a real answer. Caleb was there when Simon lifted me out of the water, and Captain Monty, Riley, Paige, and other party guests were watching and listening from a nearby fishing boat that Captain Monty had managed to navigate towards us through slush and ice.

A LITTLE RATTLED, BUT OTHERWISE FINE. I paused, my thumbs hovering over the keypad, before adding, I MISS YOU, THOUGH.

I'd barely hit Send when another text popped up.

DO YOU WANT ME TO COME OVER?

I stared at the screen. There was nothing I wanted more than to see him; before my impromptu dip this afternoon, the plan had been for Paige to spend the night with Grandma Betty while I went to the lake house, where Simon would meet me after his parents had gone to bed. But then Grandma Betty had insisted I stay with them, and I'd been too scared to argue.

IT'S LATE, I typed. HOW ABOUT AN EARLY BREAKFAST?

HARBOR HOMEFRIES, 8 A.M.?

I agreed to the meeting, then closed the phone and looked at Paige. I couldn't see her under the blanket, but the white mound rose and fell every few seconds. Satisfied she was out, I pushed aside my own comforter, got up, and started across the living room.

Paige hadn't wanted to sleep in her room – or anywhere on the second floor – and I didn't blame her. Back home, I'd offered to stay in Justine's room so Paige could have mine, and as weird as it sometimes was, and as much as it could feel like I hadn't known Justine at all, I did know one thing: she wasn't a murderer. Paige's situation was obviously very different, and I understood her wanting to keep her distance.

But that didn't mean I had to.

The only light came from the fireplace and faded as I climbed the stairs. When I reached the top step, it was so dark I couldn't see my hand on the banister. I felt along the wall for a switch, but there wasn't any.

This was normally the point at which, if I'd even made it this far, I'd bolt back down the stairs. But surprisingly, I felt okay. Calm. Strong. The feeling had started as soon as I hit the water and intensified quickly. I was submerged less than a minute, but by the time I was back on solid ground and my body had had a chance to absorb the natural salt, I felt better physically than I had since jumping off Chione Cliffs.

I'd taken only two steps down the hall when I heard a familiar voice.

'Can't sleep, Vanessa?'

I froze, then turned slowly to see Betty standing in the open doorway of her bedroom.

'You thought it was your boat, didn't you?' she asked.

I stepped towards her. 'I know it was my boat.'

'But they're dead.'

Our eyes locked. Hers were usually aimed up, but

now they found and seemed to hold mine in place. In the dim lighting, their grey clouds appeared to shift and move, just like the ones in the sky. 'How do you know?' I asked.

She stepped aside and waited. As I entered the room, I breathed in the salty ocean air blowing through the open windows. I hadn't been in Betty's room since the morning of the Northern Lights Festival last summer, and it looked different. The walls, which had been filled with needlepoint images of Chione Cliffs, were bare. The fireplace was dark. The carpet had been replaced with dark hardwood floors. Besides Betty herself, the only thing that indicated the room belonged to her was the purple swimsuit hanging from a hook on the bathroom door.

And an older, tired-looking man, sitting in a rocking chair by the windows.

'Hi, Oliver,' I said.

He looked up from the open notebook in his lap. I wondered if he was working on another volume of *The Complete History of Winter Harbor*. He'd written several over the past thirty years – mostly, he claimed, to distract Betty from her own fears with stories of the adopted home she loved.

'Vanessa,' he said, and returned his gaze to the notebook.

That was odd. When I'd first met Oliver, he'd been cool, even cranky. But he'd slowly warmed up as he had helped us figure out what was going on in Winter Harbor, and couldn't have been nicer after he and Betty had reunited following a years-long separation. This greeting, unaccompanied by 'hello' or a smile, was one the old Oliver would've given.

Before I could ask if I was interrupting, Betty sat in a velvet armchair by the fireplace and continued speaking.

'I'd hear them,' she said. 'Their voices fell silent the second the water froze, and they never spoke again.'

Not wanting to bother Oliver, who was now writing, I stepped towards her and lowered my voice. 'But it *was* my boat. Mine and Justine's. It was worn in the same places, and one oar had –'

'Red anchor stickers.' Betty tilted her head. 'Just like the kind Winter Harbor pharmacy sells at the register, the kind every child begs her parents to buy. If you look closely, you'll find them all over town – on garbage cans, newspaper bins, street signs.'

I frowned. Now that she mentioned it, I could picture them. And the pharmacy was where Justine had bought hers the day she decided to decorate the oars.

'If Raina and Zara were alive,' Betty continued, 'and if they were planning some kind of revenge, I would know.'

'But they'd try to keep it from you, wouldn't they?

They'd know you could hear their thoughts and be careful to control what they think.'

'I'd still hear their efforts to focus on other things. All sirens are connected, so it's possible to hear a stranger's thoughts if you try hard enough, though it isn't easy. But you can always hear family. Even if you don't want to.'

I looked away, like she could actually see the doubt on my face. My eyes fell on the bed on the other side of the room; it, too, looked different, covered in one thin sheet instead of layers of blankets, as if Betty hadn't slept in it since the day I'd found her lying there, her dried skin flaking, so thirsty she couldn't speak.

'She was kind.'

I looked at Betty. She motioned for me to sit in the chair across from hers.

'Your mother, Charlotte Bleu, owned a small bookstore on the outskirts of town. She'd let people read there for hours, never caring whether they finished books without buying them. She carried an impressive collection, too – lots of rare and first editions that she could've sold for a great deal of money, but that she gave away if a customer was interested and couldn't pay the asking price.'

It took a second to find the words for my next questions. 'Is that where she met my dad? At her bookstore?'

Betty paused. 'I don't know.'

'Did you see them together? Did they ever come to the restaurant?'

'No. But as far as I understand, they weren't together long.'

Now that we were actually talking about her, the questions came faster than I could ask them. 'Did Raina say anything else? She obviously knew about them, since she had their picture. Did she take that picture? If not, whoever did must know more about –'

'Vanessa, I'm afraid I've told you all I know. If Raina knew more, well . . .'

I sat back. If Raina knew more, we'd never find out.

We were silent for a long moment. The only sounds were the light flapping of fabric as the curtains lifted in the breeze, and the rustling of paper as Oliver turned pages. I had countless questions about Charlotte, Dad, the first year of my life, the inconsistent effects of my abilities. But there was one question I needed to ask above all the others. One that, at this point, only Betty could answer.

I glanced at Oliver. He was engrossed in his work and didn't seem to be paying attention to us, but I leaned closer to Betty and lowered my voice to a whisper anyway.

'I drink salt water,' I said. 'Constantly. I take two salt-water baths every day. That helps, but I still get so thirsty

121

and hot. And now I'm having these terrible headaches that won't go away no matter how much aspirin I take.'

I paused, giving her a chance to tell me what I needed to know without my having to ask. But she didn't. Her face, like her eyes, remained blank.

'Betty,' I continued, my voice trembling, 'how do you do this? How do *I* do this?'

There was a loud, single knock behind us. I jumped. Betty didn't.

'It's late,' Oliver said, suddenly next to us. The rocking chair, which had apparently hit the wall when he stood, moved forward and back, forward and back, like it was still occupied. 'We should all get some sleep.'

His head was turned towards me, but his eyes aimed over my shoulder.

'Paige is waking,' Betty added coolly. 'She'll worry if you're not there.'

Torn between wanting to try to learn more and getting out of there as fast as possible, I finally stood and walked across the room. At the door I turned to say something – to thank Betty, to assure her that Paige was doing well, or to offer something else that kept this brief visit from ending awkwardly – but then I saw her standing perfectly still before the open window, the wind whipping her long grey hair around her head. Like she was listening intently to something only she could hear.

'Goodnight, Vanessa,' Oliver said evenly.

I stepped into the hallway and closed the door as fast as I could without slamming it. I had one hand on the stairwell banister and was about to start down when it occurred to me that I shouldn't be able to see the banister. The hallway was brighter than it had been when I came upstairs, and the new source of light seemed to be coming from behind me.

It's a lamp, or candle, I told myself. *You just didn't notice it before. . . .*

But it wasn't a lamp or a candle. It was a glowing, silver stream rippling across the floor at the other end of the hall.

I glanced towards Betty's room; her door was still closed. I listened for Paige, but she was silent. So was the rest of the house – even the wind seemed to have stopped. All I could hear as I headed slowly down the hallway was the ancient floorboards creaking beneath my feet.

Reaching Zara's old bedroom, I stopped and looked down. The cool, silver light streamed out from under the door and washed over my bare feet like water on the beach. The last time I'd stood in this spot, Justine had encouraged me to go inside. I waited for similar encouragement now, but it didn't come.

I grabbed the glowing doorknob – and yanked my

123

hand back when the brass scalded my palm. It felt like I'd just touched an open flame, but the knob wasn't hot. It was ice cold. It burned a shimmery blue and seemed to pulsate in time to my pounding heart.

Closing my eyes, I pictured the inside of the room as I'd last seen it. White furniture. Crystal perfume bottles. A million bursts of light reflected in floor-to-ceiling mirrors.

I took the knob, twisted, shoved the door.

The silver light went out.

I fumbled for the cell phone in my sweatshirt and flipped it open. I aimed it inside the room, but the dim beam was swallowed by blackness.

I glanced down the empty hallway. The crack beneath Betty's door, lit just seconds ago, was also dark.

I exhaled. The power must've gone out. Lamps had been turned on in Zara's room, and my overactive nerves had simply transformed their normal light into something else. Which was completely understandable, considering everything I'd learned in the Marchands' house – and this was my first time back there since the day Winter Harbor froze.

Just to be sure, I moved further into the room. The air grew thicker, heavier. It smelled stale, like the door and windows hadn't been opened in months. The darkness brightened slightly when I neared the wall of windows, thanks to a high full moon. Reaching the first window, I looked out at the ocean crashing onto the shore a hundred feet below, then turned and peered around the room.

My eyes had adjusted enough to see several feet in front of me, and I didn't know whether to be reassured or disappointed when I saw that the room was empty. There was no furniture, no dresser for crystal perfume bottles to line. The mirrors had been removed from the walls, exposing peeling wallpaper. And just as it had in Betty's room, the carpet had been ripped up, revealing dull wooden planks.

If she'd somehow come back to life, this wasn't where Zara was hiding.

'Sleep,' I said quietly, starting back across the room. 'You need it. Now.'

My eyes were fixed on the door as I walked, so I didn't see the lamp in the middle of the room until my right leg knocked into it and sent it clattering to the floor. The sudden noise shattered the silence, and I lunged for the lamp to keep it from rolling and waking Paige downstairs. My fingers grabbed the base, and I gently turned it upright and placed it on the floor.

My entire body ached to run back downstairs, but I stayed put long enough to tug on the lamp's thin, short chain.

The bulb glowed white. In its illuminated circle I could see a cord that ran from the lamp base and plugged into an outlet on the nearest wall.

And lying on the floor nearby, a rowing boat oar, its trail of shiny red anchors glittering like garnets in the bright light.

CHAPTER II

'It's raining rats and spiders.'

I stared at the windscreen. The wipers fired back and forth, but the water streamed down the glass like they were still.

'Rats and spiders?' Paige repeated.

Dad smiled at her in the rear-view mirror. 'Way back when, Vanessa didn't like the idea of cute cats and dogs falling from the sky. She was, however, indifferent to rodents and creepy bugs. We've been using the phrase to describe heavy rain since.' He paused. 'Isn't that right?'

I could tell he wanted me to share the story of *how* we had eventually decided on rats and spiders – which included a lengthy family process of elimination involving charts and lists that had taken place over two nights and lots of Chinese food – but I wasn't in the mood. I was tired, achy, and still trying to make sense of everything that had happened over the weekend.

'Yes,' I said instead.

'Well,' Paige said, 'it's definitely an accurate

description of what's going on out there. Thanks again for the ride, Mr Sands.'

'Thank you for taking the scenic route with me while I dropped off books to a colleague. And if the weather's still this bad after school, just call and let me know. I –'

He slammed on the brake. I jerked forward, hard enough to make the seat belt lock and tug me back.

'Dad, what –'

The car swerved to the left, cutting me off. It swung back to the right, and then left again. As Dad spun the steering wheel, fighting to regain control on the slick road, I dug my feet into the floor and grabbed the ceiling handle. In the back seat, Paige squealed; I glanced in the side-view mirror just as she covered her face with both hands.

A second later, the front left tyre hit a kerb. The car rocked, then stopped.

'Oh no,' Paige breathed.

My fingers shook as I tried to unbuckle the seat belt. The latch gave on the third try, and I twisted in the passenger seat to look in the back. 'Are you okay?'

She, too, was looking back, through the rear window.

'Paige,' I said. 'What is it?'

'It's bad,' Dad said. 'Call nine-one-one. I'll be right back.'

'Wait –'

But he was already gone.

Paige's eyes were wide as she turned back and slid down the seat. 'There's a bus. Turned over, on the pier. Its front end looks like a giant accordion.'

'Did you see what happened?'

She shook her head. 'The rain was too thick.'

'Can you please watch my dad?' I asked, rummaging through my backpack. I found my phone and reported the accident. After I hung up, I climbed between the two front seats and stood on my knees next to Paige.

The bus's back end was hanging over the side of the pier by the aquarium. It was hard to tell what had caused the accident, as dozens of cars now filled the road in front of the pier. Many people approached the bus to try to help, and others stayed near their vehicles, talking on their cell phones and gesturing wildly.

It didn't take long for the police to arrive. Ambulances came next. Then fire trucks. Dad talked to several officers, apparently telling them what he'd witnessed. Paige and I watched through the window until the emergency workers emerged from the bus with the first passenger on a stretcher. From our position fifty feet away, I couldn't tell if it was a man or a woman, but one thing was clear: the passenger wasn't moving.

Dad returned moments later, completely drenched, and we took a long, slow detour around the accident. By the time we pulled up to Hawthorne, first period was half over.

'If we hurry, we can still make the alumni assembly.' Paige threw open her door and dashed through the rain, using a copy of *The Winter's Tale* as an umbrella.

'Vanessa . . .'

I'd started sliding across the back seat but stopped when Dad spoke.

'You'll be careful?' he asked.

I looked at him. 'With what?'

'With . . .' He looked out at the school, through the windscreen, and back at me. 'I don't know. Never mind. Have a good day, okay?'

I climbed out of the car and closed the door. Standing on the pavement, I watched him drive away, hardly feeling the rain soak my hair, my clothes, my shoes.

Did he know something? Did he know that *I* knew something? Or was his cautionary request simply a result of seeing an entire busload of people, all of whom had mothers, fathers, family who cared about them, careen towards tragedy?

'Vanessa!' Paige shouted. 'Come on!'

I waited for the Volvo to round the corner before turning and running up the steps. Paige held open the door for me and then hurried down the hall. I wanted to ask what the big deal was, but Paige was too fast. The distance between us grew as we neared the auditorium, and when she reached the entrance, I was so far behind she pointed inside, waved, and disappeared.

I was still several feet away and considering spending the rest of the period in the girls' bathroom when Ms Mulligan poked her head out of the auditorium.

'Vanessa,' she whispered loudly. 'You're just in time!'

In trying to avoid eye contact, I caught sight of the flyer hanging next to the auditorium doors.

'The Annual Alumni College Roundtable?' I read out loud.

'The most anticipated event of the entire application season,' Ms Mulligan said.

'It sounds great,' I said, backing away, 'but I actually have a huge AP Calc test later that I need to study for. And I need to keep up the grades if I'm going to get into a great college, right?'

'I can help.'

I spun around to see a boy I didn't know standing by a nearby water fountain. He used the end of his tie to wipe his mouth before smiling at me.

'I have study hall this period, and I'm an excellent tutor,' he said. 'I've been studying calculus since sixth grade.'

'How long ago was that?' I asked.

'Three years.'

A freshman. He couldn't have known Justine, so he wasn't offering out of sympathy. And I'd never seen him before let alone talked to him, so chances were slim that he was confusing me for someone he actually knew.

'I'm also fluent in four languages,' he continued, stepping towards me. 'Do you take French? Spanish? How about –'

'Thanks, but I think I'm okay. And I probably should check out the roundtable for at least a few minutes.'

His face fell. Consoled by the fact that students were expected to be quiet during assemblies, which meant I could use the time to sort out my thoughts in a notebook, I followed Ms Mulligan inside the auditorium.

'I saved you a seat.' She took my elbow and steered me towards the faculty and staff section.

Hoping for an alternative, I scanned the room for Paige, finally spotting her, seemingly transfixed, in the front row. Several empty seats surrounded her, but I wasn't about to sit that close to the stage or be so exposed to the rest of the senior class. The back row would be ideal, but a quick check showed only one empty seat.

Right next to Parker King.

'I'm going to sit with friends,' I whispered, pulling away. 'But thanks.'

I didn't wait to see if she was disappointed, surprised, or both. Instead, I veered towards the back row before

I could change my mind. I excused myself as I climbed over a dozen pairs of feet and ignored my classmates' annoyed looks. At least they were all girls, which was one benefit of sitting by Parker.

'Hi,' I said when I finally reached the empty seat.

'Hey,' he said, not looking up from his iPod.

'Do you mind . . . ?'

He glanced at me, then at the chair. 'No,' he said with a shrug. 'Whatever.'

Puzzled, I sat down. Part of me was relieved that Parker wasn't instantly smitten like so many other guys seemed to be . . . but a bigger part was confused. He'd talked to me on the first day of school, supposedly without knowing about Justine. He'd made a point of trying to find me when he'd found a picture of her. And we'd spent quite a bit of time together in the park last week.

Not falling at my feet was one thing. But after all our recent interaction, now he acted like he didn't even know who I was.

I sat back and watched his thumb move around the iPod's small white dial, turning up the volume. Caleb had used music to tune out Zara and encouraged Simon to do the same. Was that what Parker was doing? Trying to drown out some sort of signal I didn't know I was sending – or how to control?

I took out a notebook and turned to a blank page. As I pretended to write down what the guest speakers were saying, I sneaked quick glances at Parker. His hands weren't shaking. His knees weren't trembling. His forehead wasn't perspiring. If being near me made him uncomfortable enough to turn up the volume until I could hear it coming from the plastic buds in his ears, he didn't show it.

'Freshman year's many things.'

The familiar voice caught my attention. I looked up to see Justine's friend Natalie Clark, whom Paige and I had run into in the Common on the first day of school, at the podium on stage.

'It's fun.'

I sank lower in my seat as she smiled and addressed the crowd.

'Exciting. Intellectually stimulating.'

I raised my notebook to hold in front of my face.

'It's also really hard. Especially when you're dealing with external challenges.'

I was too late. She'd spotted me. Our eyes met, and her head tilted.

'College can be difficult all on its own, but when you're also struggling with personal issues on top of classes and homework, the way I've been, the way others in this room certainly are and still will be months from now, it can be unbearable.'

She didn't look at anyone else while speaking, so I knew these words were meant for me. I looked down at my notebook and scribbled quickly, hoping she'd think I was appreciatively transcribing her helpful speech.

'Hey.'

I was so determined to avoid Natalie's sympathetic stare I didn't realise Parker was talking to me until his thumb was on my hand. The gesture stopped my pen instantly.

'Want to get out of here?' He'd removed one earphone and now leaned towards me, his face blank.

'Yes.'

He looked past me to the faculty and staff sitting a few rows down. When they appeared to be sufficiently distracted, he climbed onto his seat and dropped over the back of the chair. I hesitated before doing the same, and took his hand when he offered it. He released mine as soon as my feet hit the floor, which helped ease my nervousness. His female fans started whispering once they realised what we were doing, but if their disapproval tipped off Ms Mulligan or any of her guidance-counselling cohorts, we were out of the auditorium too fast to find out.

In the hallway, he walked ahead of me, not bothering

to make sure I followed. And I almost didn't; when we neared the library I was tempted to go inside without alerting him, but I was curious. About where he was going, why he'd asked me to come, and why he acted around me the way he did. So I trailed him through several other hallways and to a set of wide, dark wood doors.

'The Eric C. King Water Polo Lounge?' I asked, reading the sign above the doors.

'It should be empty now.' He took a key from his pants pocket, then unlocked and opened the door. 'After you.'

I stepped into the large room. It was filled with leather couches and chairs, sleek silver tables, and a flat-screen TV so wide it took up the entire length of a wall. Floor-to-ceiling windows overlooked the swimming pool. Banners, trophies, and team photos were displayed throughout the room.

'Your dad must be proud,' I said, nearing a framed photo of Eric C. King himself. In the picture he was cutting a satin ribbon that hung across the very doors we'd just passed through.

Parker ignored the question. 'You know, you're only the second girl I've had up here.'

I shot him a look.

'Not like that. I swear. Despite popular opinion, I

actually *don't* spend all my free time hooking up.' He paused. 'Do you know Felicia May?'

'The gymnast?'

'Right. After she came to a match last year, she wouldn't leave me alone. She e-mailed me twenty times a day and followed me all over school.'

'What a hassle.'

'Thank you. Not everyone is as understanding.' He grinned. 'Anyway, one morning last March, Felicia followed me to what had been up until then a guys-only haven. I tried to get her to leave, but she wouldn't, and once we were inside I had to bring in reinforcements. She didn't last very long with the rest of the water polo team up here, watching and critiquing the girls' swim team practising down below.'

'Critiquing?'

'After spending so much time in the water, we're all excellent judges of form.'

I rolled my eyes as he took two bottles of water from a refrigerator. He handed me one, then flopped on the couch and turned on the TV. I still didn't know why he'd asked me to come here with him, but he certainly wasn't acting like it was because he couldn't wait for us to be alone together.

'Are you seeing anyone?' The question was out before I knew I wanted to ask it.

Something flashed across his face – disappointment, or regret. But it was fleeting, and in the next moment he winked at me. 'Why? You interested?'

'I have a boyfriend,' I reminded him, my face flushing.

'And?'

'And my locker's next to Sarah Tepper's. I overheard her talking about you the other day, so I just wondered if you guys were going out.'

'Nope.' He raised the remote, changed channels. 'I'm not going out with Sarah Tepper – or anyone else. Nor do I want to. Feel free to post that on the school website. Maybe they'll leave me alone.'

He said this casually, easily, not like he was harbouring deep, secret feelings for someone. And being in love was the only reason he'd be immune – or whatever you wanted to call it – to the signals other guys responded to.

There went that theory.

'Wow.'

I followed his gaze to the TV – and a live image of a toppled bus, its front end scrunched like an accordion.

'The driver died,' Parker said, reading the text running along the bottom of the screen. 'Four are missing and eight others are in critical condition. Bummer.'

He raised the remote and changed the channel.

'Wait,' I said, heart thudding. 'Go back.'

He looked at me curiously but did as I asked. I walked across the room, my heart pounding in my ears.

'Vanessa?' he asked when I stopped inches from the screen. 'What is it?'

It was a girl, talking to a police officer. A girl with long, dark hair. A white dress.

And silver eyes.

CHAPTER 12

'What do you think about Chicago? Or Denver? Or Honolulu?'

I glanced up from the *Boston Globe*. 'Honolulu?'

Paige took a booklet from the stack on the table between us. 'University of Hawaii. Home to palm trees, rainbows, and turquoise water.' She opened the pamphlet and frowned. 'Actually, its proximity to the ocean, regardless of colour, is a pretty big negative.'

Since our arrival at the Beanery, I'd been reading and rereading the paper's coverage of yesterday's bus accident, scrutinising the accompanying photos for the girl from the news broadcast, but the mention of water reminded me I was thirsty. Again. Less than a week later, the strength I'd felt after dropping into Winter Harbor was fading fast.

'Ms Mulligan must be thrilled that you've fallen under her spell so fast,' I said before draining my iced tea.

'I'd just never really thought about it before, you know? Back home, college is optional. Those who go don't go far, and they usually come back when it's over and end up doing what they would've done if they'd never left.'

'Like managing popular tourist restaurants?' I asked.

She shrugged. 'I just figured if that's what I was going to wind up doing anyway, why waste time pretending I had another choice?'

'But you do have other choices.'

'Yes. I could be an architect. A graphic designer. A doctor.' She grinned. 'Okay, probably not a doctor. That's too much school – and blood.'

I took a long draw on the straw until it sputtered in the empty glass. 'I think that's great, Paige. Really. But isn't Honolulu kind of far?'

'That's just one option.' She sifted through the pamphlets. 'There's also Phoenix, Des Moines, and Houston, which are –'

'Closer, but still really far away.' I leaned towards her. 'New England's the college capital of the United States. You don't like any of the choices around here?'

Her smile faltered. 'They're too competitive. My grades are decent enough that Hawthorne let me in, but I'm not cut-throat enough to endure four years of crazy academic pressure.'

I knew her current preferences were due to other factors – like wanting to put thousands of miles between herself and everything she wanted to forget – but the discussion would have to wait until later.

'It's almost time,' I said. 'Be right back.'

She raised her mug. 'I'm getting a refill. Do you want one?'

'Please. Thanks.'

As she stood and started for the counter, I took my backpack from the floor and wove through the small tables and chairs crammed in the tiny coffee shop. The only restroom was all the way in the back and occupied when I reached it.

I leaned against the wall to wait and wondered how much I was going to have to lie in the next half an hour. I considered trying to get out of the interview, but I knew Ms Mulligan would've just rescheduled for a time when she could attend, too. And as much as I didn't want to feign enthusiasm and try to talk myself up, I wanted even less to be critiqued afterwards.

Two minutes passed, then three, then four. After five minutes, I knocked lightly. When there was no answer, I stepped closer and brought one ear to the door. It was hard to hear anything over the buzz of people talking and laughing, but I thought I could make out the sound of running water. I waited another few seconds and knocked again, harder.

No answer.

I turned to flag down a server and ask if the restroom had been locked accidentally when a faucet squeaked and the quiet rush stopped.

'Sorry,' a guy said, opening the door. I didn't recognise him, but he was wearing a Hawthorne uniform, which was about as wrinkled as my own. His eyes were red. Before leaving the restroom he ducked back inside and yanked a wad of paper towels from the dispenser.

'No problem,' I said.

He blew his nose and shuffled past me. Sinking into a chair at a table near the coffee shop's entrance, he placed his head in his hands and stared at the screen of an open laptop. The only times he released his head were to wipe his eyes and dab at his nose. Not wanting to be among the customers who might make him feel worse by watching curiously, I darted into the restroom and closed and locked the door behind me.

The room was tiny; there was barely any space between the toilet and sink for my feet. I balanced my backpack on the edge of the sink as I removed the clothes I'd packed that morning.

This is your chance! a recent e-mail from Ms Mulligan had declared.

Stand out from other applicants and show this Bates alum the wonderful, unique individual you are. I'd suggest wearing something mature and memorable (i.e., ditch the school uniform). Knock 'em dead!

Another note had followed a minute later.

My apologies for the well-intentioned yet highly insensitive encouraging phrase. I wasn't thinking. Good luck! – KM

I didn't need luck. What I needed was someone else's life. But since that wasn't going to happen, I'd decided to make the best of a bad situation and at least try to be presentable, if not memorable. This wasn't in hopes of being accepted to Bates, but of making a nice enough impression on Ms Mulligan's contact that he or she gave a good report and she eased up. I could always come up with some reason not to apply later.

I changed quickly, putting on a black pencil skirt; a crisp, white button-down shirt; and a fitted black cashmere cardigan with pearl buttons. I gathered my school uniform and sweatshirt and shoved them in my backpack, redid my ponytail, and reached towards the sink.

I'm so sorry . . . I hate that I'm writing this . . .

I'd just leaned down to splash water on my face when my eyes fell on what looked to be a printed-out e-mail. It sat folded on one corner of the sink, the paper thin and wrinkled with wear.

I wish things could have been different . . . we're simply not meant to be . . .

The guy who'd used the restroom before me. This must be his note, its message the reason he'd seemed so upset. Feeling guilty for unintentionally intruding on his privacy, I looked away and dried my face with a handful of paper towels.

There was a knock on the door. I lifted my backpack, then refolded the note so that the paper's blank side was exposed, and tucked it behind the soap dispenser. It would be harder to see for someone who wasn't looking for it, and easy for someone who was.

Back in the coffee shop, my heart sank when I saw a man sitting with a maroon Bates folder on the table in front of him. In between checking his BlackBerry, he glanced up and around the room.

My interviewer was male. For some reason, when I'd practised my responses to the anticipated questions earlier, I'd imagined a woman doing the asking. Even worse, he was fairly young. Talking to a grandfatherly type might be manageable, but this guy, dressed in trendy dark-wash jeans and a tan wool coat, appeared to be in his early thirties.

Heading towards him, I tried to get a look at his hands. The best I could hope for now was that he was married and completely, hopelessly in love with his wife.

'Vanessa?' He stood as I neared and held out one hand.

No wedding band.

'Matt Harrison.' We shook hands, and then he pulled out my chair, hitting the back of the one behind it. The seated young woman gave him a look before scooting forward, but he didn't notice. 'It's so nice to meet you.'

'You, too.' I sat, feeling ridiculous in my mature and memorable outfit.

'Can I get you anything? Coffee? Tea? Muffin?'

'I'm fine, thank you.' I caught Paige's eye across the room. She still stood at the counter, waiting for her order. When she saw me, she gave me a quick thumbs-up.

'So,' he said, sitting down and crossing his arms on the table. 'Senior year.' He looked at me expectantly, like I was supposed to elaborate.

'Yup.'

'Kathryn says you're an excellent student.'

'I do okay.'

'Modest, too. That's refreshing.'

The table was small, and he sat so close I could smell his aftershave. I tried to lean back, but the tables and chairs were so near to each other I didn't have far to go.

'Why don't I tell you about my experience at Bates?' he asked. 'Then you can ask me any questions you may have, and we'll go from there.'

'That sounds great, Mr Harrison.'

'Matt. Please. Mr Harrison is the old guy filling my parents' house with Revolutionary War memorabilia.'

I half listened as he talked about admissions, lecture size, accessible faculty, and job-placement rates. Not that it mattered, but he didn't tell me anything I hadn't already heard from Simon. The monologue, however, relieved me of having to speak, which I appreciated.

'What do you need?' he asked twenty minutes later.

I tuned back in. 'I'm sorry?'

'As far as I'm concerned, Bates would be privileged to have you. I'll do everything I can to make sure you're confident that if you enrol with us, you'll want for nothing. Financial assistance, your own dorm room, off-campus housing . . . all are possible.'

He talked as though I'd already been accepted, but that decision was up to Admissions, not him. Plus, this interview was just one small part of the application process – and I hadn't said more than ten words. Which meant Matt Harrison thought Vanessa the siren, not Vanessa the student, would be a great match for Bates.

'Paige,' I said, catching her eye across the room.

'Excuse me?'

'My best friend.' I gave him the biggest smile I could muster. 'She's also a senior at Hawthorne. If I attend Bates, I'll need her to as well.'

He sat back as Paige approached the table and pulled up an empty chair. Sensing I wasn't thrilled about the idea of interviewing, she'd asked earlier if I'd like her to come in case I needed back-up or an excuse to cut the meeting short.

'Paige is an outstanding student,' I said. 'She just transferred to Hawthorne from the Winter Harbor School in Maine, and she's already all caught up.'

'It's no big deal,' Paige said, easily jumping into the conversation without knowing where it was going or why. 'The curriculum wasn't that different.'

'It's a *huge* deal. Harvard's already knocking on her door. And Yale, and Brown.' I looked at her. 'What did they offer again? Full tuition? A furnished apartment?'

'Two bedrooms,' she said with a nod. 'Jacuzzi tub.'

Matt glanced at me, and I smiled. Then, as my draw made him more interested in my wants than those of his alma mater, he picked up his BlackBerry and started typing. 'I don't know that Bates has ever awarded such a package, but let me see what I can do.' He stopped typing and looked at the phone's screen. A second later, he stood and started backing up, towards the door. 'Be right back,' he said, bringing the phone to his ear.

'Thanks,' I said when he was outside.

'He must've been really grilling you,' Paige said.

'Not terribly. I just needed a break from the spotlight.'

'Is that why you're sweating like you just sprinted the Boston Marathon?'

I brought one hand to my forehead; it was hot and damp. So was the rest of my face and neck. Blotting my skin with paper napkins only made a fresh layer of perspiration appear.

'Why don't you go have a drink and regroup?' Paige asked. 'If you need more time, I'll ask for a private jet or a petting zoo or something and get Mr Bates back on the phone.' She paused. 'By the way . . . why am I making such hijacker-like demands?'

I improvised quickly. 'I think straight-A Simon gave a glowing recommendation, because I've pretty much already been accepted. And Bates alumni who come from Hawthorne must make some sizable donations, because Matt seems very determined to bring me on board and keep me happy. But I told him there was no way I was going without you.'

'Does Bates have a satellite campus in, like, San Diego?'

'Two, actually. You'll have your pick.'

'Fabulous,' she said as I retrieved my backpack from

the floor and stood up. 'Oh, you might want to go say hi to your friend.'

'What friend?'

'The one who works here.'

I looked across the room. 'I don't know anyone who works here.'

'Well, someone who works here knows you. I didn't get her name, but she was asking all sorts of questions – including how you were feeling, like she'd heard you were sick or something.'

The counter was lined with stools, all of which were occupied. I could make out only one employee through the crowd: a young guy who ran the counter's length between trips to the cappuccino machine.

'I'll say hi,' I said, wanting to get out of there before Matt returned. I leaned down and gave Paige a quick hug. 'And thank you again. You're the best.'

Back at our table, I took my sweatshirt from my bag, put it on over my clothes, and pulled up the hood. The additional warmth only made me sweat more, and I had to squeeze the iced-tea glass with both hands to keep it from slipping out of my grasp.

The cool liquid tasted so good I struggled to drink it without gulping. It wasn't until I'd swallowed the last drop that I realised that this iced tea was different from the one I'd finished before changing in the restroom.

It was salty. My last drink hadn't been because I'd run out of salt earlier in the day.

Keeping the hood pulled low, I peered over my shoulder. If Paige had put salt in my drink after noticing how often I added the secret ingredient to anything I consumed, she wasn't watching for my reaction. She was chatting away, probably rattling off additional demands to Matt, who had returned and was taking notes on a legal pad.

I turned back and flipped through the packets in the ceramic bowl in the middle of the table. Raw sugar, Equal, Splenda.

I went to the counter, wedged myself between two female customers, and waved for the barista's attention. It took a few tries for him to see me, but finally he came over.

'Iced tea, please,' I said.

'Sweetened or unsweetened?'

I hesitated. 'One of each?'

He opened a refrigerator under the opposite counter and took out two pitchers. He filled two glasses and returned to me.

'How much?' I asked, reaching into my sweatshirt pocket.

'Don't worry about it.'

'What? But –'

I stopped when he spun away and darted towards the hissing cappuccino machine. After he'd moved on to his next customer and it was clear he wasn't coming back, I put a ten-dollar bill on the counter, then took a sip from each glass.

Neither was salty.

'Your friend told him not to charge you.'

The low voice was near my ear. I turned and pressed my back against the counter, relaxing only slightly when I recognised the sad Hawthorne student from the restroom. He stood inches away, holding an empty plate with one hand and wiping his eyes with the other.

'What friend?' I asked.

'The woman who works here. She told him she'd cover you.'

I scanned the room, then craned my neck to check behind the counter and peer into the kitchen. Besides the barista, the only visible employees were a dishwasher and a baker. Both were male. 'Did she say why?'

Before he could answer, a splitting pain shot from one ear to the other, passing through my skull like a bullet.

I struggled to keep my eyes open. Somehow, in the reflection of a glass muffin dome, they locked on another pair that shone like sunlight glittering across the ocean's surface. When those eyes found mine, a new source of pain burst in the centre of my head and stayed there, pulsating.

I didn't have to turn around to see who watched me.

'Zara,' I breathed.

And then I collapsed to the floor.

CHAPTER 13

The following Saturday morning, I lay in bed with the comforter pulled over my head, listening. For Zara and Raina. For Justine and Betty. For someone to tell me something, anything about what was going on.

But all I heard was music coming from my old bedroom. Dad singing somewhere downstairs. Mom banging pots and pans in the kitchen.

Giving up, I threw off the covers and reached for the water bottle on my nightstand. I'd been thirstier than usual all night and had refilled the bottle four times before dawn. It was almost empty again now, so I finished it off, went to the bathroom for another refill, and then followed the loud country music down the hall.

My old bedroom door was closed. I knocked, but the sound was lost in the strumming and singing coming from the other side. I tried again, louder.

'Paige?' I called out. 'Can I come in?'

No answer. No change in music volume either.

Still knocking, I cracked open the door. Paige was sitting at the desk with her back to me. I said her name again, but her head remained lowered. Guessing she was working on college applications – though not sure how she could concentrate with the music so loud – I crossed the room and tapped her shoulder.

'Vanessa!' She shot up in the chair. One hand flew to her chest, the other over the open book before her.

I pointed to the iPod dock station on the dresser. When she nodded, I reached over and turned down the music.

'Sorry,' I said. 'I knocked, but you didn't hear me.'

'No, *I'm* sorry. I shouldn't have had it so loud.' She looked around quickly, like she'd misplaced something, then lifted her messenger bag from the floor by the chair and placed it over the book. Before it was covered, I glimpsed small, neat handwriting, a flash of white. 'What's up?'

She smiled at me, but her eyes kept flicking back to the bag, like it might suddenly slide off the desk and expose the book.

'Everything okay?' I asked.

'Of course.' She waved one hand. 'I was just journaling. Lots on the brain: college stuff, Riley . . . you know.'

Sensing she'd be more comfortable with some distance between her private thoughts and me, I went to the other side of the room and sat on the bed. 'Speaking of stuff on the brain,' I said carefully, 'I keep thinking about what you said a few weeks ago. About Raina and Zara.'

For half a second, her face froze. In the next instant, she stood up and joined me on the bed. 'The day in the park? When my mind was playing terrible tricks on me?'

I nodded. 'That's just it. I know they weren't really there because there's no way they could've survived the harbour freezing . . .' I hesitated, debating how much to say.

'But you can't help wondering . . . what if?' she finished.

'Exactly.' There was certainly more to it than that, but maybe we could talk about the possibility without my divulging what – or who – I'd seen at the coffee shop yesterday.

'I wonder, too.' She stretched out, hugged a pillow to her chest. 'Sometimes it scares me so much I lie here, wide awake, just waiting for them to appear at the window or jump out of the closet.'

I frowned, thinking of the countless nights I'd done the same thing in this very room. Although then I'd been waiting for the bogeyman, and Justine had been there to help coax me to sleep.

'But you know what I tell myself?' Paige said.

I shook my head.

'That Grandma B would know. She'd hear them, or

sense them, or something, and she would tell me long before anything could happen. And she said that she hasn't heard them –'

'Since the harbour froze.' Seeing the surprise on her face, I added, 'We talked about it a little when you and Oliver went out to get breakfast. She told me the same thing.'

'Oh.' She lowered the pillow to her lap, traced an embroidered flower with her finger. 'Did you guys talk about anything else?'

'Not really.' Now wasn't the time to reveal what else I'd hoped to learn from Betty. 'To be honest, she seemed a little . . . off.'

Paige's eyes met mine. 'Off how?'

'I don't know . . . tired. Distant. Not quite herself. You didn't notice?'

'No. But it'd be understandable. Between her physical and emotional recoveries she's got a lot going on.' She added lightly, 'Maybe *she* should keep a journal.'

I smiled. 'And Oliver seemed okay to you? Not extra uptight or anything?'

She considered the question. 'He seemed even more protective of her than usual, but I thought that was nice – not weird.'

'You're right. It's great that they're looking out for each other. And Betty does seem to be doing amazingly well physically. She looked a million times stronger last weekend than she did at the end of the summer.'

'Well, she *is* Winter Harbor's favourite super senior citizen.'

I forced myself to ask the next question before I could chicken out. 'Do you know if she's doing anything special to regain strength? Besides swimming?'

'Eight times a day? I don't think so. That doesn't leave much time for yoga and weight lifting.'

'No special diet? Vitamins or supplements?'

I'd hoped for hints as to how I might build up my own strength, but I'd gone too far. Paige's eyebrows lowered as she tilted her head.

'Not that I know of,' she said. 'Why?'

My face flared. 'No reason. I just –'

'Knock, knock!'

This time, Paige and I both jumped. I must not have closed the door all the way because Mom poked her head into the room without actually knocking or waiting for a response.

'Morning, girls!' she sang. 'Just wanted to let you know that there are fresh goodies – and lots of fun – waiting for you downstairs.'

'Thanks, Mom. We'll be right there.' I waited for her to start down the hallway before turning back to Paige. I was prepared to mumble my way through some sort of explanation for wanting to know the secret to Betty's health success, but she was already sliding off the bed and reaching for her robe.

'I'm starved. Do you mind if we eat first and chat more later?'

I swallowed a disappointed sigh. 'Not at all.'

In the hall she hurried towards the back staircase that led to the kitchen. I started to follow, but something by the window at the opposite end of the hall stopped me.

A fleeting flash of silver.

'Vanessa? You coming?'

I gave Paige a quick smile and motioned to the bathroom. 'Be there in a second.'

As her footsteps faded down the stairs, I dashed towards the light. I told myself it was just the sun reflecting on a passing car, but I couldn't shake what Paige had just said about waiting for Raina and Zara to appear outside the bedroom windows.

Reaching the end of the hall, I held my breath, slowly pulled open the sheer white drape . . . and exhaled when I spotted the cluster of silver balloons tied to a lamppost across the street. A neighbour having a birthday party was no reason to freak out.

Simon, however, was.

He was standing just down the pavement from our house, looking around like he wasn't sure where he was.

My heart hammered in my chest and my entire body burned as I flew down the main stairwell, across the living room, and through the front door. He was scanning the row of brownstones and somehow looking better than I'd ever seen him in jeans, a grey sweater, and a navy blue peacoat. He wore real shoes – brown leather ones, with laces – instead of his regular sneakers, and his dark hair was shorter than the last time I'd seen him. It was shinier, too, like he'd used some sort of styling gel.

Those appearance changes were enough to process, but one thing really got me.

'Where are your glasses?' I asked.

His head snapped in my direction. When he saw me, relief washed over his face. He pocketed a piece of paper (directions, I assumed, since he'd never visited me in Boston before), and walked towards the steps, stopping before the last one.

'I got contacts,' he said.

'Why?'

'To get that much closer to a microscope lens.'

I smiled. That *would* be the reason.

'I got your messages. I'm sorry I didn't respond, but I was working in the lab and didn't get them until late last night, and I figured you were already sleeping, so . . .'

'So you just decided to get in your car and drive a hundred and fifty miles?'

He looked down at his feet, then back up at me. 'To see you, Vanessa . . . I'd drive a lot further on much shorter notice.'

I ran down the steps and into his arms. 'Do me a favour?' I said into his neck. 'There's a coffee shop on the corner of Newbury and Exeter. Meet me there in twenty minutes?'

Simon's arms tightened, and I knew he worried something was wrong.

'Full house today. I'd rather have you all to myself.'

He kissed my forehead. 'Twenty minutes.'

He watched me run back up the stairs. I waved from the doorway, then peeked through the curtains to make sure he headed in the right direction.

I've never showered faster in my life; I didn't even bother with salt. I did take the time, however, to put on lotion, dry my hair, and find the right outfit. The last task was particularly challenging, just like it always was, since I wanted to look good for Simon without looking too good for anyone else. I sifted through the clothes spilling out of the red suitcase and onto the carpet, but they were all too plain and wrinkled.

My heart beat faster as I faced Justine's closet, which was still filled with vibrant shorts and tank tops, skirts and sundresses. If she were here, she wouldn't hesitate to loan me her clothes – in fact, she'd probably insist on it.

She used to encourage me to wear bright colours instead of the neutrals I usually gravitated towards. But it still felt strange opening her closet door, especially because no one had since the day we'd left for Winter Harbor at the beginning of last summer.

I took the thin handle and pulled gently – then harder. I stared at the closet's contents, not sure what I was seeing.

Her summer clothes were gone. In their place were wool skirts, flannel pants, and cashmere sweaters. They were organised by type of clothing and colour, with the reds and oranges on the left fading to tans and ivories on the right.

No one but me ever came into this room. Had Mom asked the housekeeper to put away Justine's things without telling anyone? If so, had the housekeeper been confused and accidentally unpacked Justine's fall clothes?

Or had Mom unpacked them herself?

I was hot again. And sweating. I closed the closet, mopped my face and arms with the towel I'd used after the shower, and redid my make-up. I found a pair of clean jeans and a white T-shirt that wasn't too badly wrinkled in my suitcase, and a fitted red velvet blazer that had magically appeared in a Nordstrom shopping bag at the foot of my bed earlier in the week. My guess was that Mom had found it in one of her boxes of old yet hardly worn clothes while searching through the basement.

'Don't you look lovely?' she said when I entered the kitchen a minute later. 'I knew that jacket would look fabulous on you.'

'Why aren't they in the basement?' I asked.

My tone made her smile fall, then freeze. 'Why aren't what in the basement?'

'Justine's fall clothes. They're hanging in her closet.'

She turned to Paige. 'Is that knife sharp enough, sweetie?'

'Did you unpack them?' I walked to the table and stood right by her. 'Did the housekeeper?'

'Cheese?' She got up like I wasn't there. 'Crackers? I got a great Brie at the market the other day . . .'

I looked at Paige, who sat at the table, holding a miniature pumpkin in one hand and a carving knife in the other, clearly unsure what to do. I tried to reassure her with a quick smile before heading for the refrigerator.

'It's a pretty simple question, Mom. I just want to know –'

She yanked her head out of the open fridge and slammed the door. 'Yes, I hung up her fall clothes. I went up there to put away her summer things, but I just couldn't do it without replacing them. I couldn't leave her closet like that – so empty, so . . .'

Her voice trailed off as her breath came faster. Her eyes were wide and watery, her hands tight on the wedge of cheese. She squeezed so hard, the soft white mass bubbled between her fingers.

'It's okay.' I stepped towards her, opened my arms to pull her into a hug. 'It's hard, I know. I didn't mean to –'

'Cauliflower.'

I stopped. Mom looked up at Dad.

'For hair. For the jack-o'-lanterns.' He held a spear of cauliflower next to his head so we could see the resemblance. 'What do we think?'

'Dad, now's not really the time to –'

'Brilliant.'

I grabbed the counter to keep from lunging for Mom. Still squeezing the Brie, she turned away from me and joined Dad at the sink.

'We think that's brilliant.' She beamed up at him. 'Thank you.'

He kissed the tip of her nose, then placed the cauliflower in the sink and gently prised the cheese from her grip.

I watched him guide her hands under the faucet and turn on the water. He said something quietly, and she laughed. My gaze travelled from them to the empty cider mugs on the counter, to the pumpkins on the table, to Paige, still holding a carving knife.

And I realised this was how it had always been. The vacations, game nights, family dinners. It had all been to keep us from dealing with anything real. To distract us from the fact that Mom worked a hundred hours a week and Dad wrote about as much in between teaching and reading other people's books so that there would be less time to fill with lies.

All those years, I hadn't been the only one pretending. The only difference now was that I was ready to stop, and Mom and Dad clearly weren't.

'I'm going out,' I said, backing away. 'I'll have my cell if you decide you actually want to talk.'

CHAPTER 14

On my way to the Beanery, I decided I needed to confront Dad. He was the one who'd created the uncomfortable, embarrassing situation that everyone wanted to ignore. Of course, if he'd never had the affair, I wouldn't exist, but given everything that had happened, I thought my absence would be a fair trade-off. If I'd never been born, Mom and Dad could have had a normal, happy marriage. Justine would be alive. And if they still carved pumpkins every fall, it'd be because they genuinely wanted to spend time together – not because they felt the need to strengthen the happy-family façade.

So we'd have it out. That was all there was to it. I'd tell him what I knew and make him talk about all we'd been ignoring for seventeen years.

But first, Simon.

He was sitting at a corner table in the coffee shop, his back to me. I hurried over, relieved to see that only a few tables were occupied. When I reached him, I put my arms around his shoulders and pressed my cheek against his.

'You have no idea how happy I am to see you,' I said.

He was smiling as I sat down, but his expression quickly turned to concern. 'Is everything okay?' he asked, his eyes travelling from my damp forehead to my damper chin.

Instantly self-conscious, I took a paper napkin from the dispenser and blotted my face. 'It's better now.' When his frown deepened, I added, 'Just more family drama. Mom's trying to resurrect the past via fall produce, and Dad's enabling instead of helping her move forward. You know – a typical Saturday in the Sands household.'

He placed one hand on my free one, which rested on the table between us. His fingers curled around mine and his thumb stroked my palm. 'You're warm.'

That was an understatement. My body felt like it'd just rolled across a bed of burning coals. 'I was so excited to see you I practically ran the whole way here.'

The corners of his mouth lifted slightly, then dropped. 'Paige told me what happened the other day.'

'What other day?'

'When you fainted.' His eyes met mine. 'I'm guessing you didn't tell me because you didn't want me to worry. I was going to ask you about it when you came up this weekend, but then when you cancelled, I worried way more than I would have if you'd just told me up front. Hence the impromptu road trip.'

'I'm sorry.' I looked down at our hands. 'It was no big deal. I woke up as soon as I hit the floor.'

'People usually don't pass out for no reason.'

I was vaguely aware of a bell jingling, the coffee shop door opening.

'I was just a little tired,' I said, still focused on our hands. 'School's been busy, and this college stuff is –'

'A piece of cake,' a familiar male voice said.

'Parker.' Startled to see him standing right by our table, I sat back and pulled my hand from Simon's. 'What are you doing here?'

'Pre-meet caffeine fix.' He nodded to Simon. 'Hey. Parker King. I go to school with Vanessa.'

'Simon Carmichael. Vanessa's boyfriend.'

Parker didn't bat an eye as he turned towards me. 'Matt said you totally killed the interview.'

New beads of perspiration grew in the heat of Simon's questioning gaze. 'How do you know Matt?' I asked.

'Who's Matt?' Simon aimed this question at me. 'What interview?'

'Matt Harrison,' Parker said. 'Bates class of 2000. He meets with all the Hawthorne applicants. My dad's pretty connected to all the college happenings, so I found out about Vanessa's meeting through him.'

'You applied to Bates?' Simon asked quietly, like Parker wouldn't hear him.

I started to shake my head, but stopped when I felt Parker's hand on my shoulder.

'The actual application's inconsequential,' he said. 'At least it is for a very lucky few – including our lovely Vanessa here. Matt said he's never been more impressed by such a bright, beautiful prospect.'

'Okay,' Simon said, his eyes focused on my shoulder, 'first of all, she's not *our* Vanessa. Second of all –'

'Excuse me.' I jerked away and scooted backward so fast the chair legs squawked against the floor. 'Sorry. I'll be right back.'

I knew they both watched me walk away, but I didn't turn around. My head was pulsating, my throat dry. My limbs felt like I was wading through pools of Jell-O. It was all I could do to get to the counter without falling to the floor and convincing Simon that something was seriously wrong.

'Water, please,' I said, my voice no louder than a whisper. 'And salt.'

The barista hesitated, apparently puzzled by my second request, but he put down the glass and disappeared into the kitchen. I glanced behind me to see Parker had moved on and was chatting up a table of teenage girls, and Simon was absently fiddling with sugar packets.

I turned back as the barista emerged with two glasses: one tall, the other short, like a shot glass.

'You're in luck,' he said. 'Willa said she knew just what you needed.'

'Willa?' I croaked.

'Your friend. My manager.' He placed the glasses on the counter before me. 'I think the green one's wheatgrass.'

He headed for customers at the other end of the counter before I could ask anything else. Not that I would've been able to even if he'd stayed. From my chin down, it felt like sand had replaced all the liquid in my body. Talking was impossible.

I drained the salt water in three gulps. My eyes welled as the cool sensation travelled down my throat, into my stomach. Feeling stronger immediately, I reached for the shot glass. I had no idea who Willa was, but she obviously knew me – or at least something about me. If she'd meant me harm, she wouldn't have added salt to my iced tea without my requesting it the other day.

So I took the shot glass, tilted my head, and threw back the green liquid. The taste was so unexpected, so unlike the fresh, mild one I'd imagined wheatgrass would have, I almost spat it out. But then I realised what it was.

Seaweed.

I'd had seaweed only once before, when Paige insisted I try Betty's famous Sea Witch sandwich. Mistaking the goopy green strands for spinach, I'd swallowed a heaping forkful without hesitating – and choked so hard on the bitter plant that Louis the chef had swatted me on the back with a spatula. This green liquid tasted just like the seaweed had then, only stronger, saltier.

How did Willa know? Was she one of them – one of us? Was this some kind of lure designed to lower my defences?

My heart raced, and my hands shook. I was torn between leaping over the counter and fleeing the coffee shop.

'Is Willa in the back?' I asked the barista. 'Can I talk to her?'

'She already left,' he said, taking a broom from a narrow closet.

'Will she back tomorrow?'

As he swept, he tilted his head towards a nearly empty tip jar on the counter. It was labelled POOR COLLEGE STUDENT PROVISIONS.

'This should do it.'

I looked down at the hand on my sleeve – and at the two chubby fingers holding a fifty-dollar bill.

'Good tips get good results,' said the man sitting on the next stool as he lightly tapped my arm. He was older, probably in his late forties, and his forehead gleamed beneath the brim of his stained Red Sox hat. When our eyes met, he winked.

My stomach turned. I glanced at the barista, who shrugged like he could not care less what I did, and then I backed away. 'Thanks . . . but I'll just stop by and see for myself.'

Whatever reason I'd been given, the salt water and seaweed shot must've been working fast, because my head was surprisingly clear as I hurried back to Simon. When I sat across from him and saw the range of emotions – concern, jealousy, love – cross his face, I started talking before worry about his reaction could stop me.

'I saw her.'

'Her?' His eyebrows lifted. 'Her, who?'

'Zara.'

His chin sank towards his neck. 'Vanessa –'

'I know you think it's impossible –' I leaned towards him – 'you're sure that they're dead, that we never have to worry about them again. But, Simon . . . I saw her. Right here, in this coffee shop. That's why I passed out.

Because she wasn't there one second, and in the next, she was.'

I reached for his hand. He didn't pull away, but his fingers were still as mine slid across them.

'I saw her another time, too. There was a bus accident, and in the news coverage that followed, I swear I saw her talking to a police officer. And there was the rowing boat on the harbour, and the oar in her old bedroom, and –'

I stopped when he slid his hand out from under mine. He reached into a leather satchel I hadn't noticed earlier and removed a folded newspaper. As he placed the paper between us, I recognised the anchor-shaped *W* immediately.

'The *Herald*?' I asked, my heart fluttering. Afraid of what I'd find, I hadn't checked the website in days.

The paper was like a wall between us. He didn't make a move to cross it, and neither did I. I couldn't even if I'd tried; I was as frozen as the covered bodies in the black-and-white photo on the front page.

'According to the article,' Simon said, sounding tired, resigned, 'two recreational deep-sea divers found a break in the ice near Chione Cliffs and followed it to an "underwater holding pen" – the reporter's words, not mine.'

'A holding pen for what?' I asked – or at least I thought I did. My thoughts were beginning to spiral

173

again, and I wasn't sure if the question made it through the inner cyclone in my head and out of my mouth.

'At least eight deceased women who were embedded in the ice, and probably more. The divers' tanks ran low, and they had to cut the swim short.'

'And they . . . the women . . . are . . . ? They were . . . ?'

'I don't know. They haven't been identified. Not publicly, anyway.'

I closed my eyes, tried to process this new information. When I opened them again, the newspaper was gone. Simon's hands were in its place, palms facing up. I placed my hands over them, and this time his fingers automatically curled around mine.

'I love you.'

The words were like daggers in my chest. 'Simon –'

'Please.' One corner of his mouth lifted in a quick, sad smile. 'I've waited so long to say that again. You don't have to say anything back . . . but can we just let it linger there for a second? Without automatically brushing it aside?'

I didn't want to brush it aside. I wanted to say it back, because I loved him, too, more than I'd thought I could ever love anyone. I wanted us to go somewhere we couldn't be found, and talk and laugh and kiss all day, every day, for the rest of our lives. But I couldn't. We couldn't. What he felt, what he *thought* he felt . . .

it wasn't real. And I cared for him too much to let him waste his life like that.

'There was something else I wanted to talk to you about this weekend,' he said.

I looked up from our clasped hands. Without the glasses, his brown eyes were darker, warmer.

'Boston University has a great science department.'

I didn't know what I was expecting, but that wasn't it. 'Okay . . . ?'

'The professors are excellent, and their research is impressive.'

This sounded like something he'd say on one of our fake campus tours. 'You want me to apply to BU?'

'Only if you want to.' He paused. 'I already did.'

His fingers tightened around mine before releasing them. He pulled a red folder from his bag and placed it where the *Winter Harbor Herald* had been only moments before. He flipped past brochures and pamphlets to a piece of white paper.

'It's a transfer application.' He watched me carefully. '*My* transfer application.'

The beads of sweat burst, sending thin, salty trails trickling down my face. Beneath my clothes, my skin warmed and moistened. My throat started to close. 'You love Bates,' I said, trying to declare but whispering instead.

'I love *you*,' he corrected me. He leaned forward and reached for my hands, which were moving on their own, inching away from his. 'I've never been as happy as I am when I'm with you. I think about you all the time. I miss you so much when you're gone that I can't concentrate. I even blew a huge test last week because I forgot about it – it completely slipped my mind. That's never happened before.'

'So you want to transfer to keep up your GPA?' I tried to joke. It was all I could do.

'I want to transfer so I can meet you after class. And walk you home from school. And see you on the weekend without either of us having to drive a hundred and fifty miles. I want to be *with* you, Vanessa, as often as possible, for as long as possible. After everything that happened last summer . . . I just don't want to lose another second if I can help it. And I can. By moving to Boston.'

A firestorm of 'if onlys' erupted in my head. If only I were normal. If only his feelings were genuine. If only we could plan a future like any other young, happy couple.

If only, if only, if only.

'I know it's a lot to process,' he continued when I didn't say anything, 'and it probably seems to have come out of nowhere. I'm sorry for that. You know I won't do anything you don't want me to.'

I nodded, blinked back tears.

'And you don't have to give me a definite answer now . . . but maybe you could give me a hint? One small, harmless hint as to what you think?'

The hot tears spilled onto my cheeks. I brushed them away, but that only made them fall faster. Unable to meet his hopeful gaze, I looked towards the windows. Three sets of eyes burned through my clothes; I didn't have to look to know that in addition to Simon, the Red Sox fan at the counter and Parker King watched and waited for my response.

Focusing on the fuzzy orange leaves floating from the trees to the pavement, I took a deep breath and answered his question.

'I think we should break up.'

CHAPTER 15

'"Emily Dickinson is wicked bad."'

I glanced up from my history textbook. Dad sat at the picnic table on the other side of our small backyard, squinting at his laptop screen.

'What do you think that means?' he asked.

'Is the student from around here?'

'I teach at Newton Community College,' he reminded me.

'Then "wicked" doesn't mean evil. It means very.'

He gasped. 'Very bad? How can she say that about one of the greatest American poets of all time?'

'What's the next sentence?'

His eyes lowered back to the screen. '"Her words flow like hot buttah" – b-u-t-t-a-h. Whatever that is.'

'Butter,' I explained. 'So "bad" in the first sentence actually means good. She likes Emily Dickinson.'

He leaned back, eyes wide, like the words on the screen had just formed a small army and threatened to assault his scholarly vocabulary. 'Well then, why didn't she just say so?'

I hid my small, quick smile behind my textbook. I'd joined Dad outside because Mom was baking again and the oven made it too hot to do homework inside, but that didn't make us study buddies.

'I'm going to get some tea.' He stood and stretched. 'Would you like anything? Maybe a sweater?'

It was a valid question. It couldn't be more than fifty degrees out, and while he was bundled up in a thick wool sweater and corduroy pants, I wore a thin T-shirt and jeans with the cuffs rolled to my knees.

I was about to decline, but then I heard something click.

His laptop. He was getting tea, which shouldn't take longer than five minutes, including boiling time . . . and he'd closed his computer.

'My blue fleece would be great.' I lowered the textbook and widened my smile. 'It should be in my – Paige's – closet.'

He beamed like he'd just been granted tenure at Harvard. The fact that I'd asked him for anything made him so happy I almost felt guilty – especially since my blue fleece was in the laundry room waiting to be washed, not in Paige's closet, and I knew he wouldn't want to come back empty-handed.

But at this point, what was one more lie?

I watched him trudge up the steps and open the door.

Several seconds later, the back stairwell window illuminated. I pretended to read as he climbed past the window, and waited another minute to give him time to reach the landing and start down the hallway.

And then I hurled myself out of the hammock and lunged towards the picnic table.

His computer was old and took a while to shut down so the desktop appeared right away, no password required. I guided the cursor to the start bar and then glanced over my shoulder to make sure Mom wasn't watching from the kitchen. Her back was to me as she commandeered the stove, so I turned to the laptop and pulled down the recent documents.

It was a short list. There was only one document, labelled W1011. I clicked on it before I lost my nerve.

Given Dad's attempt to hide whatever he was working on, I didn't expect W1011 to be a student paper on Emily Dickinson. But I never would have guessed what it actually was.

A log. Twenty pages long, with dated entries that went back weeks. Some sections consisted of a few sentences, others of several paragraphs.

All were about me.

I checked the windows again. Mom was rummaging through a kitchen cabinet, and the back stairwell was still lit, which meant Dad hadn't come down yet.

I quickly skimmed the most recent entry.

I'm afraid my relationship with Vanessa is still recovering. I continue to give her space while trying to make sure she knows I'm available if she needs me, but all I receive in response is curt conversation and the occasional smile. And in that expression, which once was one that could've lit the entire city of Boston in the middle of a blackout, I see disappointment. Sadness. Resentment. I know she's suffering, and why wouldn't she be? In their brief time together, she and Justine were closer than two sisters with decades of shared time and experience between them.

My eyes stuck on that last sentence. He didn't understand. If Justine and I really had been that close, she'd still be here.

Somewhere above me, I heard Dad call for Mom. His voice was followed by light, muffled footsteps hurrying upstairs. Guessing I still had a few minutes before they gave up on the fleece search, I continued reading.

I just wish she'd let me in. I wish she'd talk to me the way she used to. If only she would, I think our healing could improve tremendously. And unfortunately, I can't broach the subject with Jacqueline. She's barely functioning as it is, drowning her sorrows in meaningless chores and tasks, and I fear making a bad situation worse. Goodness knows how she'd react if she actually realised we were losing our other, living daughter.

I'm a desperate father, running out of ideas. If you have any advice, I'm all ears – or eyes, as the case may be.

This prompted countless questions, like, Why was Dad keeping this journal, or log, or whatever it was? Was he writing to a real person, as suggested by his request for advice, and divulging our – my – private troubles to someone who had no idea who I was or what was really going on? It didn't sound like Mom had any idea what he was doing when he claimed to be grading papers or working on his book, so why was he lying? If this was just his way of sorting out thoughts, which was the only logical explanation I could imagine him giving, why the big secret? Why go to such lengths to hide what he should be able to say out loud if he truly cared about our family?

And could he really, possibly not know why I looked at with him disappointment? Hurt? Resentment?

The answers would have to wait. A quick glance behind me showed the back stairwell dark and the laundry room lit.

'Come on,' I whispered, clicking on the Internet Explorer icon. The blue 'e' turned like it was waking from a long nap. 'Come on, come on, come *on*.'

Finally, a new window filled the screen. I automatically clicked in the address bar and started typing Hawthorne's web address. I had about thirty seconds to sign onto the school server, get into my e-mail account, send Dad's log to myself, and erase his browser history. It'd be a tall order on a brand-new, superfast laptop, and nearly impossible on this one.

I would've risked it . . . but then I registered the Internet's home page.

Gmail. It wasn't the regular landing page, where you had to sign in with your username and password. It was the inbox page, like Dad had forgotten to sign out – or hadn't bothered to, since he'd planned to return to it soon.

I stared at the screen. He'd never told me he had a personal account, which might've been useful information to have for the times when Newton Community College's server went down.

But then, maybe I shouldn't have felt slighted. It wasn't like he'd told everyone *but* me. In fact, judging by the long list of e-mails filling the inbox, he'd told only one person. One person who appeared to write to him every day. Who'd written to him as recently as twenty minutes ago.

Someone with the initials W. B. D.

'What aren't you telling me?'

I slammed down the laptop screen. 'Paige.' I grabbed my chest as she came around the table and sat across from me. 'Don't scare me like that.'

'Sorry. I won't ever again – as long as you tell me what's going on.'

I'm snooping. Dad's divulging family secrets to strangers. Mom's clueless. Oh, and by the way? Mom's not really my mother, and you and I are more like sisters than we realised.

'What do you mean?' I pushed away the laptop.

She held out her open cell phone. My eyes froze on the familiar number before continuing down the small screen.

V NOT ANSWERING CALLS OR TEXTS. IS SHE OKAY?

'He also left three voicemails asking the same thing.' She closed the phone and reached into her jeans pocket. 'I didn't want to answer without talking to you first, then when I went to your room, I heard a strange buzzing. It took me a while to figure out where it was coming from, but finally I did: a sneaker in the bottom of your suitcase.'

She held out my cell phone. The flashing red light indicating new messages was like a strobe light atop a police car.

'Since Saturday, Simon has called you twenty-four times and sent thirty-one texts. But you wouldn't know that because you somehow lost your phone inside the toe of an old shoe.' She placed the phone on the table when it was clear I wasn't going to take it. 'What happened? Did you have a fight?'

'Sort of.' I looked at my hands, imagined them in his.

'Sort of? What does that mean? He swung and you ducked?'

I closed my eyes, took a deep breath. I'd said the words to myself countless times over the past three days, preparing for the moment when I'd have to say them out loud . . . but that didn't make this any easier.

'We broke up.'

Paige's face fell. 'You *what*? Why?'

'It was just too hard. The long-distance thing, I mean.'

'The long-distance thing?' she repeated, exasperated. 'That's not hard.'

'Of course it is. People break up because of it all the time.'

'Some people, yes – the ones who weren't supposed

to be together in the first place. But they're not you and Simon. Call it fate, soul mates, divine intervention, whatever, but you were put on this planet for him, and vice versa. A few miles can't change that.'

I didn't answer. I was afraid I'd break down if I did.

'I can't believe this,' Paige finally said, resting her elbows on the table, her forehead in her hands. 'You guys were so perfect together. When I was with Jonathan ... when I think about the time we spent together ... I think that's the closest I'll ever get to what you and Simon have.' She paused. 'What you ... had.'

What we had. Past tense. Over and out.

'Maybe this is just temporary?' she suggested. 'Maybe it's a small freak-out that'll eventually blow over? So he can focus on fruit flies and lab rats, you can enjoy senior year, and next summer, when you're both back in Winter Harbor, you can have a passionate reunion that will last, like, for ever.'

I was glad the outside light shone from behind me so she couldn't see tears form. My eyes had been watering every morning and night – and sometimes in the afternoon, usually when I passed by the science labs at school. They never spilled over so that I was actually crying, making me happy for perhaps the very first time that my body depended on every drop of salt water it could find to function.

186

'It's a nice idea,' I said softly. 'But I don't think so.'

She sniffed and fanned *her* watering eyes with both hands. 'Come to Winter Harbor this weekend.'

'What?'

'Grandma B asked me to visit. I'm going to take the bus to Portland and meet Riley there, and he's going to drive me the rest of the way.' She paused. 'If you come, you can call Simon, and maybe he'll meet you. And then you guys can talk and try to come up with an alternative to breaking up.'

Simon aside, getting out of town was tempting; if I was alone here this weekend, I knew I'd replay in my head everything that happened last weekend a thousand times.

'Success!'

I jumped at Dad's voice. Swivelling on the bench, I saw him standing on the top of the back stoop, holding my blue fleece triumphantly overhead like it was a trophy.

'It was a challenge,' he said, starting down the steps. 'One that, had I faced it alone, would've ended with your turning into a human Popsicle.'

I glanced at Paige. She looked at her phone.

'But your mother, the all-knowing woman that she is, found your favourite blue fleece buried in a mountain of clean clothes in no time.'

He reached the picnic table and held out the jacket. I looked at it, then up at his proud, smiling face, then at Mom. I could see her through the kitchen window, washing dishes like everything was normal. Like this was any other night. Like her husband hadn't ruined her family seventeen years earlier and didn't talk about her to perfect strangers.

'Actually,' I said, turning to Paige, 'I think a trip to Winter Harbor is exactly what I need.'

CHAPTER 16

The next morning, we got to school early. Paige wanted to ask Ms Mulligan about a new restaurant-management program she'd found online the night before, and I wanted to spend some time on the *Winter Harbor Herald* website in the privacy of a near-empty library.

As soon as we stepped into the main lobby, it was clear we weren't the only ones getting a jump start on the day.

'They're up to something,' Paige said as two teachers brushed past us like we weren't there. They walked quickly, closely, talking in hushed voices. 'Has Hawthorne ever given a school-wide, all-day pop quiz?'

'Never.' But she was right. If the faculty wasn't up to something, something was definitely up. In a matter of seconds, a dozen more teachers flew past, and not one stopped to ask what we were doing there so early. They all hurried in the same direction.

'I'm going to try to catch Ms Mulligan before the guidance department evacuates,' Paige said. 'Meet outside the gate in the event of a real emergency?'

As she turned left, I headed right, narrowly avoiding

a four-person pile-up as a trio of history teachers darted out of a classroom and into hallway traffic. I tried to decipher the whispers, but there were too many, and they moved too fast. As soon as I made out a cluster of words – 'sudden,' 'sad,' 'damage' – the speakers were five feet ahead of me and out of eavesdropping range.

When the library doors appeared, I slipped inside, noting as I did that the traffic slowed to a crawl at the end of the hall before trickling inside the auditorium.

I found a computer station behind a tall shelf filled with dusty reference books and signed into my e-mail.

ALERT!!!

The message at the top of my inbox greeted me like a roadblock. The subject was in all capital letters. The type was red, the font bold. Hawthorne prided itself on proper e-mail etiquette, and this one word broke every rule. I would've thought it spam and deleted it, but it had been sent from the president's office less than ten minutes before. In all my time at Hawthorne, there was only one other instance when an important mass e-mail had come from the president's office instead of the vice president's. That e-mail, which I'd deleted without reading as soon as I realised what it was, had announced Justine's death.

Holding my breath, I clicked on the e-mail.

To Members of the Hawthorne Community:

It is with great regret that I report the passing of our dear friend and Hawthorne Preparatory sophomore Colin Milton Cooper.

For those of you who were fortunate enough to spend time with Colin, you know that he was one of the brightest, kindest individuals ever to grace our halls. For those of you who weren't, I'm sorry to say that you missed the chance of a lifetime.

I expect that as representatives of a centuries-old, world-class educational institution, you will conduct yourselves accordingly during this transitional period. If you have any questions or concerns, my door is always open.

One final note: In today's digital age, news travels fast – and, oftentimes, erroneously. That is why I ask you to refrain from discussing this development with anyone outside of the Hawthorne community. All media inquiries should be directed to Mr Harold Lawder, public relations manager.

With condolences and warm regards,

Dr Martin O'Hare, President

Colin Cooper had been a current student. That must've been why the school was panicking. His death alone would've been reason for mass e-mails and staff assemblies, but Justine had been an alumnus for all of a week when she died, which meant Hawthorne had basically lost two students in a matter of months.

I reread the note, trying to picture Colin. I didn't know many lowerclassmen and couldn't put a name to the face.

Keeping the e-mail up, I opened another window and googled 'Colin Cooper.' When that turned up thousands of responses, I added 'Milton' and 'Hawthorne Preparatory.' I was just about to hit enter when my eyes fell to the last entry on the first page.

Meet COLIN MILTON COOPER and other single professionals at IVY TRAILS, your first step down the pathway of intelligent matchmaking!

Intelligent matchmaking? As in an online dating service? This Colin Milton Cooper couldn't be the same one; if he was a sophomore he'd have to be sixteen years old, max, which just seemed too young to be matchmaking online. It also seemed too risky. If anyone else at school ever found out, they wouldn't let him forget it. Hawthorne kids might've had more money than a lot of other kids their age, but that didn't make them more mature.

Determined to rule it out, I clicked on the link.

'Oh, no,' I breathed.

According to the education history listed on his profile, the Colin Milton Cooper on Ivy Trails was a current Hawthorne student. But that wasn't what got me.

It was his picture. Because as it turned out, I was among those who'd spent time with one of the brightest, kindest students ever to grace our school's halls. Not much – but enough to recognise his curly brown hair and green eyes.

Colin Milton Cooper was the guy from the Beanery restroom. The one who'd been crying, whose e-mail I'd found.

'He jumped off a bridge.'

I leaped out of the chair.

'Sorry.' Parker leaned against a bookcase, holding a coffee cup. 'You looked curious.'

Heart pounding, I dropped back into the chair and reached for the mouse. 'Then you're seeing things.'

'I take it you got *el presidente*'s cease and desist?'

I signed out of my e-mail, closed the search results window.

'It's ridiculous the things they're scared of.'

I was about to click out of the Ivy Trails window, but something in his tone made me stop. 'Like what?'

He stepped closer and perched on the edge of the desk. 'You know what they say about bad publicity?'

'That there's no such thing? Because any publicity's good publicity?'

He nodded. 'Know what Hawthorne says?'

I was suddenly very aware of his eyes on mine. I couldn't think of anything else – including an answer to his question.

'Kill it or be killed. That's why the mass e-mail and early-morning staff meeting. They want to keep the story as quiet as possible before the press has a field day.'

'And what would that story be?' I asked, wanting to know as much as I didn't want to know.

He nodded to the computer screen, where Colin Milton Cooper still smiled. 'The MIT crew team was out practising early this morning and spotted poor Colin on the bank of the Charles.'

I looked at my lap, fiddled with my sweatshirt sleeve, pictured Simon rowing on Lake Kantacka. 'How do they know he jumped?' I asked. 'Did anyone actually see him? Maybe he fell, or was –'

'There was a note. On Longfellow Bridge. Attached to a single white balloon and weighted down with a glass paperweight.'

For the thousandth time that week, my eyes watered.

'Apparently, he let some girl get the best of him.' He dropped into the desk chair next to mine and crossed his arms behind his head. 'They're known to do that.'

'How do you know all this?'

'My dad. Connections. The usual ways.' He took his cell phone from the pocket of his blazer. 'Want to know the creepiest thing?'

I didn't, but he was already leaning towards me, pressing buttons.

'When they found him, his mouth was all twisted. Contorted.' He held out the phone. 'Kind of like he was smiling.'

I stared at the photo, struggled for words. It wasn't a full smile, not like the ones the victims had last summer, but it was close enough. 'Where did you . . . how did you . . . ?'

'Police sent it to O'Hare, who sent it to Dad, who left his cell unattended while taking his morning bubble bath.'

Tearing my eyes away, I turned back to the computer. 'Hey.'

He was next to me now. Our elbows brushed together as I grabbed the mouse. Our skin was separated by four layers of clothes, but the touch still sent a fast, fleeting charge up my arm and down my spine. My hand shook so much I couldn't hold the cursor steady long enough to close the picture.

'I'm sorry.' His voice was gentler, softer. 'And stupid. I don't know why I showed you that.'

'It's fine. I just want to – I can't seem to –'

His hand covered mine. The mouse stopped. Barely breathing, I watched the cursor glide steadily towards the corner of the screen. His index finger slid over mine and rested there briefly before pressing down.

Colin Milton Cooper disappeared.

I looked from the screen to our hands. He didn't move his. Even worse, I didn't move mine.

'I have to go,' I whispered.

'What?' He squeezed my hand, snapping it out of its hypnosis. 'Where?'

I yanked my arm away and jumped up.

He reached for me, but I lunged back. I felt him watching me as I snatched my bag from the floor.

I didn't know where I was going. Not at first. I just ran – out of the library, down the hall, through the front doors. Reaching the pavement, I turned left and kept running, my legs pumping harder, faster. I darted between people, flew across streets without glancing at traffic lights. Orange and red leaves swirled around me, but I hardly saw them, barely felt their dried edges flit across my skin. Over my thudding heart I barely heard horns honking, wind rushing past my ears . . . and eventually, the Charles River lapping against dirt.

I didn't stop until cold water splashed around my ankles. Then I looked up, surprised to see where my body had led me without my brain consciously directing it.

Longfellow Bridge. It spanned the river, connecting Boston to Cambridge a half mile away. Five hundred feet overhead, morning commuters rushed by, oblivious as to what had transpired only hours before.

A crew team passed by. The rowers' chants jerked me back to the present.

What was I doing? And why? Yes, Colin Milton Cooper drowned after jumping in the river. Yes, he'd had his heart broken only days before. But that didn't necessarily mean that Raina and Zara . . . that they had anything to do with . . .

Simon. I rummaged frantically through my backpack for my cell phone. I still hadn't returned any of his texts or calls, but I needed his voice of reason now more than ever. I needed to hear him swear that it was impossible, that there was no way they were involved because they were completely, totally, one hundred per cent –

Dead. His battery must've died, because his phone went right to voicemail.

I closed my cell and scanned the river's surface,

looking – hoping – for some sort of sign. A flash of light, a sudden splash, a pair of silver-blue eyes. Anything to indicate that what I was thinking was possible, that I wasn't crazy.

Without thinking, barely feeling the chilled water soak through my tights, I took another step, and another. The water rose to my knees, crept up my thighs.

I could do this. I'd stopped them before, and I could do it again.

I hadn't gotten far when a hard, fast force slammed into my stomach, shoving the air from my lungs. I lunged against it, reaching my arms forward and digging my heels into the mud, but it was too strong.

'Stop!' I gasped. 'Please, let me –'

My calves collided with something and I toppled backward, landing on my left shoulder. The pain made me see white – and I temporarily forgot what I'd been about to do.

'It's okay,' a male voice soothed.

The light dulled as the pain eased, and the river slowly came into focus. My head was spinning, and it took a second to register the arms around my waist, the khaki-clad legs enclosing mine like a fortress.

'You're okay...'

My heart lifted.

Simon. Despite everything I'd said, despite not returning his texts and phone calls . . . he was here. He'd been so worried when he didn't hear back that he'd come all the way down from Bates to check on me.

Closing my eyes against the fresh welling of tears, I climbed to my knees, wriggled around, and threw my arms around him.

'Thank you,' I whispered into his neck.

His hands pressed protectively against my back. Ignoring the small warning voice sounding deep inside my head, I pulled away slightly and kissed him.

His lips tensed.

'It's okay,' I breathed against them. 'I'm okay.'

His lips were still hesitant, but they responded, relaxing more with each brush of mine. Soon the kisses came harder, faster, deeper, until I forgot where we were and why. When he lay back on the ground, gently pulling me with him, I didn't even open my eyes to see if anyone watched. I didn't care.

'I'm sorry.' My mouth trailed across his cheek, towards his ear. 'I don't know what I was thinking.'

He pulled me closer, his hands moving from my waist to my hips.

'I missed you . . . so much.'

His hands stopped. 'You what?'

My breath caught. I opened my eyes. Slowly lifted

myself up. I saw the white shirt collar. Navy blue blazer. Gold-embroidered shield.

'I just saw you at school ten minutes ago.'

My eyes spilled over when they reached his. They weren't brown, or warm, or comforting.

Because they weren't Simon's.

They were Parker's.

CHAPTER 17

'And I thought Z was an exhibitionist.'

The reference to Zara made me jerk the steering wheel, which I'd been clutching tightly since leaving Boston for Maine an hour before.

'Sorry,' Paige said. 'But that must be a good sign, right? That I can refer to my dead sister's PDA in casual conversation?'

I focused on breathing – and driving in a straight line. Not wanting to worry her unnecessarily, I hadn't told Paige about what had happened. It was the right thing to do, but keeping it to myself was becoming more of a struggle every day.

'PDA?' I asked.

'Public displays of affection.' She studied her cell phone screen. 'I could count on a football team's fingers and toes the number of times I caught her making out with random guys. But even she had limits.' She shot me a quick glance. 'When it came to PDA. Not when it came to life and death. Obviously.'

'Who doesn't have limits?' I reached for the water bottle in the cup holder between the seats.

'Parker King.'

I jerked the steering wheel again – this time because the open water bottle was in my lap.

Paige handed me a stack of napkins left over from our last pit stop and took the wheel. 'Want me to drive?'

'Nope.' I sopped up the water, tossed the wet napkins in a plastic convenience store bag, and took back the steering wheel. 'Why do you say that? About Parker, I mean?'

She held out the phone. I glanced at it, then swallowed and kept my eyes glued to the road.

'I know.' She turned it back to her for another look. 'Gross, right?'

I tried to agree, but the best I could do was nod. Considering that the photographic evidence in question was of Parker sprawled out on the ground with me on top of him, I thought that was pretty good.

'And who's the girl?' She squinted and brought the phone closer. 'His face is totally clear, but hers is hidden behind her hair.'

Thank goodness for small favours. I'd left Simon's sweatshirt home that day to be washed by the housekeeper. Had I been wearing it, Paige – and everyone else at Hawthorne – would've identified me right away.

'Don't know,' I said. 'Who took the picture?'

She snapped the phone shut and tossed it in her purse. 'No idea. But it's on Prep Setters, that private-school gossip site. I signed up for text alerts – I thought it'd be a good way to get to know my new classmates.'

I'd heard of Prep Setters but had never visited their site. 'Does the website give names?'

'Usually. This picture didn't have any – the caption referred to them only as "Hawthorne's happiest couple", so whoever submitted it probably doesn't go to Hawthorne since everyone there knows Parker. But I bet it's only a matter of time before someone recognises them and writes in with the ID.' She paused. 'Um, Vanessa?'

'Yeah?'

'If I wanted to fly, I would've taken a plane.'

I glanced at the speedometer; the needle hovered at eighty. 'Sorry,' I said, taking my foot off the gas. 'I guess I'm a little distracted.'

'Are you sure you want to drive on to Winter Harbor by yourself? Why don't I call Riley and ride the rest of the way with you?'

'I'm fine. Promise.'

She reached over and squeezed my knee. As we drove in silence, I focused on road signs and tried to ignore my heart thumping faster with every turn. I knew Paige would've alerted me if Simon had said anything about him coming to Portland, too . . . but what if he'd changed his mind? What if he'd decided at the last minute to confront me in person? What would I say? Especially when all I really wanted to do was take back what had already been said?

I barely had enough time to think of the questions, let alone their answers. The restaurant we'd agreed to meet Riley at was closer to the highway than I'd thought, and before long we were pulling into the near-empty parking lot. When he saw us, Riley hopped off the hood of his Jeep and waved.

'Do you think this is okay?' Paige asked softly.

'What do you mean?'

She looked at me, her eyes suddenly sad, worried. 'Hanging out with another guy? Even just as friends?' She paused. 'Am I a terrible person for looking forward to seeing Riley today?'

I stopped the car, leaned over, and pulled her into a hug. 'You could never be a terrible person.'

We were still hugging when Riley tapped on her window.

'Hey, cutie,' he said when she opened the door. He leaned in and gave her a quick kiss on the cheek, then offered me an even quicker smile. 'Vanessa.'

'Hi,' I said.

He looked down. Paige frowned at me. I looked past

them both, feeling both relieved and disappointed when no one else got out of the Jeep.

'Have a great time,' I said, forcing brightness into my voice. 'Paige, I'll see you in Winter Harbor tonight.'

Concern clouded her face, but she gathered her stuff from the floor and took the door handle. 'At least try to stay under triple digits?'

'Done.'

I watched them start across the parking lot. He took her hand casually, easily, and she tensed and glanced back at me. I waved once, motioned for her to turn around, and drove away before I could make either of them more uncomfortable.

After all, it wasn't their fault Simon hated me.

It was mine.

The Volvo's ancient thermometer read sixty, which meant it was more like forty degrees outside, but I rolled my window all the way down and turned on the air conditioner. The further I drove the hotter I became, until sweat ran down my neck and my clothes clung to my skin. But I didn't stop to buy more water. I was afraid if I did I'd stop heading north, towards Winter Harbor, and go west, towards Bates.

What should've been a three-hour drive took two hours. I breezed past the sailboat-shaped sign announcing Winter Harbor's entrance and sped into town and down Main Street. It wasn't until I reached Betty's restaurant that I finally slowed to a stop in the parking lot.

I retrieved my phone from my purse, and my heart sank when there were no messages.

YOU PROBABLY HATE ME. I DON'T BLAME YOU.

I'd barely finished typing when I started deleting.

I'M SORRY FOR NOT CONTACTING YOU SOONER.

I deleted again and stared at the blank screen. After our last conversation, which had ended with my running out of the Beanery and Simon sitting at the table, stunned, words were falling short.

HI. HOW ARE YOU?

I pressed Send before I could change my mind, then watched the screen and waited for a new message to pop up. After a few seconds, I checked the sent folder and called my voicemail. Everything seemed to be working fine.

I slid the phone into the pocket of my jeans, climbed out of the car, and zipped up my jacket. It was ten degrees colder in Winter Harbor than it had been in Portland, and the breeze felt like swirling snow against my perspiring skin. By the restaurant's staff entrance, I redid my ponytail and patted my face, hoping people would assume my skin was red from the cold.

'City slicker!' Louis the chef declared as I entered the kitchen. 'Studying hard and partying harder?'

'Something like that.' I smiled, reminded of the first time I visited Betty's last summer, after a near-sleepless night in the lake house. It had been two days after Justine's funeral and my first full day all alone in Winter Harbor. I'd gone to Betty's for breakfast – and anonymity among strangers. When I'd told Garrett the valet that I'd had a rough night, he'd taken that to mean I was nursing a hangover and had asked Louis to prepare me his special culinary cure. The supposed reason for my initial visit had been a constant source of teasing ever since.

'You're in luck. I've just perfected this year's pumpkin-spice pancake recipe. Instant remedy for all that ails you.' He grabbed a fork, speared a piece of pancake on the griddle, and cupped one hand beneath it as he came towards me.

'Amazing,' I said, savouring the warm, sweet taste. 'I feel better already.'

'Of course you do.' Louis dropped the fork into his apron pocket and crossed his arms over his chest. 'Now what's wrong? Really?'

I brought one hand to my face. 'What do you mean?'

'I mean, it's October. You should be curled up in your

fancy brownstone, reading fancy books in preparation for your fancy college.' He glanced around the kitchen, then stepped closer to me and lowered his voice. 'It's Betty, isn't it?'

My heart skipped.

'You're worried about her,' he continued. 'We all are. She hasn't been here in weeks, and any time that guy of hers comes in – what's his name? Mortimer? Lucifer?'

'Oliver.'

'Right. Any time he comes in, he's white as a ghost and shaking like he's just seen one. And as soon as we ask how Betty is and if she's coming by soon, he clams up and leaves.'

'Why?'

'If I knew that, honey, I'd trade in the spatula for a crystal ball. Lord knows the money I could make telling rich tourists about the few things they can't control.'

'Well,' I said, making a mental note to talk to Paige about Oliver later, 'when I see Betty, I'll let her know the restaurant misses her.'

After Louis filled me in on the staff (including Garrett, who was back at college but apparently still talked about me whenever he e-mailed) and loaded me up with bagels and fresh orange juice, I took a deep breath and asked the one question I'd come there to ask.

'Hey, Louis? Speaking of fancy books . . . do you remember a small bookstore that used to be on the out-skirts of town?'

He didn't look up from the pot he stirred. 'You mean Cather Country?'

'Maybe?' Betty hadn't mentioned a name.

'That's the only bookstore I've heard of. I didn't live in Winter Harbor when it was open, and I only know about it because locals still talk about it. People were so upset when it burned down they didn't read for weeks.'

When it burned down? Betty had left out that im-portant detail, too. She'd lived in Winter Harbor for more than sixty years so she had to know. And if she'd somehow missed it when it happened, she would've heard about it from the locals – or from Oliver, who was the town's resident historian.

So why hadn't she told me? Why hadn't Oliver, who'd been in the room when she brought it up?

'Any idea what happened to the owner?' I asked.

'She was supposedly filing papers in the basement when the fire started and couldn't get out. The store was so far away from town, no one knew until it was too late. By the time they did, there was no longer a body to find.'

I started to ask if he knew when this happened, but then the dining-room door swung open and a dis-gruntled waiter burst through. As Louis became engrossed in a debate over that morning's special, I waved and ducked outside.

The air was even colder now. I shoved my hands in my jacket pockets and lowered my head against the wind. Hurrying towards the car, I struggled to process everything I'd just learned and thought of who else I could talk to in order to learn more.

If Betty knew more than she'd claimed, she clearly didn't want to share. That meant Paige probably couldn't help. Oliver wouldn't tell me anything Betty didn't want me to know. Mr and Mrs Carmichael might be able to fill in a few holes, but I didn't feel comfortable talking to them now. The same went for Caleb, who'd probably slam the door in my face as soon as he saw me. Simon would research until he could tell me whatever I wanted to know, but I couldn't ask him to without explaining why – and apologising until I could no longer speak.

Or maybe he wouldn't. A quick check of my phone showed that he still hadn't answered my text, so he might not want to talk about anything yet.

I'd just slid the phone into my jeans pocket when two car doors slammed nearby.

'Are you kidding me?' a male voice demanded. 'Please tell me this is your twisted idea of a practical joke – a Halloween gag to jump-start your old man's ticker.'

Reaching the car, I took the door handle and peered

over the roof. A middle-aged man in khakis, a brown suede coat, and a Red Sox hat stood behind a gleaming black Land Rover a few spots down, waving his arms around like the SUV was an aeroplane preparing to land. Whoever he was upset with stood on the passenger's side, out of sight.

'Well, congratulations. You just blew your old stupidity record out of the water.'

The man spun around. I yanked open the door and dropped into the driver's seat. In the rear-view mirror, I watched him bark into a cell phone as he headed towards the restaurant's entrance. A teenage boy followed several feet behind, his head down, his ears plugged with small white earphones. My eyes followed the iPod cord to a familiar leather messenger bag.

'Parker?'

His head snapped up. I shot down my seat. Squeezing my eyes shut, I waited and wondered what he was doing here. Summer was over and half the harbour was still frozen; the only tourists who visited Winter Harbor now were leaf peepers checking out the foliage, and Parker didn't seem the type.

I waited a few more seconds before looking around. Relieved to find no one standing next to the driver's-side door – or anywhere else around the car – I sat up, started the engine, and hit the gas.

The Winter Harbor library was on the other side of town. As I drove the familiar route, I thought of the last time I'd been there – and why. Simon, Caleb, and I had gone to talk to Oliver, who was a regular patron, the day I'd learned that he was the love of Betty's life. We'd hoped he'd be able to provide insight into the rest of the Marchands, including Raina and Zara, whom we'd suspected were involved in Justine's death and the other mysterious drownings. He'd answered many of our questions and prompted countless more we never would've thought to ask when he revealed that theirs was a family of sirens.

Given Oliver's recent odd behaviour, I was reluctant to initiate another face-to-face conversation. But what I was wary of trying to learn from him directly, I hoped to find in his multivolume *The Complete History of Winter Harbor*.

There was only one other car in the library parking lot, which I assumed belonged to Mary the librarian. I pulled into an empty space near the front door, put my phone on vibrate, slid it into my jeans pocket, and headed inside. After waving to Mary, who didn't seem to recognise me from my summer visits, I found the small local-interest section – and four books by Oliver Savage. Mary had once kept them up front so Oliver would stop asking why no one was borrowing them, but apparently he had bigger things to worry about now.

I took the books to the reading area by the old stone fireplace. I'd spent quite a bit of time with them over the summer when looking for information about fleeting storms and related deaths, and I didn't recall reading anything about Cather Country. But that could've been because I hadn't known to look for it.

There was nothing in the first three volumes. In the fourth, I discovered one small paragraph in a chapter about successful local businesses – the same chapter in which Betty's Chowder House was mentioned. The bookstore's paragraph, however, was even less revealing than the restaurant's had been.

Cather Country, a cosy book nook located off Lawlor Trail, opened in May 1990 to rave reviews. Owner and Winter Harbor newcomer Charlotte Bleu offered customers new, used, and rare works in a warm, inviting setting. The store, which quickly became a regular must-stop shop for residents and vacationers alike, burned down in November 1993. The fire's cause was never determined, and Cather Country was never rebuilt.

My eyes lingered on the second-to-last sentence. Something else happened in November 1993.

I was born.

'Hey, stranger.'

I slammed the book shut. 'Caleb. Hi.'

He came over from the DVD section. As he neared I prepared for a barrage of questions about the break-up, but he simply smiled and kissed my cheek.

'Simon didn't tell me you were going to be here this weekend.'

That obviously wasn't the only thing Simon hadn't told him. Caleb's greeting would've been very different had he known his brother and I were no longer together.

'It was an impromptu trip,' I said. 'Paige wanted to see Betty, and I tagged along.'

'Nice.' He nodded to my lap. 'Couldn't you write your own Winter Harbor book by now?'

'Not one that anybody would want to read,' I joked.

He looked down, his smile faltering.

'What about you?' I asked. 'Why the library on a sunny fall day?'

'Movie night with the guys. The DVD collection's surprisingly good here.'

I nodded, unsure what to say next. I knew Caleb and I would always be connected because of his connection to Justine, but because things with Simon were different, talking to Caleb felt different, too.

'How long are you around?' he asked after a long pause. 'Want to grab breakfast tomorrow?'

'I think we're leaving pretty early. But next time?'

'Absolutely.' He checked his watch. 'I hate to chat and run, but I was supposed to be at the marina ten minutes ago. Now that the harbour's totally thawed, customers are anxious to get their boats back in the water.'

'Of course.' As I stood to give him a hug goodbye, I registered what he'd just said. Seeing my body freeze and face flush, he stepped towards me.

'You didn't hear?' he asked quietly.

I tried to shake my head, but it wouldn't move.

'We had a crazy heat wave last weekend. It melted the last of the ice.'

'Have you –' I whispered. 'Have they –'

'No one's seen anything. Because there's nothing to see.'

'Right.' I managed to nod. 'I know.'

'Vanessa, you know how Zara felt about me. If she'd somehow survived . . . don't you think I'd be the first one she'd try to find?'

My eyes watered – partly because he was right, but also because he sounded so calm, so quietly confident, that he reminded me of Simon.

He held out his arms, and I stepped into them. We hugged for several seconds before I pulled back. As he walked away, he shot me a quick smile and called over his shoulder.

'That brother of mine better be taking good care of you!'

Which probably would've made me break down completely if my cell phone hadn't buzzed right then. My fingers, slick with perspiration, slid across the phone twice before getting a good enough grip to pull it from my jeans pocket.

V, GRANDMA B CALLED. SHE'S UPSET, WANTS TO HAVE NIGHT ALONE WITH ME TO TALK. FEEL TERRIBLE, BUT DO U MIND??? XO – P

P. Not S.
Sinking back into my chair, I texted her back.

COURSE NOT. HOPE SHE'S OK. WILL STAY AT LAKE HOUSE. CHECK IN LATER. – V

A second later, the phone buzzed again.

SAW YOU IN TOWN. AM STUCK HERE TONIGHT. WANT TO HANG OUT?

CHAPTER 18

I agreed to meet Parker for three reasons. The first was simple: I didn't want to be alone. Paige was with Betty, and even if I went to their house and tried to stay out of the way so they could have time together, I knew Paige would insist on including me.

That meant going out, which led to the second reason: I didn't affect Parker the way I did other guys. Yes, we'd made out by the river, but only because I'd thought he was Simon, and because as everyone on the New England prep-school circuit knew, he wouldn't refuse any girl who threw herself at him. As long as I kept my eyes open, we should be able to hang out without another awkward situation, and I shouldn't have to deal with the kind of unwanted attention I'd get in public.

Of course, that didn't mean I could simply pretend like our impromptu lip-locking session hadn't happened. And so, reason three: I'd explain the misunderstanding and ask him to get Prep Setters to take down the picture before more damage was done.

They were good, sound reasons. Unfortunately, as I

stood in the Lighthouse Resort parking lot, they didn't stop me from feeling guilty.

'They're coming for you.'

I looked up. Parker stood on the top deck of the two-storey yacht, holding a bottle of wine and two glasses.

'Seriously,' he said. 'You've been out there so long security just called and asked if I needed them.'

I glanced over my shoulder. Two men in Lighthouse Resort and Spa jackets eyed me from a nearby golf cart. 'I don't drink,' I said, turning back.

'Neither do I.'

I waited for him to smile or laugh, but he didn't. Reminding myself that this was the best of all my options, I forced my feet down the dock and up the ramp leading to the main deck. He met me at the top. His hands now empty, he held one towards me.

'This isn't a date,' I said.

'You have a boyfriend.'

This, too, was said without a hint of a smile. Somewhat reassured – and not about to correct him – I took his hand and stepped onto the deck. The second my feet hit the floor he let go and headed towards the cabin. I followed him – mostly because he didn't seem to care whether I did.

'Closing up for the winter?' I asked once inside. The cabin, which had multiple rooms and looked more like an apartment, was filled with covered furniture. The only pieces not hidden by white sheets were the bar, two stools, and a TV.

'We never opened.' He removed two water bottles from a refrigerator and gave me one.

'Why the trip now?' I asked.

He reached into a trash can next to the bar and pulled out a red sweatshirt.

'The Annual Live Like a KING Fish-Fest?' I said, reading the front.

'Also known as the two days of the year my dad clears his calendar for some quality one-on-one time. Or at least finagles his calendar so that he can conduct all appointments via e-mail and cell phone. His assistant gets assorted memorabilia made so it seems like more of an event.'

He tossed the sweatshirt back in the trash. It landed on top of several wine bottles.

'Is he outside?' I asked. 'Upstairs?'

'Not any more. He's at the resort, having dinner. After a gourmet lobster feast, he'll retire to the beach house and stare at ESPN until slipping into an alcohol-induced slumber.'

'Why aren't you with him?'

He looked at me, his eyes narrowing slightly.

'Sorry. That's none of my business, I don't know why –'

I was interrupted by a phone ringing. Parker took his cell from his pants pocket, told whoever was calling to come aboard, and hung up. Before I could figure out what to say next, the deck door slid open and a delivery guy entered the room.

'I got half cheese, half pepperoni. Hope that's okay.' Parker gave the pizza guy cash and me a quick smile. 'You can pay for your share, if you want. Since it's not a date.'

A few minutes ago that smile plus teasing combo would've sent me running for the Volvo. But now, it was relaxing. Reassuring. Given the little he'd said about his dad and their weekend, it was clear that he'd just wanted company – not *my* company, specifically.

We decided to eat outside, and I followed him out of the cabin and down the long main deck. At the deck's end, he hopped over a white chain and stepped onto the bow. He didn't offer his hand to help me or even look behind him to make sure I was still there, so I stepped over the chain without hesitation.

'Nice view,' I said, joining him at the bow's tip. Across the harbour, the lights of downtown Winter Harbor glittered.

He set down the pizza, took a slice, and lowered himself to the edge of the bow, letting his legs hang over the side. 'Why'd you say you were here again?'

I sat a few feet away, my back to the railing, my legs pulled to my chest. 'I didn't. I'm checking on my family's lake house.'

He nodded. We ate silently, him staring off at the dark horizon, me wondering what he was thinking. He seemed distracted, removed. Whatever had happened with his dad earlier must've been pretty bad. I thought about bringing up our time by the river, but it didn't feel right. I didn't want to make him feel worse, and clarification didn't seem as pressing now, since making out with me was clearly the last thing on his mind. In fact, rather than worrying about putting him in his place, the longer we sat there, the more I wanted to help him feel better.

'So,' I said, my heart rate quickening. 'College applications are due soon.'

'Rumour has it.'

'Do you have a first choice?'

'You mean besides taking a boat – a real boat, not a floating McMansion – down the East Coast then up the West Coast after graduation? Stopping at random ports, meeting people who know nothing about my family or me? For a year, maybe longer?'

I paused. 'Yes?'

'Then no. But I'll probably end up at Princeton. I don't have the grades, but Dad has connections.'

'I hear the campus is beautiful.'

He laughed once. 'Okay, Ms Mulligan.'

A fresh wave of warmth spread across my face. I was glad it was dark so he couldn't see.

'What about you?' he asked. 'Joining the crimson tide? Barking like a bulldog? Roaring like a lion?'

As he referred to Ivy League mascots, I looked across the harbour, recalled the other lights that had broken up its darkness a few months ago. 'None of the above.'

'Ah, a trendy liberal arts college. Intellectually stimulating, yet highly impractical,' he said, lowering his voice like he was repeating something he'd heard many times before. 'So Williams? Amherst? Or are you going to make Matt Harrison's dreams come true and go to Bates?'

'I'm not going to college.' It was the first time I'd said it aloud, the first time I'd admitted it to anyone but myself. I almost expected Ms Mulligan to storm the bow, grab me by the shoulders, and try to shake sense into me.

'But you go to Hawthorne,' Parker said.

'And?'

'And everyone who goes to Hawthorne goes to college. That's why our parents shell out gobs of money – to secure our futures before we've given them any thought.'

'Well then, I guess I'm bucking tradition.'

He looked at me, really looked at me, for the first time

since my arrival. 'Is it because of what happened? With your sister?'

His assumption was wrong, but I gave him credit for asking the question other people would've only thought to themselves.

'It's because I don't see the point,' I said.

'What did your parents say when you told them?'

'That it's my life. That they respect and support any decision I make.' This, I knew, was what Justine would've wanted to hear if she'd ever summoned the courage to tell them the truth. 'That they love me, no matter what.'

My voice hitched on the last word. Fortunately, if Parker noticed, he didn't say so. Shifting his gaze to the invisible horizon, he gave me space to get past the moment.

'Today,' he said some time later, 'when my dad got an e-mail from my coach saying that I quit the water polo team, he told me I wasn't *allowed* to make a joke out of him like that. He said that, besides my last name, water polo was one of the few things I had going for me – and that he was proud of me for.'

Any surprise I felt learning he'd quit the team was quelled by his dad's reaction to the news. My parents would be upset when I finally told them I wasn't going to college – but for what they thought it meant for me, not them.

'You know what he'd say if I told him I wasn't sure about college? That I didn't know if it was right for me?'

Our eyes met. I expected his to flash anger, but they were dulled, sad.

'He'd tell me to leave, to not even think about coming back until I had proof that I'd applied to and been accepted to one of his pre-approved schools.' He looked out at the water. 'I don't know what's worse. Getting kicked out . . . or being too scared to tell him what he doesn't want to hear.' He hesitated. 'You just might be the bravest person I've ever met, Vanessa Sands.'

'Actually –'

I was cut off by a sudden swell that caused the yacht to drop then lift. The movement was so sharp I grabbed the railing to keep from sliding off the bow. In the next second, a long, narrow speedboat roared past us and out of the harbour. Squinting through the darkness, I could just make out the name painted on the back of the boat: *Deep Sea or Die*.

I was still clutching the cool metal when I heard a light thud and the fibreglass trembled beneath me. Forcing my eyes from the rippling water, I glanced in the direction of the noise – and saw Parker standing there, wearing only cargo pants. My eyes travelled from his bare chest to the shirt, shoes, and socks by his feet, and then past him, to the lights glowing downtown.

'What are you doing?' I asked, gripping the railing even tighter.

'Going swimming.'

'The water's freezing.'

He stepped to the left – and into my line of vision. 'I haven't been once since quitting the team. It's the one thing I miss.'

I stared at his olive skin. White spots burst before my eyes with each heartbeat.

Fortunately, since I couldn't seem to look away, he moved out of my line of vision. Unfrozen, I released the railing, stood, and walked backwards, my sneakers squeaking on the fibreglass.

'I should go,' I said, watching his torso as it turned towards me. 'It's pretty late.'

'It's eight o'clock.'

'Simon – my boyfriend – will be calling any minute. I don't want to miss him.'

'Well, wait,' Parker said, starting after me. 'I'll walk you out.'

'Don't!'

He stopped. My gaze finally shifted to his face, which was scrunched in confusion.

'I'm fine,' I continued, trying to sound casual. 'Thanks for the pizza. See you at school.'

I spun away, hurried across the bow, and hopped over the chain. I waited until I was halfway down the deck and pretty sure that Parker could no longer see me before running the remaining distance. As I reached the top of the ramp that led to the dock, a splash sounded from the front of the boat.

I held my breath and listened. For water moving, arms paddling, legs kicking.

There was nothing. Even the wake left by the speedboat had faded, and the harbour, which only seconds before had lapped against the sides of yacht, was still.

I pictured *Deep Sea or Die*, the bold, black script like a crooked finger inviting unassuming swimmers closer. I thought of the divers who'd accidentally discovered the icy tomb. I felt pressure around my abdomen, the same kind I'd felt when Parker had pulled me out of the river.

'Don't do it,' I said quietly, stepping back from the ramp. 'He's fine. Just leave him – and everything else – alone.'

But I didn't. I couldn't. And in less time than it had taken me to reach the ramp, I was at the bow's tip again.

'Parker?' I whispered, scanning the water's dark surface. 'Parker?' I tried again, louder.

I was about to run to the cabin to look for a flashlight

when I caught sight of something long and flat out of the corner of my eye. It floated away from the yacht and towards the centre of the harbour like a piece of wayward driftwood.

I darted to the side of the bow and leaned over the railing for a better look. Barely making out Parker's profile, I raced to the deck, yanked the SS *Bostonian* life preserver ring from the wall, and ran back to the side railing. The water was as black as the sky, but I imagined it glowing, pictured tall beams of light shooting up from its depths the way they had during the sirens' final attack last summer. Then, summoning Justine's athletic abilities and all of my upper-body strength, I reached the preserver as far behind me as my arm would allow, and flung it forward.

It landed with a plop several feet from Parker. He didn't move.

You know how, when you're floating on your back on the lake, the water rises and falls against your ears? So that for half a second you can hear everything around you and then for the other half a second everything's muted? It's kind of like that.

Simon. That was how he'd described Zara's effect on him when they'd been alone in the woods . . . and it was exactly what Parker seemed to be experiencing right now. In the freezing water. Which could kill him if something else didn't first.

'*Parker*,' I hissed.

Nothing.

Gripping the railing, I searched the water for flashes of light, signs of life beneath its smooth surface. If he was under a siren's spell, what would happen if I jumped in after him? I was a strong enough swimmer that I might be able to escape a single siren, but I'd be defenceless against any more than that.

Security. They were probably still in the parking lot, monitoring activity aboard the SS *Bostonian* and making sure nothing was amiss. I could find them, tell them the truth – that Parker had decided to go swimming and might be hurt – and let them deal with it. Of course, if they weren't fast enough, or if the sirens were too powerful, then the three men would –

My eyes locked on a patch of frothy water.

He was gone. He'd been lying there, as stiff and motionless as a corpse . . . and then he'd flipped over and disappeared, shooting into the water head-first.

'No.' I didn't look away as I kicked off my sneakers, tore off my jacket and sweatshirt. 'No, no, *no*.'

I hesitated only briefly before taking off my jeans and tossing them aside. Down to a T-shirt, bra and underwear, I scrambled up the railing, climbed over the top rung, and slid down the other side. My toes stuck out over the side of the boat, and my hands grew slippery around the railing now behind me. Closing my eyes, I breathed in the moist, salty air, pictured Parker bandaging my knee in the Boston Common bandstand.

And jumped.

The instant infusion of salt was exhilarating, but the water was pitch-black. I might be able to swim for hours, but if I couldn't see my hands in front of my face, how would I ever find Parker?

I somersaulted and was about to swim towards the surface when something grabbed my ankle.

My scream created a blinding cloud of bubbles. I kicked and pulled, but whatever it was hung on, letting me drag it several feet before letting go. Once freed, I lifted my legs and flew through the harbour facedown, scanning the darkness for Raina, Zara, any of the other Winter Harbor sirens.

I was so focused on the water below me I didn't see the body in front of me until my head collided with its chest, its arms locked around my shoulders.

I squirmed and struggled, but it was no use. In seconds, my head was back above water.

'Parker!' I tried to shove his chest. This time, he let me go. 'What's wrong with you?'

'What's wrong with me?' He spat out water, wiped

his eyes, brushed back his hair. 'What's wrong with *you*? You run out of here like someone's chasing you, then come back, throw yourself in the water, and practically drown. If I hadn't been here –'

'I didn't practically drown,' I shot back before realising why he might think so. Unlike other swimmers, I didn't need to come up for air ... and hadn't before he'd grabbed me. He must've thought I'd been underwater too long. 'And I jumped in the water because *you* disappeared.'

As I spoke he shook his head, mouth open, prepared to launch into a rebuttal ... but then his head stilled. 'You thought I was in trouble?'

I reached forward, swam in the direction of the yacht. 'Forget it.'

He was by my side instantly. 'I don't want to forget it. I mean, I was fine – I got cold floating on my back and swam underwater to warm up my muscles, but ...'

He kept talking, but I no longer heard him. I'd stopped swimming to grab my head, which suddenly felt like it had been caught in a boat propeller and was now sinking underwater. The pain was so intense I couldn't seem to kick and breathe at the same time.

If not for Parker, who eventually swam next to me, then under me, with one arm across my chest and his hand cupping my shoulder, I would've drifted all the way to the harbour floor.

'I can do it,' I gasped when we reached a ladder on the side of the yacht.

I was wrong. He stayed in the water as I attempted to climb – but was next to me the second my foot slid off the first rung. We climbed the ladder the same way we'd swum to it, with his arm around me, pulling me with him, relieving me of enough of my own weight to step from one rung to the next.

On the deck, he shifted his position so that one arm was under my back and the other under my knees, and lifted me easily.

'I'm fine,' I said as he carried me down the deck, fully aware of how unconvincing I sounded. 'Really. It's just a little headache.'

'You just need to be quiet. And let me do this.'

I was too tired to argue. Plus, besides the pain throbbing between my ears, this wasn't entirely unpleasant. Parker was concerned, protective. Kind of like someone else I knew.

That's what I would tell myself later, when I wondered why I didn't protest as he carried me into a cabin and gently laid me down. Even though we were in a bedroom. On a boat, at night. Alone.

'I'll get you some aspirin,' Parker said quietly.

I closed my eyes and tried to clear my head. Gradually, the pain dulled. By the time he returned a few minutes later, I could sit up enough to take the aspirin with water.

'You should probably change out of those,' he said as I handed the glass back to him. Avoiding my eyes, he nodded towards my soaked T-shirt and then put a stack of dry clothes on the nightstand next to the bed.

'Thanks,' I said. 'Do you mind . . . ?'

I didn't have to finish the question for him to know what I was asking. He left quickly, closing the door gently behind him.

As the headache continued to fade, I took off my wet clothes and pulled on my jeans, which Parker had retrieved from the deck, and a Boston Red Sox sweatshirt. I slid under the covers and told him to come in when he knocked.

He opened the door slowly, like he was nervous about what he might find inside. Relaxing when he saw me completely covered, he took a washcloth from the stack he'd placed on a nearby desk and sat carefully on the edge of the bed.

'It's a little cold,' he said.

'That's okay.'

He pressed the washcloth to my forehead, my temples, my cheeks. When he reached my chin, I lifted it slightly and he held the cloth to both sides of my neck.

The coolness felt so good, I closed my eyes and tried to ignore the guilt percolating in the bottom of my belly.

Because I wasn't doing anything wrong. Parker was just being a friend. Even if things were perfect between Simon and me, I could still have guy friends – especially if they were immune to my abilities.

'Why don't you rest while these are in the dryer,' Parker said, nodding to my wet clothes on the floor, 'and then I'll take you home?'

'Don't.'

He looked up, surprised.

He wasn't the only one.

'Can you just stay here a while?' I hardly believed the words as they came out of my mouth. 'The clothes will dry on their own.'

I was counting on the assumption that he, like me, would rather not be alone. And it seemed I was right. He draped my wet clothes on the doorknob and across the back of a chair, and then sat next to me after I moved over to make room.

He'd changed, too, but I could still feel the coolness of his skin inches away. He didn't say anything and neither did I, and soon I was relaxing, breathing easier, no longer worrying about whether what I was doing was wrong.

The next thing I knew, early-morning light filtered

through the blinds over the bed. Parker was exactly where he'd lain down hours before, but now I was curled up next to him, my arm across his stomach. His arm was around my waist, his hand on my hip.

I lifted my head and peered past him to the night-stand, where my phone, peeking out of my purse, flashed red. Careful not to wake Parker, who breathed deeply, I slowly reached over, took the phone, and opened it.

V, AT THE LAKE HOUSE. WHERE ARE YOU?? PLEASE WRITE OR CALL.

   SIMON

CHAPTER 19

'He'll come around,' Paige said, opening the Beanery door the following Monday.

'He came around,' I said. 'Twice in person and eighteen times on the phone. And I missed him.'

'I still can't believe you slept through all that. You must've been exhausted.'

I had been, but she didn't know the real reasons why – or where I'd been sleeping when Simon had tried to reach me. She could tell something was up when I met her at her house after leaving Parker later that morning, so I told her about the visits, voicemails, and text messages. But I said that I'd missed them because I'd crashed early at the lake house – not because I'd been swimming and snuggling with Hawthorne's most notorious player.

My reasons for meeting Parker were somewhat understandable, but besides the strange, simple fact that I'd wanted to, there was no good reason for why I'd spent the night.

'He said he was sorry, didn't he?' Paige asked. 'For not getting back to you right away?'

'Yes, but when I didn't answer, his messages went from worried to frantic. And then he didn't pick up when I called him back, and he hasn't tried again since.'

'Well, when he does pick up, you'll apologise and explain what happened. No biggie.' Paige stepped aside to let me pass. 'True soul mates cannot be stopped.'

I tried to return her smile as I entered the coffee shop, but my mouth wouldn't cooperate. Because I *had* apologised. I'd given him my somewhat-but-not-entirely-true explanation. I'd tried contacting him dozens of times since waking up to his initial text two days ago. But when I called, the phone went straight to voicemail. When I texted, my messages went unreturned. So it seemed soul mates *could* be stopped – by sheer stupidity.

'I'm starving.' Paige dropped her backpack on an empty table and started towards the counter. 'Want anything?'

'My treat,' I said quickly. 'Since you drove the whole way back yesterday.'

'I would've done it for nothing, but since you're offering, chicken soup seems like appropriate compensation.'

She returned to the table as I went to the counter. I'd suggested the Beanery for lunch, and since we had the first meal period, it was barely eleven o'clock: post-early-morning rush, pre-afternoon pick-me-up. We'd never been there at this time, and I was happy that the coffee shop was nearly empty, its staff keeping busy by filling sugar bowls and napkin dispensers.

It was the perfect chance to confront my mysterious seaweed server.

'Excuse me?' I said to the only employee behind the counter, whose back was to me. 'Is Willa in?'

'Is the sun up?' the woman said pleasantly, turning around. 'What can I do for you?'

Her eyes were lowered to the napkin dispenser she held, and I took advantage of the distraction to give her a quick once-over. She was thin, about my height, and wore a brown apron over baggy khakis and a loose-fitting white button-down shirt. Her hair was tucked up under a brown Beanery baseball cap. Her hands were pale, wrinkled, and showed the first signs of liver spots. They trembled as she tried to close the dispenser.

'Can I help?' I asked.

'That's okay, I think I've –' She glanced up. Our eyes met. The napkin dispenser slipped from her grasp and clattered to the floor.

Heart thumping, I hurried around the counter to help clean up the mess. Another employee reached her first, and they squatted and gathered napkins. I tried to decipher their whispers as I backed away, but a third employee chose that moment to turn up the volume of the jazz playing overhead.

'Sorry about that.' Willa stood and patted her hands on her apron. 'Caffeine jitters. That's what I get for drinking too much free coffee.'

'No problem,' I said.

She took a deep breath and smiled at me. Her face confirmed what her hands had suggested: she was older. She was at least three times older than other Beanery staff members, most of whom were college students. Her cheeks sagged. Shallow folds lined her forehead. Her brown eyes looked out from under pale, drooping eyelids.

'What would you like?' she asked, wiping down the counter. 'Cappuccino? Espresso? We have a fantastic quiche today, right out of the oven.'

'Sounds great. I'll have a piece of that, a chicken soup, and two iced teas.'

'Coming right up.'

I watched her head for the kitchen, then looked behind me. Paige sat at the table, reading a newspaper. I waited for her to glance up so I could let her know soup was en route, but she was too engrossed.

'Are you a model?' a guy three stools down asked as I turned back.

'No,' I said, too nervous to worry about whether to respond or ignore him.

'Really?' He rested one elbow on the counter, placed

his cheek in his palm. 'I feel like I've seen you before. Like, on billboards. Wearing pretty dresses. Generously sharing your beauty with all of Boston.'

I leaned across the counter, tried to peer into the kitchen.

'You're too striking for catalogue work. What about catwalk?'

'I'm not a model,' I said, turning towards him. 'I'm a student. That's it.'

He frowned and sat back. 'Well. That's a shame.'

I was about to apologise – it wasn't his fault he was drawn to me – but stopped when I heard voices coming from the kitchen. Loud, unhappy voices. They were accompanied by what sounded like doors slamming.

Two minutes later, a male employee emerged, face flushed, fists clenched. A minute after that, Willa followed, carrying a round tray. If she had been involved in the backstage brawl, she didn't show it.

'Here we are.' She placed the tray in front of me. 'Can I get you anything else?'

I took a quick sip from one of the glasses of iced tea. When it was bitter, I tried the other. 'There's no salt.'

'Excuse me?'

'In my drink.' I leaned towards her and lowered my voice. 'Last time, you put salt in my iced tea.'

Her furry white eyebrows lifted. 'Did I? Sorry about

that, I must have confused it with the sugar. Here.' She ducked and took something from under the counter. 'Your next one's on the house.'

I looked at the complimentary beverage card without taking it. 'What about the seaweed?' I asked.

'What's that?' She cupped one ear with her hand.

My heart was beating a million miles a minute now – but out of confusion, not nervousness. 'The last time I was here, your co-worker gave me a green drink in a shot glass. He said it was courtesy of you, and that he thought it was wheatgrass.' I paused to let that sink in. 'But it was bitter. Salty. Like a seaweed smoothie.'

Her face was blank as I recalled this encounter. It wasn't until I was done that her eyes widened slightly. 'I remember now. Sometimes vendors send us new products to sample, and we try them out on customers. Last week we got in a box of all-natural energy drinks. That's what you had.'

'But the barista said it was from you, specifically. From my *friend*, Willa.'

'Hey, Marty,' she said.

The guy three stools down looked up.

'Who's your best friend here at the Beanery?'

'Wily Willa, of course,' he said with a grin.

She turned back to me. 'I've been here a long time. I've got lots of friends.'

I opened my mouth to fire off another question, but the only one I could think of was whether it was possible that I'd been wrong. Willa's thoughts on the matter were obvious, so there was no point in asking.

'Thanks,' I mumbled instead, leaving the beverage cards but taking the tray.

'Vanessa.'

Now my heart seemed to stop. I looked down at the pale, wrinkled hand on my sleeve.

'Are you all right?' Willa asked quietly.

My eyes lifted to hers. 'How did you –'

'*Are* you?'

I nodded once. 'I think so.'

Her fingers tightened around my arm before releasing it. I stood there, frozen, until she disappeared into the kitchen.

'Oh, my goodness.' Paige groaned lightly as I joined her at the table. 'Remember that accident? With the bus?'

'Yes,' I said, barely hearing her.

'Remember the confusion about whether some of the kids who were supposed to be on the bus really were? Because not everyone on the coach's roster was accounted for?'

'Right.' I glanced at the counter, the kitchen door.

'They're not confused any more.'

Paige held up the *Globe*. The glaring headline was impossible to ignore:

**Bodies of Four Missing BU Terriers
Found at Logan**

'The airport?' I asked.

'They were floating in the harbour at the end of a runway. Two pilots spotted them last night.'

I took the newspaper and flipped quickly through the pages. 'Does it say anything about what they looked like? When they were found? Were they –?'

'No,' Paige said. 'It doesn't say.'

I exhaled a small sigh of relief. If they'd been smiling, the article would've said so. That was too grotesque an image – and too valuable a detail – to omit. I folded the newspaper and slid it under the lunch tray, out of sight.

'When you were with Betty this weekend, did she happen to mention if . . . ?'

Paige took an iced tea and fiddled with the lemon wedge perched on the rim of the glass.

'Did she say if anything . . . strange . . . was going on? Or if she was maybe hearing things she shouldn't?'

She took the sugar dispenser, held it over the glass, studied the white powder as it streamed towards the liquid.

'I'm sorry,' I said, 'I know it's uncomfortable. I just –'

'Don't you think I'd tell you if there was anything you needed to know?'

I sat back. Paige had never spoken to me like that before.

Her face crumpled immediately. 'I'm sorry. I'm an idiot. It was just a hard weekend. Like I said in the car coming back yesterday, Betty was emotional, which made *me* emotional . . . and I guess I'm not ready to talk about it yet.'

'You don't have to talk about anything. And I'm the idiot. It's just, my mind automatically goes there whenever something like this happens.' I nodded to the corner of the newspaper sticking out from under the tray. 'Even if it's silly and illogical. I can't help it.'

The sound of glass breaking made us jump in our chairs. Remembering Willa's caffeine jitters and the way they'd made her drop the napkin dispenser, I stood, ready to help her pick up whatever had slipped this time and demand to know how she knew who I was.

But it wasn't Willa. It was a barista – the same one who'd served me the shot of seaweed.

'Of course,' he said, throwing his hands up in the air. 'Of course *this* on top of people crying family emergency and leaving in the middle of their shifts.'

Mumbling, he grabbed a broom and started sweeping. I looked around the coffee shop's main room, stepped towards the counter and scanned its length, and then peered into the kitchen.

Willa wasn't there. But every other employee I'd seen since we'd gotten there was.

'Vanessa?' Paige asked as I turned towards the door. 'Where are you going?'

'Be back in a second,' I called behind me.

Outside, I looked up and down the pavement. When Willa wasn't in front of the café, I found a narrow alley down the block, darted between dirty brick walls, and ran. A strip of tarmac divided the businesses running along this street and the one behind it, but tall fences made it impossible to see the back of the Beanery. I kept going, dodging trash cans and dumpsters, and shot out onto the pavement. Ignoring the appreciative smile of a middle-aged man cleaning the windows of the pizzeria next to me, I veered left – and almost slammed into another man.

His back was to me, but I recognised the frizzy white hair floating around his head and the red wool peeking out from under the hem of his jacket.

Dad was downtown. In the middle of the day. Even though he'd told us at breakfast earlier about the amazing Thoreau lecture he was giving at ten o'clock. His lectures lasted an hour, minimum, and it was just after eleven. Even if he'd kept his talk short, there was no way he could've made it here from Newton that fast.

I was about to call out to him when he raised one arm and waved to someone in front of him. I followed several feet behind, staying close to the buildings so I could duck inside if he turned around.

He's just meeting Mom, I told myself. *Or a colleague. For an unexpected lunch date.*

When he slowed to a stop, I was in front of a vintage clothing store. A long rack lined with winter jackets stood on the pavement; I took a pink peacoat, held it up so that it hid my face and torso, and peered around it. A cluster of people waiting for a bus prevented a clear view, but between their shifting heads and shoulders, I caught quick glimpses.

Of a hug. A kiss on the cheek. Two Beanery coffee cups.

One for him.

The other for Willa.

CHAPTER 20

I wanted to yell. I wanted to run over, shove them apart, and demand to know what was going on. But the second I realised who he was meeting, my mouth went dry. My legs trembled beneath me. I grabbed the clothing rack to steady myself, and when I looked up again, they were gone.

I thought of Dad's e-mail, the initials of the person he'd been corresponding with every day.

W.B.D. Could the W stand for Willa?

Their quick departure gave me the rest of the day to plan what I would say. And after school, while Paige stayed behind for extra help in maths, I went home, determined to learn what no one had told me in seventeen years – what they might *never* have told me if I hadn't first discovered part of the truth myself.

'Is Dad in his office?' I slammed the front door closed, tossed my backpack on the couch. Through the dining-room doorway I could see Mom sitting at the head of the table. 'I need to talk to him.'

No answer.

'Mom?' I was ready to storm in the opposite direction, but something about her posture stopped me. Her back was straight as a stick, her head perfectly still.

I started towards her, the calm I'd achieved during the day slowly crumbling. Did she know? That Dad had lied about where he'd been that morning . . . and, at this point, about who knew what else?

'Mom?' I asked again, standing behind her.

Still nothing. She was transfixed by the images on the small television screen before her. Leaning forward for a better look, I put one hand on her shoulder.

'Vanessa!' She jumped. 'Don't sneak around like that!'

I stood up, brought one hand to my racing heart. 'I wasn't sneaking. I slammed the door. I said your name twice. You didn't hear me.'

'Oh.' Puzzlement crossed her face. It was gone in an instant, and then she beamed up at me. 'I did the most wonderful thing today. Look.' She held up the TV, which I now saw was actually a portable DVD player. 'Recognise anyone?'

'George Clooney?' I asked, squinting.

'You might want to save that buttering up for when your father's in the room.'

'That's Dad?' The man with the dark hair looked too

young to be my father. He was also wearing a cape and vampire fangs.

'And me. And you. And lots of our friends.'

A home movie. That, from the looks of it – and us – was at least fifteen years old.

Mom replaced the DVD player on the table. 'There's a shop in Cambridge that converts tapes to discs. I found a bunch of our old home videos hidden away in the basement and had them changed over.'

'That's great,' I said, thinking this was a step forward. Maybe watching old videos of Justine would help her confront the loss and eventually feel comfortable talking about it.

'You were just a toddler, so you probably don't re-member, but for years your father and I hosted the best haunted house this side of Boston.'

'Why'd you stop having them?' I asked.

'I started working more. You kids got older. But your sister always loved them – she missed them when they stopped.' Mom paused, then beamed up at me. 'I thought it would be fun to do again this year. You can invite Simon, of course, and anyone else you'd like. Same goes for Paige.'

And there it was. Mom wasn't revisiting the past to get through the present. She was revisiting the past in hopes of re-creating it.

I was too worried to be fazed by the Simon reference. 'I don't think this is a very good idea.'

She looked at me. 'What do you mean?'

'I mean it's pretty obvious what this is about. And if you think you'll feel better by doing things that made Justine happy –'

'Your father's in his office,' she snapped. 'You were looking for *him* when you came in, weren't you? Not me.'

I slowly retreated, now noticing the tissue box next to her arm, the moist paper balls scattered across the table. 'Right. Sorry.'

My worry quickly gave way to anger as I neared Dad's office. Whatever was going on with Mom was his fault. Her behaviour might have been triggered by Justine's death, but again, if it wasn't for his relationship with Charlotte Bleu, I wouldn't be here, Justine would be, and Mom would be fine. And to top it off, after messing everything up, he still wasn't doing a single thing to help her get better.

All of which sent the cool, calm line of questioning I'd prepared right out the window.

'Who's Willa?'

Behind his computer, Dad choked on whatever he'd just sipped.

I closed the door and strode towards his desk. 'I saw

you downtown today. When you were supposed to be in class.'

'Vanessa,' he said, his face turning tomato red as he mopped up the tea with a stack of papers, 'why don't you have a seat, take a deep breath, and calm down? Then we can try to sort out what it is you think you saw.'

I sat down. It was either that or strangle him. 'Mom's planning a spectacular haunted house. Just like the ones you used to have. Do you know why?'

His hands shook as he dropped the sodden papers into his trash can.

'Because she's trying to feel closer to her dead daughter.' I paused, waited for him to take another sip of tea. 'Her *only* daughter.'

This time he dropped the mug. It hit the edge of the desk and fell to the floor.

'That's funny. Willa has slippery fingers, too. Probably just one of many things you two have in common.'

He sighed. 'Who told you?'

'Who *didn't* tell me?'

He took his time retrieving the mug, then sat back and clasped his hands over his belly. 'I understand you're angry . . . but please know it's a very complicated situation.'

'Please know that's an understatement.'

He raised his hands, as if giving me that one. 'It's a mess. And I offer you my most heartfelt apologies.'

'For which part? Hurting Mom? Lying to Justine and me? Telling my entire life story in daily installations to a total stranger?'

His eyes grew big. 'How did you –'

'Or seeing yet another woman? Now? After everything that's happened?'

'Vanessa,' he said sternly, like I'd gone too far. He sat up, leaned towards me. 'I'm not seeing Willa – or anyone else. I love your mother. I've loved her with all that I am for more than twenty years. If I didn't, you would've found out the truth a long time ago.'

My chest tightened. 'What's that supposed to mean?'

'It means Jacqueline . . .' His voice trailed off, and his head dropped. A second later, it lifted again. 'It means she wanted to protect you. She didn't want you to have to suffer from knowing something that wasn't your fault and that you could never change.'

'So, what? You really weren't going to tell me? Ever? Because it would be so much better for me not to know who I really am?'

'That wasn't my intention. I figured – I hoped – that the right time would eventually present itself. And that whenever it did . . . everyone would agree you deserved to know the truth.'

I looked away, tried to imagine how I'd react if Simon wanted to do something I didn't agree with. Would I go along with it even if I thought it was wrong? Because I loved him more than any potential consequence?

Yes, I probably would.

'Who is Willa?' I asked a moment later.

'A friend. She knew Charlotte.'

I lifted my eyes to his. It was the first time I'd heard him say her name aloud. He didn't even blink.

'Do you see her often?' I asked.

'No. Today was the first time in many years.'

'You just said she was a friend.'

'We stay in touch,' he said. 'We don't visit.'

'Is she the one you e-mail every day?'

'Yes.' If he was mad that I'd accessed his account, he didn't show it.

'And you tell her about me?'

'I do. She and Charlotte were close. I keep her informed as a courtesy.'

'A Christmas card's courteous.'

'It means nothing,' he said.

Clearly it meant something or he wouldn't be doing it. 'Does Mom know?' I asked.

'No. She wouldn't understand.'

'And that's not enough reason to stop?'

He sighed, closed his eyes. 'There was an arrangement.'

My breath caught. Finally, he was going to tell me something I didn't already know . . . and now I wasn't sure I wanted to hear it.

He looked at me, reached for my hand. Apparently thinking better of it, he sat back and rested his on the arm of his chair instead.

'Before I go any further, you must know that you are loved, Vanessa. Every minute since the one you were born, you've been adored. And when Charlotte and I made our decision, we did so with only your happiness in mind.'

'Okay . . .'

His lips parted, closed. Parted again. After all this time, he didn't know how to explain it. 'Charlotte didn't tell me she was pregnant. I found out because I accidentally ran into her in the supermarket when I was up in Winter Harbor one fall weekend, working on my book.'

His book. Back then, there probably had been one.

'At first, she tried to flee the market without talking to me. Then, when I caught up with her in the parking lot, she told me someone else was the father. But her eyes gave her away.' He paused, looked off at something across the room. 'Her eyes were . . . something.'

This I knew all too well. 'What happened after that?' I prompted, not wanting to dwell.

'She tried to brush me off. I wouldn't let her. I told her that though our . . . situation . . . wasn't something I was proud of, and though I hated every second of pain it caused my wife, I couldn't help bring a child into the world and then disappear. I demanded to be involved, to help, even if all that amounted to was annual updates and financial assistance.'

I bristled. As disappointed by him as I'd been, I still didn't want to imagine life without my Big Poppa.

'If it had been up to me,' he said quietly, seeing my reaction, 'I would have been with you more often than not. Somehow, we would've made it work. But she didn't want that.'

'What did she want?'

'For a while, not much. Throughout the rest of her pregnancy, she sent occasional notes to me at work, telling me how she was feeling. Then, when you were born, she sent another note. I went back to Winter Harbor the day I received the news and met you for the very first time.' He smiled. 'You were the prettiest baby I'd ever seen.'

'And Mom still didn't know?' I asked, quickly moving past the special moment he and Charlotte had shared.

His head lowered, his smile faded. 'Not at that time, no. She didn't find out for another year.'

I pictured the boxes in the basement, recalled Mom's explanation that she'd given away my newborn clothes. 'What happened then?'

Moving slowly, as if buying time to decide whether he was doing the right thing, he turned towards the bookcase next to his desk. He slid aside a stack of old dictionaries, revealing a plain wooden box. He removed a small keyring from his sweater, unlocked the box, and reached inside.

'I received this,' he said.

Barely breathing, I took the postcard. It was a scenic shot of Winter Harbor in fall, when the leaves glowed brilliant shades of red, orange, and yellow. Betty's was in the forefront. Behind the restaurant the water, rimmed with trees, gleamed in the afternoon sun.

My eyes lingered on Betty's. It was a Winter Harbor institution, but every store in town sold postcards featuring dozens of local scenes: the lighthouse, rocky cliffs zigzagging down to the ocean, fields of wildflowers. Yet Charlotte had chosen this one. Did she do so intentionally? Knowing I'd eventually see it, hoping it'd be some kind of hint?

Fingers trembling, I turned over the card. The blue ink had lightened with time. Some letters were smudged, like the note had once gotten wet. The handwriting was small, precise, as if trying to calm its message.

Dear Philip,

This will be the last time you hear from me. Vanessa and I are leaving Winter Harbor. I know you, like me, want only what's best for her. That's why we're going . . . and why I can't tell you where.

Thank you. You've given me an extraordinary gift for which I'll be for ever grateful.

— Charlotte

'That's it?' I asked. 'She just left?'

'She tried. Fortunately, she owned a small business and gave her employees a phone number in case they needed her. When I went back up to try to stop her from leaving, I sweet-talked the employees with some little-known Emerson trivia, and they called her on my behalf. She hung up on me, but Winter Harbor police tracked down the number's location. I found you both in a tiny apartment in Montreal.'

'You drove to Canada?'

'I couldn't abandon the only lead I had. Plus, I was worried she'd fear me doing exactly what I did and move again.'

As I pictured him racing through New England and

across the border, I felt strangely moved. He'd cared. His motives before and after my birth might've been occasionally muddled . . . but I believed he'd always cared about me.

'When I found Charlotte,' he continued, 'she gave me two choices. Either I could leave and never see either of you again, or I could take you home. And raise you here, in Boston. She said that was actually the better option for you, but that she hadn't wanted to ask me, to risk destroying my family. When I told her you could only make our family better, she agreed to let you go. Her only additional request was that she never saw you again, because she didn't think she could handle the pain of saying goodbye a second time.'

'Those were the only options?' I asked. 'What about joint custody?'

'It was one or the other. She wasn't clear about much, but she was clear about that. She said it was for your safety – not just your happiness or well-being, but your *safety*. And I believed her. I assumed she had an ex-boyfriend who she worried would do something drastic if he knew about us. About you.' He looked at me until I looked back. 'The only thing worse than the possibility of never seeing you again was the possibility of something bad happening to you. Something I could've prevented.'

'So you brought me home.' I shifted my eyes to the stack of dictionaries, willed myself not to cry.

'I did.' He paused. 'We both know your mother . . . Jacqueline . . . isn't always the easiest person to please. But Vanessa, she took one look at you and fell in love. She had issues with me, obviously – when I told her about you and Charlotte after Charlotte disappeared from Winter Harbor, she locked me out of the house for a week. But whatever disappointment or anger she felt towards me was never directed at you. And when I told her you needed a good home, she made sure you had one.'

'Just like that?' I whispered.

'Just like that.'

He said this so simply, so matter-of-factly, I knew it must be true. 'And Justine?'

'She wasn't even two years old at the time. She wouldn't have remembered your first year on earth if you'd spent it under our roof.'

'And Charlotte?'

'She returned to Winter Harbor.' His gaze fell to the postcard I still held. 'A week later, there was a fire. At her store, in the middle of the night.'

I watched his lips tremble. I was tempted to hug him but resisted.

'I don't know why she was there so late,' he said. 'No

one does. But she probably fell asleep, because she never called nine-one-one. By the time someone passed by, saw smoke through the trees, and alerted the authorities, it was too late. The building, with Charlotte inside, was gone.'

There was a dull pain in my chest, like my lungs were contracting in sympathy. I'd known this had happened, but hearing it from Big Poppa, being so near his sadness, made it much more real.

'A few months after that,' Dad said, reaching into the wooden box again, 'I received another note.'

I took the card. It was ivory, its edges worn. The handwriting was similar to that on the postcard, but looser, with more space between letters.

Dear Philip,

I'm writing on behalf of Charlotte Bleu, my younger sister. As I was sorting through Charlotte's personal belongings in her home after the tragic fire, I came upon several notes you'd written her. Knowing the brief yet important history you shared, I wanted to reach out. I hope you don't mind.

Needless to say, I'm devastated by this unexpected loss. And while I don't know you personally, and while you certainly don't owe me anything, I wondered if you would consider a trial partnership. In exchange for regular, written updates about Vanessa, I will, if and when the time comes, answer any and all

*questions she may have about her mother. As I understand it, you
and Charlotte didn't spend very much time together; I would be
pleased to share with your daughter what you cannot.*

*This is a difficult, sensitive situation for all involved, and
I understand if you'd rather sever ties completely and move
forward. However, if you're willing to attempt this arrangement,
I assure you that I will act with the utmost care and discretion.
I have no personal agenda other than to know my niece from a
distance, and to do for her what her mother would have asked
me to.*

I look forward to your response.

With kindest regards,

W. Donagan

P.O. Box 9892

Boston, MA 02135

'Willa . . . my aunt,' I said, trying out the word, 'she's
lived in Boston this whole time? And she's never wanted
to see me? To at least meet me?'

'She said she didn't want to complicate things any
more than they already were. I agreed that was best.'

I looked up. 'And now that I know who she is?'

He gave me a small, sorry smile. 'Her feelings haven't
changed. That's why we met today. She told me you'd
been coming into the coffee shop and that she thought
you knew something was up. That made her uneasy.

She's always felt very strongly that direct communication between you two would only worsen a complicated situation.'

'She's wrong.' My voice was sharp, urgent.

'Excuse me?'

I understood his surprise and did my best to rewind. After all, he didn't know everything either.

'Dad,' I said, taking a deep breath, struggling to recall some of what I'd planned to say, 'I'm not going to lie. When I first learned that Mom wasn't really my mother –'

'She *is* your mother,' he corrected quickly.

I tried again. 'When I first learned she wasn't my *biological* mother, I was shocked. And angry. And disappointed. I couldn't fathom how you could do that to her – or to Justine. Part of me still doesn't, since the one surefire way to resist a siren's call is to love another woman, and I truly believe you've always loved Mom, but maybe Charlotte's power was extraordinarily strong, or maybe –'

'Vanessa.'

I held my breath, looked at his hand, which he held up like a traffic sign.

'What did you just say?' he asked.

I'd been so focused on racing ahead to the next

thought it was hard to remember. 'That you've always loved Mom?'

'After that.'

'That maybe Charlotte's powers were really strong?'

His head tilted to one side, and his eyebrows lowered. 'What powers?'

I hesitated, then, realising the confusion, shook my head and offered a small smile. 'It's okay. I mean, it's not – it's hard and weird and unreal – but at least I know now. You don't have to hide it any more.'

'Hide . . . what?'

My lips, still lifted, froze. Images of Paul Carsons and Tom Connelly and Max Hawkins flashed through my head.

Was it possible?

'Dad,' I said, 'you knew that Charlotte wasn't normal, right? That your relationship . . . wasn't normal?'

His eyes narrowed even more. He didn't have to speak for me to know his answer.

'She was a siren. Like in one of your old books.' I paused, wishing, not for the first time, that we could re-wind, start over. 'You were her target.'

CHAPTER 21

'Do you have any special skills?'

'Special skills?' I repeated.

The man waved around a champagne glass filled with sparkling cider. 'Like playing the accordion, or competitive flame-throwing, or something else you might not think to include on your application but that could set you apart from the thousands of other seniors with great grades and standard extracurricular activities?'

I can breathe underwater. And command the attention of every guy in the room just by walking into it. And make enemies with every girl in the room the same way.

'I don't think so,' I said.

'What about your family? Maybe your uncle's a famous actor? Or your second cousin's an Olympic luger? At Colgate, your family's our family, so if the relatives are doing anything exceptional, you should definitely let us know.'

My female relatives kill men for sport. Will that win me early acceptance?

'They're all pretty average,' I said, holding up my empty water glass. 'Would you mind ... ?'

Beaming at the request, he took the glass and started backing up, towards the refreshment table. 'Don't you go anywhere! Next I want to tell you what Colgate can do to make your life –'

I knew I should warn him that he was about to collide with a waiter, but not doing so bought me about twenty seconds as he stumbled and brushed juice off his lapel. I used the time to get a head start towards the other side of the room.

'Vanessa!' a female voice called out behind me.

I glanced over my shoulder to see Ms Mulligan hurrying after me, holding a small blue Yale flag overhead. Behind her was another male recruiter in a pinstriped suit and bold red tie. He was already smiling, which made me move faster. Shielded by clusters of students, I zigzagged through the transformed gymnasium. By the time I reached the nearly empty state-school section, which Hawthorne had deigned to include for their few scholarship students, Ms Mulligan and the Yalie had given up on me and moved on to the senior class president.

I took a water bottle from my backpack and drank. I hadn't been feeling well since my long talk with Dad the day before, when I'd told him everything I knew about the Marchands and last summer and had shown him old *Winter Harbor Herald* articles online for back-up. I'd also told him I'd inherited some of Charlotte's abilities but left out a few key details, like my involvement in freezing the harbour and how unpredictable my physical health had been since then. But even without that information, we'd talked for hours. I'd left his office exhausted and thirstier than I'd been in weeks. I would've skipped today's networking event if attendance hadn't been mandatory for all seniors; I didn't need to attract even more unwanted attention by breaking rules and getting in trouble.

Plus, the event gave me somewhere to be besides home for a few hours. This was awkward and uncomfortable, but since Mom was still studying home movies and Dad had taken a personal day to hide out in his office, it was also preferable.

I wandered around the room's perimeter, careful to stay a safe distance from the long tables covered in fancy linens and bouquets of flowers. We'd been instructed to break the strict dress code so that the event felt more like the 'mocktail' party it was supposed to be, and my classmates had taken advantage of the opportunity to wear their designer best. The girls had gone for librarian-sexy in pencil skirts, silk blouses, and heels; the guys looked like Wall Street trainees in dark suits and shiny ties.

Not wanting to stand out even more in my

Hawthorne skirt and hooded sweatshirt, I'd striven for invisible while getting dressed and had finally decided on black pants, a black turtleneck, and black flats. I'd taken my hair out of its usual ponytail and let it hang down so that I could hide behind it when necessary.

As I circled the room, I saw only one other student who'd taken about as much care with his appearance. He wore jeans, a wrinkled beige T-shirt, and a brown sports coat that, with its suede elbow patches and frayed cuffs, was trendy rather than classic. Dirty Converses completed the outfit. He stood in a small circle with two older men who talked to each other like he wasn't even there.

And as he stared off at nothing, his expression blank, I knew that, in a way, Parker was somewhere else.

'I'm done.'

The salt water I'd just swallowed shot back up my throat.

'Sorry.' Paige patted my back as I struggled not to choke. 'I waved on my way over. I thought you saw me.'

I forced the water back down. 'What about your list?'

She held up a notebook. Each of the dozens of colleges she'd been interested in learning more about was crossed off with a single red line.

'They're all either too big, too small, too expensive, or too hard to get into. And I'm definitely not enough of anything for them.' Her arm fell to her side. 'The

Amherst guy asked me what sports I play, and when I said I swam for fun, he excused himself to make an important phone call – then went to the refreshment table instead.'

'It's his loss,' I said. 'These schools are so used to their stuffy traditions, they don't know what they're missing.'

'Well, I don't think I missed anything. And I'm kind of tired. I think I'll check out at the nurse and go home early.'

'Do you want me to come with you? We can get something to eat? Or see a movie?'

'Thanks, but I could use a few hours alone.' Apparently seeing concern flash across my face, she added, 'I'm fine. Really. I just want to sort through some things. College. My future. All that fun stuff.'

'Okay,' I relented, unconvinced. 'You'll call if you change your mind?'

'Absolutely.'

I watched her disappear into the crowd, then continued walking. When I came to a tall cardboard cutout of five beaming students holding diplomas from the University of Massachusetts at Worcester, I ducked between it and the wall. I lowered myself to the floor, tilted my head back until it pressed against cool tile, and closed my eyes.

'You look like you'd rather be home under the covers, too,' a soft voice said.

Looking to my left, I saw a girl not much older than me sitting on the floor a few feet away. She was behind a velvet curtain one college was using as part of its display, hugging her knees to her chest.

'Crowds aren't really my thing,' I said.

'Mine either. I'm only here to keep my job.'

I lifted my head from the wall. She looked more professional than the students in a grey wool suit and pearls, but her chubby cheeks were flushed, her blonde hair was pulled back into a sloppy ponytail, and black flecks lined her eyelids, like her hand had shaken when she was putting on mascara. She had to be nineteen. Twenty, max.

'Your job?' I asked.

'I work for –' She hesitated before shifting into a squat and peeking around the edge of the curtain; apparently deciding the coast was clear, she raised herself just enough to dash the short distance between her hiding spot and mine – 'Dartmouth,' she finished, sitting next to me.

Justine's answer to the personal essay, the one confirming Mom's greatest fear – that her eldest daughter, her *only* daughter, wasn't going to college – flashed before my eyes.

I don't know . . . but neither do you . . .

'I'm an admissions counsellor,' the girl continued, fanning her face with one hand. 'And a Dartmouth alum. When I graduated last spring, I didn't know what I wanted to do – the school's amazing at teaching you how to think, but it doesn't offer one course that tells you exactly how to survive in the real world.'

'You graduated? From college?'

'I look like I'm twelve, I know. I'm actually twenty – I graduated high school early, too. That's also why I didn't know what to do with myself. I was so busy cruising at mach speed, I never slowed down long enough to think about where I was going.'

'And when you did, you decided Admissions was it?' I asked, genuinely curious. For all the reasons Hawthorne said we should go to an Ivy League school, staying there post-commencement was never one of them.

'My parents did. It was either that or come home and live with them until I figured out something else, and they worried that if I did that, I'd get a job at Starbucks to pass the time and end up frothing milk for ever.'

'That would be their worst nightmare?' I guessed.

'Pretty much. And as it turns out, working in such a public position is mine.' She peeked out into the gym again before turning back to me. 'I'm supposed to be talking up all these students and telling them how great Dartmouth is, but I'm wired for studying, not socialising. I'm just no good at it.'

'You're doing fine right now.'

She'd been biting her bottom lip between sentences, but now her mouth relaxed into a smile. 'I'm Alison Seaford. And you're . . . ?'

'About as fond of socialising as you are.' I didn't want to give my name in case Ms Mulligan had shared my situation with all of today's recruiters.

'Right. Well, I don't know what your plans are, but Dartmouth really is a fantastic school. Gorgeous campus, top-notch facilities, award-winning professors. And a totally supportive community.'

She seemed so nice I was tempted to tell her about Mom's love of Dartmouth, but I didn't know how to do that without prompting other questions. 'Thanks for the info,' I said instead. 'I'll definitely keep it in mind.'

'Great.' She took a deep breath and released it slowly. 'I should probably get back out there. But it was nice meeting a fellow wallflower – you don't see many of those at schools like this. And if you ever have any questions about Dartmouth or college in general, please feel free to shoot me an e-mail.' She took a business card from her suit jacket pocket and handed it to me. 'I'm *great* behind the computer.'

It wasn't until she was gone and I was alone again, staring at the shiny green shield on her business card, that I realised what I'd said.

I'd keep it in mind. Like it was really an option.

For the first time, I was disappointed by the idea of not going to college rather than simply scared because of the reasons it was impossible. The feeling was so uncomfortable – and pointless – I emerged from behind the cardboard graduates and started for the gymnasium entrance. If Paige hadn't gotten too far, maybe I could still convince her to join me for a movie.

I was halfway around the room's perimeter when a searing pain exploded in my head. It started between my eyes and shot back, like an electric drill burrowing into my forehead, through my brain, and out of my skull. I clamped my mouth shut to keep from crying out and fell against the wall to prevent myself from collapsing. The pain was blinding, the urge to close my eyes overwhelming, but somehow, I held them open. I wasn't in the middle of the room, but I was still exposed to anyone looking this way; I didn't want to alarm them before the white light faded.

Which it did, finally, several seconds later. Just in time for me to see Parker follow a girl into the hallway.

I started after them, glancing once behind me. Across the room, Parker's dad still talked with the Princeton recruiter like nothing was wrong, like Parker had just excused himself to give his dad time to seal the deal.

But something was very wrong. Because I'd felt pain like that before. I knew what it meant.

Zara was here.

I burst through the gymnasium doors. My head snapped to the right, then the left, but the hallway was empty. They were already gone. I tried to listen for her, to feel her presence, but all I heard was the buzzing of conversation from the gym. All I felt was the pain still throbbing, less intensely, inside my head.

Using that as a guide, I headed in the direction of the main entrance, thinking Zara would want to take Parker out of the school and away from witnesses. The ache dulled then sharpened. When it became more bearable, I quickened my pace until it struck again, slowing me down. Twice it seemed to disappear completely, so I backtracked and turned left instead of right, right instead of left. Eventually, the pain strengthened and steadied, and I stopped.

I was so worried – and terrified – it took me a second to realise where the pain had led me.

The swimming pool.

Through the glass door I watched Parker take off his shoes and socks, roll the cuffs of his pants to his knees, and sit at the edge of the Olympic-size swimming pool. Zara was nowhere in sight, and for a brief moment I thought – hoped – that she'd left him alone. But as he lowered his legs into the water, she came out of the girls' changing room, wearing a black bikini and a sheer black sarong. Her dark hair hung loose down her back and the sides of her face, hiding the gleaming silver eyes I knew were aimed right at him. She touched Parker's shoulder, made sure he appreciated her appearance before slowly untying the sarong and letting it drift away from her waist, down her legs.

The pain swelled against the base of my skull and started down my spine. I twisted the doorknob, but it didn't budge. She'd locked the door.

I opened my mouth to yell but stopped when she sank slowly into the water, keeping her back to me. Once all the way in, she turned towards him, placing her hands on the tiles on either side of his legs. His torso blocked her face, but I knew that her silver eyes were warm and cold at the same time, her pink mouth was partially open in invitation, and her head was coyly dipped to one side.

I knew she looked just like she had when she'd targeted Caleb, then Simon, in the woods. When her beauty had been like a pendulum that hypnotised with a single swing. Later Simon had told me how strong her power over him was, and the one thing that had snapped him out of it.

Me. I'd yelled his name and broken her spell.

But Parker didn't love me the way Simon did – the way Simon had. I wasn't even sure he liked me that much. My voice wouldn't have the same effect on him.

I still had to try.

'Parker!'

Nothing.

'Parker!'

Still nothing. His head lowered as hers lifted, and stayed there as they kissed.

I banged on the glass with both fists. Pounded harder when she helped him take off his jacket and pull off his T-shirt. As he started to slide across the pool's edge, towards her and the water, I spun away from the door and across the hall. I opened the glass display case and grabbed trophies, plaques, and medals. And then I hurled them, one after the other, at the swimming-pool door.

On the third trophy, the glass cracked. A gold medal finished the job, sending shards flying on both sides of the door.

'Stop!' I yelled, lunging across the broken glass. I threw one arm through the opening and fumbled for the knob. 'Get away from him!'

My hand shook, making my fingers slip off the lock. I was still trying to get a good grip when another hand – larger, wider – gently squeezed my arm.

'Vanessa?' Parker asked.

My head snapped up. Through a haze of fear and pain, I registered his green eyes, narrow with concern, and then her . . . brown eyes, wide with shock.

'Georgia?' I said.

The girl Parker had just been making out with stood a few feet behind him, soaking wet, shivering, clutching her sarong to her chest. I saw her face for the first time and was stunned when her eyes weren't silvery blue, when she didn't look anything like I'd imagined.

Even now my head pounded, but this girl wasn't Zara. She was Georgia Vincent, a smart, pretty junior who was in my study hall . . . and who apparently had a thing for Parker.

'Yes?' She shot him a confused look.

'I'm so sorry.' I tried to pull away. 'I thought you were . . . I thought he was . . .'

'It's okay,' Parker said gently. 'Everyone's okay.'

My arm, suspended above the broken wedges of glass still in the door, was tired, heavy. I wanted to yank it back and use whatever energy I had left to run down the hall and out of the building, but Parker's fingers tightened around my flesh, refusing to let go.

'Actually,' Georgia said, 'I'm not. What *was* that, Vanessa? What's wrong with you?'

'Nothing,' I said, not believing it myself. 'I just . . . thought you were someone else.'

'An axe murderer?' She held out both arms, exposing her practically naked body. 'Look at me. Where would I hide it?'

I lowered my eyes and stared at the floor.

'Whatever. I'm going to dry off and get my clothes.' She paused. When she spoke again, her voice was softer, flirty. 'Come with me?'

'I don't think so,' Parker said.

Her bare feet slapped the tile floor as she stormed away. I waited until I heard the changing-room door open and close before daring to look at Parker.

'I'm so sorry,' I said.

'You mentioned that. And don't be. You saved me from doing something I would've regretted the second I'd done it.'

'I yelled and knocked first.' As if that made it better.

'The pool's right next to the English wing. The glass is soundproof.'

His eyes held mine. I wanted to look away as much as I wanted to stand exactly like that. For better or worse, my aching arm made the decision for me.

'Sorry . . . do you mind?'

He glanced at his hand, then immediately released his fingers, like he was surprised to find them still touching me.

I stepped back, the soles of my shoes crunching against the broken glass. 'I should go. Find someone to help clean this up, I mean.'

'Don't.'

I stopped.

'It's still going on, isn't it?' Parker asked. 'The net-working thing?'

I nodded.

'Why don't we just hang here for a while? I mean, we might not be able to keep out all the recruiters who are probably scouring the halls for us right now' – he nodded to the hole in the door – 'but I'm willing to risk it if you are.'

I was. Partly because he wanted me to, partly because it might give me a chance to explain my strange beha-viour without revealing too much, but mostly because I was completely drained. I doubted I could even make it back to the gymnasium without napping first.

When I didn't make a move to leave, he unlocked the door, opened it, and offered his hand to help me walk across the shards of glass on the other side.

I followed him to the edge of the pool, where his clothes still sat. He put on his T-shirt and offered me his jacket. When I thanked him but declined, he left the jacket on the floor and continued walking towards the deep end of the pool.

'He's all yours!' Georgia shouted, fully clothed and hurrying towards the swimming-pool entrance. 'And by the way – he doesn't live up to the hype!'

He stopped at the bottom of a diving-board ladder. Coming up behind him, I raised my eyebrows.

'Your first dissatisfied customer?' I asked.

'Don't know.' He gave me a crooked grin. 'I'm still waiting on the report from another one.'

I was grateful when he started up the ladder so he couldn't see my face burn. Strangely, despite the embarrassing reference, I felt a tiny rush of energy. It started at my toes and seemed to swim up, through my veins. It was enough to make me take a metal step in both hands and climb after him.

I'd made it as far as the second step when I pictured Simon waiting for me on the other side of the iron fence surrounding Winter Harbor's Camp Heroine. For a second, I clung to the cool metal and considered climbing back down.

'There is a girl,' Parker called down.

And there was another rush. It made my skin tingle – and me keep moving.

'Remember that day in the water polo lounge? When you asked me if I was seeing anyone?'

'Yes?' I focused on my movements. Right hand, left hand, right foot, left foot.

'Well, I lied. Or maybe I didn't. Not technically, anyway. You know Amelia Hathaway?'

'Sure,' I said, grateful when he didn't mention my spying on them in the library a few weeks ago.

'We hooked up at a party over the summer and I thought I wasn't interested in anything else – until I was.

We hung out a few times, and while I liked her more and more, the feelings weren't exactly reciprocated.'

'That's too bad.' Right hand, left hand, right foot, left foot.

'It was. Especially because when she insisted she didn't feel the same way, I just stopped caring about what I did and who I did it with.' He grabbed the railings at the top of the ladder and hoisted himself onto the board. 'Until now.'

Right hand, left hand, right foot, left –

I stopped, my hands on the railings, Parker's hands on mine. I peeked down, saw how far away the floor was, and didn't resist when he helped me up onto the board. We faced each other, our bodies separated by inches, our fingers overlapping on the railings. The combination of his nearness, a lifelong fear of heights, and standing twenty feet above the pool should've made me too terrified to breathe, but I felt surprisingly steady. Strong.

The feeling only intensified when Parker spoke again.

'I don't know what you thought was going on in here,' he said quietly. 'But I know you were worried about me. Whatever it was, you thought I was in some kind of trouble and wanted to help. Just like that night in the harbour . . . right?'

I swallowed, nodded, looked past his shoulder to the water below.

'Vanessa, no one's ever cared about me that much before. And I'm not sure why you do, but I'd love –'

'Parker.' My voice was a whisper.

'No, please. Let me get this out before I lose my nerve. We don't know each other that well, but I'd love to –'

'*Parker.*'

He stopped. His fingers pressed against mine as he turned and followed my gaze.

He leaned over the railing. 'Is that –? Doesn't he look like –?'

'Yes,' I said, tears filling my eyes.

It was Matt Harrison. The Bates recruiter. Floating on his back, and drifting towards the centre of the pool.

As Parker waved and called out, trying for a response, I sank to my knees, knowing he wouldn't get one.

Because Matt Harrison was dead.

And smiling like he'd never been happier.

CHAPTER 22

After alerting school security, Parker and I spent an hour talking to the police. He tried to get me to go before they arrived, to save me from having to deal with the messy aftermath, but I refused. He did most of the explaining anyway, but I wanted to confirm that we'd been together when we found the body. If he'd said he'd been alone, the police might've suspected him of being involved, and I couldn't allow that.

I stayed for another reason, too. While Parker filled in his dad and President O'Hare, both of whom looked more concerned about how they were going to handle this potential bad publicity than the fact that a college recruiter had just died on the premises, I excused myself to call my parents – and then went outside instead.

Hawthorne and the Boston Police Department must have had some sort of pre-arrangement, because by the school's main and rear entrances, life continued undisturbed. The networking event had ended, and seniors and recruiters mingled in separate groups on the steps and pavement, the recruiters talking about where to grab an early dinner, the students eavesdropping in hopes of 'accidentally' joining them. They appeared to have no idea about what was transpiring on the other side of the building. And besides a few straggling lower-classmen, there was no activity by the rear entrance.

I was about to go back inside and try tailing a police officer until he was alone when a white truck got my attention. It was parked half in, half out of the narrow delivery entrance driveway several yards down the block from the building's rear doors. COLONY BAKERY was written on its sides in blue script, and a darkened strobe light sat on the dashboard. As I approached, I could hear the static of walkie-talkies, men speaking in hushed voices. The truck took up most of the driveway, blocking my view of what was going on behind it, but I caught quick glimpses of red medical bags, a stretcher.

'You lost?'

I jumped at the woman's voice. She stood just behind me, wearing dark pants and a long white baker's coat, and carrying three water bottles she'd apparently just bought at the deli next door. A Commonwealth Emergency Medical Team badge peeked out near the collar of her jacket. Seeing my eyes linger there, she quickly fastened the button with one hand.

'Nope,' I said too brightly, nodding to the truck. 'Just hungry. Do you have any scones?'

'There's a bakery across the street.'

'Yes, but the scones in there are hours old by now. The ones in your truck are probably right out of the oven.'

She gave me a slow once-over. Then, deciding I was simply annoying and not a threat, she brushed past me. 'This is a private entrance. You'll want to move along.'

I'd been two feet down the driveway and now moved to the pavement. I took a book from my backpack, leaned against the wall, and hoped I appeared to be reading while waiting for someone. Each time I heard footsteps heading down the delivery driveway or a truck door open, I casually peered around the corner. The next EMT I saw was another woman, and the two after her were older married men.

But the fourth was promising. He was young, probably in his early twenties, and his left ring finger was bare.

'Excuse me?' I asked, swapping the book for a notebook and pen.

'What's up?' The upper half of his body was behind the open passenger's-side door as he leaned inside the truck.

I waited to make sure no one else was coming before venturing down the driveway. He finished whatever he was doing inside the truck, pulled out, and closed the door.

'Hi.' I offered him what I hoped was a friendly yet suggestive smile.

It seemed to work at first – he returned the expression and even took a step towards me – but then his mouth set in a straight line as he remembered where he was. 'You shouldn't be back here,' he said.

'But I've been waiting for you.'

He'd started to turn away but stopped. 'You have?'

'I'm researching a story. For the *Globe*.' That was a stretch, but at least I wasn't wearing my school uniform.

He still seemed unsure, but he was listening. 'What about?'

'Creepy local deaths for a Halloween special feature. I figured as one of Boston's best emergency medical responders, you've probably seen some pretty strange things.'

This was an even bigger stretch. He was wearing the bakery disguise, too, and unlike the first woman I'd spoken with, his badge was hidden. So how would I know he was an EMT at all, let alone one of the best? I braced for another reprimand.

But it didn't come.

'Actually, I have,' he said, sounding pleased as he leaned against the truck and crossed his arms over his chest. 'But are you sure you're a reporter?'

My breath hitched.

'You're way too cute to be stuck behind a computer, writing all day.'

I laughed lightly. This seemed to make him even happier, and he immediately launched into various cases of murder, suicide, and a combination of both. I pretended to take notes, pausing every now and then to smile or move closer, but when none of his stories were about the city's recent victims, I helped him focus.

'What about the guy who jumped off the bridge a few weeks ago?' I asked. 'The one who left the note and the balloon?'

'That was pretty standard. His girlfriend broke up with him, and he couldn't go on without her.' He winked. 'Understandable, depending on the girl.'

My stomach turned. 'And there was nothing . . . unusual . . . about him when he was found? No weird marks or expressions?'

'Not that I can recall.'

'What about the accident with the bus of BU athletes? Nothing strange?'

He shook his head. 'They found the last four missing students, and the others are recovering well in the hospital. Unfortunate, but also pretty standard.'

I took another step towards him, rested one hand on his arm. 'I've heard that in certain circumstances, people can die with their mouths frozen open and their lips turned up. Almost like they're happy. Have any of the recent victims looked like that?'

'Now that you mention it, that bridge jumper didn't look entirely devastated when they found him.' He looked behind him and then leaned towards me. 'And off the record? Some guy just drowned in this fancy school's pool. When they brought him out, he was grinning like a Cheshire cat.'

He jumped back as a door slammed somewhere behind him. I looked over his shoulder to see the original female EMT coming towards us.

'Thanks so much,' I said, backing up. 'You've been really helpful.'

'Wait.' He started after me. 'What's your name? How can I –'

The female EMT grabbed his arm. As she demanded to know what he'd told me, I spun around and ran.

I sprinted past the school, across the street, and through the park. As I dodged pedestrians and baby strollers, I tried to make sense of everything I'd just learned. I reached our brownstone barely winded and took the steps leading to the front door two at a time.

'Oh, good,' Mom said as I burst into the foyer. She was in the living room, sorting through more cardboard boxes. When I glanced her way, she held up two

286

black capes. 'What do you think? For costumes? For you and –'

'Sorry.' I swung by and gave her a quick peck on the cheek. 'Can't talk now. Is Dad still in his office?'

'He's at work. He felt well enough to make his afternoon lecture.'

This sounded like another lie told for Mom's sake, but there was nothing I could do about that now. I flew through the room, up the stairs, and down the hallway.

'Paige,' I said, knocking on her bedroom door. 'I know you said you wanted to be alone, and I'm sorry to interrupt, but –'

I stopped as the door swung open under the weight of my fist, releasing a blast of hot air.

'Paige?' I stepped into the room. It was dark except for the soft glow of my old night-light plugged into the wall by the desk. 'Are you okay?'

She didn't answer. Thinking she'd fallen asleep – and still wanting to talk – I tiptoed over to the bed. I felt through the darkness, aiming for the pillow, hoping to gently wake her by stroking her hair. My palm grazed the pillow . . . but her head wasn't there. I felt my way along the bed's length. In addition to Paige, the blankets and sheets were missing.

I went back to the head of the bed and turned on the small lamp on the nightstand. In the dim light I saw that the bed was completely stripped. The blinds were down, the curtains pulled tight across them. That was strange, but even stranger was what was in the middle of the room.

Eight portable heaters were arranged in a wide circle, their cords connected to three separate power strips. The heaters surrounded blankets and sheets from the bed as well as what appeared to be the entire contents of the upstairs linen closet: old comforters, wool throws, and even guest towels. The bedding was also arranged in a circle and resembled some sort of nest. In the middle of the nest were pillows – from the bed and extras from the closet – and a plastic jug of water. The pillows were fluffed, like they hadn't been touched since being placed on the floor, and the water jug was full. The rest of the room looked like it always did, with one exception.

Paige wasn't in it.

I used my sleeve to wipe the sweat forming on my face, then ran back down the hallway. I stopped in my room, thinking she might be waiting for me there, but it, too, was empty.

There was only one other room on the second floor: the bathroom. I approached it slowly; my energy was finally waning, and I was wary of what I might find. The door was closed, and no light shone out of the thin space between it and the floor, but I could hear water running, like someone was taking a bath.

I'd found Paige in a bathtub once before. She'd been pregnant then, and sick. Untransformed, her body had been unable to give the life growing inside her what it needed. Raina and Zara, rather than taking her to a doctor, had cared for her at home, making her drink gallons of ocean water and take hot baths. They'd been in the bathroom with her the day I'd watched through the cracked door, holding her pale, shaking hand, guarding without speaking.

As I walked towards the bathroom now, I pictured her body writhing and twitching. I imagined the noise she'd made, which had been something between a moan and a shriek and had sounded like nothing I'd ever heard before. I remembered her eyes, her beautiful silver-blue eyes, shining towards the ceiling, seeming to stare at nothing and everything at once. And I prayed that that wasn't what waited behind this closed door.

I knocked once. Twice. Three times.

'Paige? It's Vanessa. Can I come in?' I held one ear to the door and listened. There was nothing except for the steady rush of water. 'Please,' I whispered, taking the knob in one hand. 'Please let her be okay . . .'

Like the bedroom, the bathroom was lit only by a

night-light. But it didn't need to be any brighter for me to see that she wasn't okay, that I was too late.

Her motionless body was held underwater by heavy iron doorstops resting on her stomach, arms, and legs. Her skin was white, her lips blue. Water streamed into the overflowing tub from the showerhead, making her hair float around her bloated face.

Containers of table salt lined the porcelain shelf on the wall next to the tub. A small white book drifted across the flooded tile floor, its gold letters glittering in the dim light.

My body went numb as my eyes locked on the small French script.

La vie en rose.

Zara's diary.

*

The hospital waiting room smelled like disinfectant and potato chips. The nauseating combination didn't help my stomach, which had been churning since I'd opened the bathroom door forty-five minutes earlier.

'You should eat something.' Mom put one hand on my knee.

'I'm not hungry,' I said.

'You're sweating and shaking. Food will help.'

I didn't answer. Across the waiting room, a little girl watched me curiously. I tried to smile, but the failed attempt made her bury her face in her mother's sweater.

'Salad,' Mom announced, standing. 'I'm going to get you a salad, and I'm going to call your father.'

'You've called him twelve times in the past five minutes,' I protested weakly.

'And I'll keep calling until he picks up.'

I had to admire her determination . . . and her unflappable calm. I didn't remember much of what happened after I'd found Paige. I knew I screamed and lifted her out of the tub, and at one point I was vaguely aware of Mom there with us, but that was all. Yet somehow, we were in the hospital waiting room. Paige was with doctors. It was like the second I screamed, Mom had woken up from her strange daydream and re-entered reality the way she'd left it.

It was a small miracle as far as miracles went, but it wasn't lost on me.

As Mom disappeared into an elevator, I stood and shuffled over to the reception area.

'Excuse me,' I said, leaning on the counter for support. 'Have you heard anything else yet? About Paige –'

'Marchand.' Barbara the receptionist, an older woman with big blonde hair, eyed me over the top of her rhinestone-rimmed glasses. 'I remember from the first twelve times you asked.'

Apparently, Mom wasn't the only determined one.

'She's hanging in there,' Barbara said. 'Still critical, but hanging in.'

'Thank you. And you'll let me know if her condition changes?'

She crossed her heart. 'But if you want to check in again before then, I won't mind.'

I'd started walking away when she spoke again.

'You feel okay? You're looking a little wobbly.'

'I'm fine,' I called back with a wave. 'But thanks.'

I was about to turn back into the square of chairs when the little girl who'd been watching me saw me coming, leaned into her mother, and whispered, 'There's that lady again. What's wrong with her?'

I knew I'd better get used to the question, since there was going to be something very wrong with me every day for the rest of my life, but that wasn't going to happen now. Ducking my head so my hair hung down the side of my face, I passed the chairs and shuffled as fast as my feet would carry me through the automatic doors. Outside, I tuned out the smokers and worried family members updating relatives on their cell phones, and dropped onto an empty bench set apart from the emergency room entrance.

Paige is fine. She's just here for a check-up. She'll be done in no time, and we'll go home and talk and watch movies like it's any other night.

As I silently lied to myself, my blood ran faster, my head grew fuzzier. Afraid I'd pass out before doing the one thing I knew I needed to, I opened my cell phone, closed my eyes, and focused on breathing. When I thought I could say what needed to be said without crying, I opened my eyes and dialled.

The answering machine picked up on the second ring. I debated hanging up and trying again in a little while, but then left a message. Because who knew what shape I'd be in later?

'Hi, Betty, it's Vanessa. I'm calling about Paige. There's been . . . an accident.'

This was another lie. In my dazed state I'd managed to retrieve Zara's diary from the flooded floor, and in the waiting room, while Mom had gone off to call Dad, I'd read Paige's careful, blurry notes. Though the outcome had been unexpected, she'd acted intentionally. She'd turned on the water, filled the tub with salt, weighted down her body. She'd known what she was doing.

She'd been trying to turn herself into one of them. Into one of *us*. I could only guess that the reason it didn't work was because she hadn't been submerged in natural salt water.

293

'She's in intensive care at the Commonwealth Medical Center,' I continued quickly. 'We don't have much information yet, but I thought you'd want to see her. Maybe Oliver can drive you down?'

I relayed the address and hung up. A few yards away, an ambulance flew up to the emergency room entrance. My eyes froze on its spinning lights. In between flashes, I pictured Justine.

I missed her. Right now especially, but also every minute of every day, even when I wasn't consciously thinking of her. I missed her smile, her laugh, her ability to make everything bad somehow good again. I missed running into her in the upstairs hallway, when she was still waking up and too cranky to say good morning. I missed talking with her every night, about Mom and Dad, school and boys, until I was tired enough to fall asleep without worrying about the dark. Sometimes, when I missed her so much I couldn't breathe, I let myself believe that she was just away, that she'd come back when she was ready.

If I lost Paige too, I thought, I'd never breathe again.

As tears filled my eyes, I was overwhelmed by the sudden need for someone to tell me it was okay. And if that wasn't possible, I wanted someone here with me, someone whom I loved and who loved me, who wouldn't make me talk if I didn't want to, who'd just stay with me on this bench until I felt strong enough to get up again.

I needed Simon.

I texted him, my fingers moving on their own. Tears rolled down my cheeks, but fresh ones replaced them, making it hard to see the small screen. I kept the message short, certain he'd know what I was asking without my actually posing the question.

PAIGE IN ICU @ COMMONWEALTH MED. CTR. SHE'S OK FOR NOW. NOT SURE ABOUT ME.

I hit Send, closed the phone, and slid down the bench until my head rested against wooden slats. I watched the ambulance lights turn until my eyelids grew too heavy to hold up, and then I let them fall. The sounds of people talking, cars passing, and horns honking in the distance slowly faded to silence.

I must have fallen into a deep sleep because the next thing I knew, someone was on the bench next to me. His arm was around my shoulders, pulling me towards him, and my cheek was pressed against his warm chest. Instinctively, I slid one hand across his stomach to his waist and left it there.

I felt better. Calmer. Stronger. My head was clearer. I was thirsty, but no more so than I'd be after waking from a nap.

Of course, if I were thinking instead of feeling, I'd realise how unlikely it was that I'd been sleeping on a bench for three hours, which was how long it would take Simon to drive here from Maine. Two, if he ignored speed limits. I'd think that there was no way Mom had left me alone in the cold that long, especially not in her current role of calm leader.

But I wasn't thinking. I was too happy he was here.

'Thank you for coming,' I whispered.

'Thank you for wanting me to,' he said, curling his free arm around my abdomen.

My eyes opened. Without moving, I looked at his arm, registered the brown jacket, the frayed cuffs. I looked down to the pavement, saw the dirty Converses.

Simon didn't wear Converses.

Parker did.

Too tired to dial the number earlier, I'd responded to a text instead. In my haze, I must've accidentally responded to Parker's text instead of Simon's.

'What do you need?' he asked quietly near my ear. 'Can I get you anything?'

Go away. Please go away and leave me alone.

But I didn't say this out loud. I didn't pull away either; my body wouldn't cooperate. Instead, it continued to act on its own, moving even closer to his, its desire to be near him muting the alarms sounding in my head.

As Parker's arms tightened around me, I thought of Simon. I loved him. More than anything or anyone. When we were together, I felt closer to whole than I ever did when we weren't.

But to my surprise, something about Parker felt right, too.

CHAPTER 23

Paige would be okay. She was extremely weak and had to stay in the hospital for observation, but her doctors said she'd be well enough to come home in a few days. I saw her in the morning, at lunch, and after school, often staying until after visiting hours ended and the nurses kicked me out. Because she was so tired we didn't talk much, and when we did we stuck to light, safe topics, like whatever was on the TV that hung above the foot of her bed. I wanted to know why she'd done it, but I didn't want to upset her or make her feel worse than she already did. She'd tell me when she was ready, and as her friend, I'd wait however long that took.

But that didn't mean I couldn't try to get answers elsewhere. Which was why, the following Saturday, I got up before dawn, left Mom and Dad a note saying I had an all-day study session, and went to Winter Harbor.

It had been less than a week since the morning I'd woken up on Parker's boat, but as I drove through town, it looked as if months had passed. The trees were nearly bare, their colourful leaves now brown and blanketing the ground. The sky was grey, the sun hidden by a low-lying layer of clouds. With nothing to do between swim and ski seasons, tourists had gone home, leaving the streets empty and storefronts quiet. I'd never been to Winter Harbor this time of year and was surprised at how lonely it felt.

Anxious to be with other people, I went straight to Betty's house. It, too, seemed different. Its turquoise exterior was dulled, the paint chipping and peeling. The long porch sagged in the middle, and the railing that ran its length was missing at least a dozen wooden rungs. Several shutters had fallen to the ground, and those that remained were cracked and cockeyed. It looked like a hurricane had barrelled through, attacking the structure and leaving disrepair in its wake.

And given the sudden, fleeting storms last summer, maybe it had.

I parked the car and dashed across the lawn and up the porch steps. I'd planned what to say during the six-hour drive up, but before ringing the bell, I took another minute to run through it once more.

'What are you doing here?'

I flew back, grabbing the railing to keep from toppling down the stairs. Oliver had flung open the door unprompted. He seemed angry, and I was about to apologise for coming over unannounced when he continued speaking.

'They didn't say you were coming.' His eyes, aimed somewhere behind me, flicked back and forth. 'They didn't say you were coming, and I don't have room for you.'

'That's okay.' I followed him as he turned abruptly and hurried inside. 'I didn't tell anyone I was visiting, and I'm not staying. I just wanted to update Betty about Paige.'

He stopped short and spun around. His eyes continued to shoot from one side to the other, never looking directly at me – or anything else in the room. He was hunched over, as if buckling under great, invisible pressure. His mouth was slack, and his bottom lip drooped towards his chin.

'Betty's fine,' he said. 'She doesn't need your help. People need to stop worrying about her and focus on more important matters.'

He was scolding me. I started to reiterate my reason for being there, but he turned back before I could. He hobbled through the living room and into the kitchen, murmuring and fiddling with his hearing aids. I waited there, thinking he'd return, but soon there was a soft, distant click, like a door closing, and his voice fell silent.

I'd been less thirsty the past few days, but now my

mouth was dry, my throat tight. I was tempted to follow Oliver, but with him distracted, this was the perfect chance to talk to Betty. Heading for the stairs before my legs could give, I took my cell phone from my jeans pocket and typed quickly.

SIMON, I KNOW YOU'RE MAD & I DON'T BLAME YOU, BUT SOMETHING'S GOING ON IN WH AND WE NEED TO TALK. CALL ME. PLEASE.

I sent the text just as my right knee slammed into something hard. I jumped back, biting my lip against the pain. As I did, I registered the living room for the first time since entering the house.

The drapes lay in a heap beneath the windows, their thick fabric torn to shreds. The old shag rug was cut up into large, haphazard pieces. The couch and chairs were turned on their backs, the stuffing ripped out, the wooden legs sawed off. The coffee table was completely shattered. Next to where it had once stood, the sharp edge of an axe was wedged into the hardwood floor.

They're just redecorating . . . finally giving the old house an overdue makeover . . .

I pretended all the way upstairs and down the hall. It was the only way to make my feet keep moving.

Betty had a perfectly good reason for not coming to see

Paige in the hospital . . . she wasn't feeling well, or Oliver was busy and couldn't drive her . . .

Stopping outside Betty's bedroom door, I took a deep breath and tried to focus. I raised one hand, prepared to knock, but waited when I realised the door was cracked open. Betty was standing near the wall of windows with her back to me. She held a phone to her ear and seemed to be listening intently. I pressed against the door, widening the gap two inches, and stood as close as I could without stepping into the room.

'My dear, there's no need to apologise,' Betty said, her voice soft, soothing. 'You did your best. Next time, you'll do better.'

Next time? What next time? Was she talking to someone at the restaurant? Managing from a distance?

'A few weeks?' Betty's voice hardened. Her back stiffened. 'I don't think that's such a good idea. As we discussed last weekend, there's no time to waste.'

I watched her grab the window frame with her free hand. Her fingers gripped the wood so tightly they turned purple, then white.

'I understand you're nervous – it's a big change. But you have nothing to worry about. You'll feel weak immediately afterwards, and then, with time and training, you'll be stronger than ever.'

I held my breath.

'Don't you want to have the life you were destined to live? To be part of a family again? *Your* family?'

There was another long pause. Betty's head shook slightly as she listened, reminding me of Oliver's flicking eyes.

'Don't you see?' she sneered. 'She doesn't care about you. Not really. You're just a fill-in, a substitute for her dead sister.'

Justine.

I gasped lightly as her name shot through my head. It was Betty's voice, but Betty hadn't said it out loud.

Eyes wide, I watched her lower the phone to her side. She continued to face the windows. I stood there, frozen, trying to decide whether to give in to the urge to flee. Before I could, she tilted her head back . . . and emitted a single, high-pitched note.

I slammed against the wall as if thrown by a tidal wave, squeezing my eyes closed and covering my ears, but the noise only grew louder, as if its source was inside my head instead of outside. When I tried to open my eyes, a silver light brighter than the sun forced them closed again. I stumbled, deaf and blind, propelled by fear and an invisible force pushing me down the hallway. Nearing where I guessed the stairwell would be, I released one ear to feel through the light for a railing. My fingers grazed something hard, and unable to see if it was the railing, I grabbed it anyway and used all my strength to pull myself over.

I half ran, half tripped down the stairs, the noise and light dimming the further I went. My phone buzzed as I reached the first-floor landing, and I slowed down to yank it from my pocket. My vision was too distorted to make out the words and numbers on the small screen. I blinked quickly, and my sight cleared just enough for me to see the mirror hanging on the wall at the base of the stairs. In its reflection, a short, balding man lunged towards me, teeth bared, axe raised overhead.

'Oliver, what –'

There was a loud crack as the axe handle connected with my head.

The lingering silver light went out.

The next thing I became aware of was water. It was salty and cold and felt so good, it took me a second to realise I wasn't swimming in the ocean but submerged in some sort of makeshift tub. The dull throbbing in the back of my head reminded me what had happened, and my tethered neck, wrists, and ankles confirmed that it wasn't over. I tried to sit up, lifting my head and pulling hard against the restraints. They wouldn't give.

Without moving my head, I looked to the right, then the left. I recognised the intricate floral print of Betty's couch, the wet velvet of the living-room drapes, the soft fuzz of Zara's bedroom rug. The wooden container was assembled and padded with the former contents of Betty's house. Above me, I saw Oliver's head as he read a thermometer, noted its temperature in a book, and dropped the thermometer back in the water; the cool, narrow instrument slid down the tank, tickling the side of my foot.

It's okay . . . You're okay . . . If he wanted to kill you, he wouldn't have locked you up in the one place where you're strongest . . .

It was hard to believe, but for once I tried to allay my fears with the truth. Yes, Oliver had knocked me unconscious, tied me up, and, I now realised, removed all of my clothes. But despite how I'd gotten here – and the fact that I couldn't get out – I felt good. If Oliver had meant me serious harm, he would've hit me with the other end of the axe or locked me up somewhere dry, with nothing to drink and no access to water.

Somewhat reassured, I tried the restraints again. They were thin, but tight. They loosened only slightly when I pulled as hard as I could.

But that was a start. I pulled and relaxed, pulled and relaxed, careful not to disturb the water so much that it attracted Oliver's attention. Eventually, I could move my left hand until it touched the side of the wooden tub. There I felt around with my fingers, grateful for Oliver's unpolished handiwork. The wood was uneven, its edges jagged. Finding a sharp point, I twisted my wrist until the rope caught on the wood. I pulled and pushed, moving my hand like a saw.

'Vanessa Sands.'

I held still. Oliver stood above me again, writing in his book. His voice was muffled, but I could tell he spoke casually, easily, like he was talking to himself.

'They said you'd be hard to catch. They said you wouldn't come willingly.'

I struggled not to flinch as he reached into the water, pressed two fingers to the inside of my right wrist. He held them there for a few seconds, apparently taking my pulse, then removed his hand and patted it on his shirt.

'Either they were wrong, or they underestimated my Betty.' He chuckled, made another note. 'That's something I would *never* do.'

Closing my eyes, I thought back to last summer, when Oliver had told Simon, Caleb, and me about his feelings for Betty, and the history of their relationship. He'd spoken of her so sweetly, with such reverence, it was clear there was nothing he wouldn't do for her . . . including, apparently, kidnapping her granddaughter's best friend.

But why was Betty doing this when she'd helped us defeat the sirens last summer? Why was she trying to convince Paige to transform? Why would she want to subject her granddaughter to a life of thirst and pain? And why did she want me held captive? Was she worried I'd try to stop Paige?

And Betty aside, who was the 'they' Oliver referred to?

Several minutes later, I had at least one answer. I continued sawing until the thin rope snapped, then used my freed hand to untie my other hand. After undoing my neck, I slid down the lined wooden tub until I could reach my ankles. Once they were released, I sat up slowly, bringing only my head out of the water.

The room held at least fifteen wooden bins like mine, maybe more. They were made from broken furniture pieces and ripped carpeting, and reminded me of caskets at a funeral parlour, except that whoever – or whatever – was inside was still alive. This was clear by the bubbling throughout what I assumed was Betty's basement, which looked more like a cave with a slick floor and rocky walls. The sound of bubbles releasing was rhythmic, just like it was when I breathed underwater.

Oliver was across the room, sitting with his back to me at a small metal table. He seemed to be writing in his book. To his right was an open laptop with the *Winter Harbor Herald* website on display on the screen. Squinting, I could just make out the main headline.

Deep Sea or Die Sinks; Bodies of
Divers Gordon Yantz, 28, and Nick
Lexington, 32, Found

Deep Sea or Die. That was the name of the boat I saw when I was on Parker's yacht last weekend. And hadn't Simon said divers had discovered the female bodies in an icy chamber? Were Gordon Yantz and Nick Lexington those divers?

My hunch said yes, and when I saw what was scattered on the damp floor around the desk, I was convinced.

There were dozens of articles, some from the *Herald*, but more from the *Boston Globe*. I recognised many I'd studied myself: about the bus accident; and the students who'd been found in the water by the airport; and Colin Milton Cooper, who'd jumped to his death from the Longfellow Bridge. There were printed e-mails and lots of pictures – close-ups of the victims as well as other familiar faces.

Like Paige, reading on a bench in the Common. Parker, playing with his iPod at the Boylston T stop. Simon, standing by a newsstand, consulting a map of Boston.

Me, drinking water. Fanning my face. Pulling a sweatshirt hood over my head. Running through the park, towards the bandstand.

We were being followed. Tracked. I didn't know

exactly why or how, but of that much I was certain. Especially because amid the articles and pictures sat a thick scrapbook with a quilted cover . . . just like the ones Zara and Raina had kept of their conquests.

I had to get out of there. And fast. I scanned the room, relieved to spot my clothes, neatly folded, on the last step of a narrow flight of stairs. My cell phone sat on top of the pile, its red message light blinking.

Oliver was still writing, humming quietly. I grasped the edge of the wooden tub with both hands and slowly pulled myself into a squat. I waited, my head ducked low, for several seconds. When Oliver didn't seem to hear my movement over the other noises in the room, I stood hunched over in the tub. There was a metal step stool on one end; I climbed out of the tub and tiptoed down the stool, cringing with every drop of water that hit the rocky floor.

Shivering, I crept that way, hunched over, arms across my bare chest, towards the stairs. I kept one eye on Oliver the whole time, but he was too engrossed in his book to notice. When I neared the papers on the floor, I paused. I waited for the bubbling in the room to swell before reaching forward and carefully lifting from the floor as many papers as I could before the noise softened. Then I continued on, sneaking quick glances at the wooden tubs every few steps.

I didn't recognise any of the sleeping women. The sirens I'd seen the night the harbour froze had been as beautiful as Raina and Zara. They'd been tall, with warm bronzed skin; long, thick hair; and healthy, toned figures. But some of the women here were pale, others blue. Their bodies were thin and frail. Their breathing was unnaturally slow. I thought two were actually dead and lingered to make sure, but then the water shifted as they inhaled.

Passing the last tub, I risked running the remaining distance to the stairs. I grabbed my phone and clothes and took the steps two at a time.

'Stop!'

The familiar voice exploded in my skull like a torpedo. I fell against the cold wall.

'She's getting away!'

'There, there,' Oliver soothed. 'Everything's fine. Everyone's here.'

My pulse thundered in my ears. When Oliver didn't immediately come running after me, I leaned down and peered out from behind the stairwell wall.

She sat straight up in a tub near the desk, her black hair slick against her head, her silver eyes shining like fading stars and aiming right at me. She was thinner than I remembered, and her skin was bluish-white instead of golden. If I hadn't memorised her every feature out of fear, I might not have known who she was.

But I did. And thin or not, pale or not, she was still Zara.

Oliver seemed to think she was dreaming, and though she appeared to look right at me, she must not have seen me. He stroked her hair and gently pressed on her shoulders, and soon the lights in her eyes extinguished as she closed them. She lay back without protest.

My legs ached to charge, but I restrained them as I hurried up the stairs, through the kitchen, across the living room, and out of the house. I slowed down on the porch to pull on my jeans and sweater, but the second my bare feet hit grass, I sprinted. I could've cried when I saw the car where I'd left it and found the keys in my jacket pocket, but there was no time for that. I jumped in and flew down the twisting driveway without looking back.

I drove for ten minutes, putting nearly as many miles between the Marchands and me, before stopping to check my phone. There were no texts, but there were four voicemails. Unfortunately, two were from Mom, one was from Dad, and the last was from Parker. Mom's were updates about Paige and dinner, Dad's asked me to call him when I had a chance, and Parker's was just to say hi and that he hoped he could see me later.

As upset as I was that Simon hadn't answered me and despite everything that had just happened, I was still pleased to hear Parker's voice. At least *he* still cared. Yes, I'd messed up with Simon, but I'd apologised countless times and received no response. I'd worry that he was in trouble, that the sirens had already gotten to him, but Paige talked to Riley every day, and Riley always mentioned what he and Simon were doing that night. I'd worry that the sirens had gotten to Riley, too, but if they had, he wouldn't still be calling Paige.

If Simon was determined to ignore me, even when I called him about something bigger than him, or me, or us, what else could I do to make it better? Especially when he wouldn't talk to me?

Fortunately, there was one other person who needed to know what was going on, who'd agree that we had to do something before the situation got even more out of control.

'Caleb!' I yelled through the open window as I sped into the marina parking lot.

He was hacking barnacles off the bottom of a raised boat. When he saw me, he looked confused, then happy, then mad. I threw the car in park and ran towards him.

He turned away and continued chopping, harder than before.

'Caleb, thank goodness,' I said breathlessly when I reached him. I held out the papers I'd taken from the basement. 'You'll never believe what I just –'

'You're soaking wet,' he said without looking at me.

'I know, that's part of what I have to tell you. I was just at Betty's, and –'

'Stop, Vanessa.'

I did.

He lowered the long metal rake and looked at me. 'How could you do it?' he asked quietly. 'After everything you've both been through, after everything that happened last summer . . .' He lowered his gaze to his work boots. 'In a million years, I never would've thought you'd be capable of something like that.'

The break-up. 'Caleb, trust me. I didn't want to. I *had* to.'

'Really.' It wasn't a question.

'Yes.' I stepped towards him. 'It's complicated, and I'll tell you everything eventually, I promise, but right now –'

'Quantum physics is complicated. Predicting Captain Monty's mood swings is complicated.' He paused. 'Sleeping with some prep-school loser while Simon's running around like a madman looking for you, so worried he can't see straight?' He shook his head. 'That seems pretty simple.'

'Caleb,' I said, my face going white, my legs numb, 'I don't know what you heard, but I swear I didn't –'

'The SS *Bostonian*? Ring any bells?'

I pictured the life preserver on Parker's dad's yacht. 'Yes,' I whispered.

'Simon saw you there. In bed, with some guy. After you tried to reach him and he drove all night trying to find you. He finally found your car in the Lighthouse parking lot, and when you didn't answer your cell, he thought you were in trouble and went up on the boat to look for you.'

'But I didn't – we didn't –'

'No?' He pulled out his phone, pressed a button, and held it towards me. 'How about that? Does that ring any bells?'

I couldn't answer even if I'd known what to say.

I was paralysed by the image of me lying on top of Parker by the river. The picture was from the Prep Setters website, but now a new caption ran along the bottom of the photo.

Parker King teaches fellow Hawthorne senior Vanessa Sands how to live like social royalty.

CHAPTER 24

Back in Boston the following Monday, I cut school for the first time ever. I woke up early, waited for Dad to take a shower, and broke into the locked wooden box in his office. Then, already dressed, I told Mom I had an early appointment with Ms Mulligan and left the house before Dad came out of the bathroom. I stopped at the post office, where I smiled and cooed at a young mail sorter until he told me what I needed to know and then took two buses away from the centre of the city. After asking for directions half a dozen times and getting lost about as often, I finally stood in front of a narrow, red-brick building at the easternmost edge of South Boston.

I checked the address in my hand against the rusty numbers nailed to the front door. The box number on the back of the old postcard featuring Betty's restaurant was linked to 134 Fourth Street. Unless there was more than one, I was at the right place.

I started up the crumbling steps. At the top, I looked to the left and saw patches of blue-green water between rooftops. I breathed in the salty air and held it in my lungs before slowly releasing it. Still nervous but slightly calmer, I raised one fist and knocked. A few seconds later, the door inched open – and slammed shut.

I waited, but it didn't reopen. I knocked again, louder. 'Please,' I called through the closed door. 'I know you don't want to see me, but I wouldn't be here if it wasn't important.'

Nothing. I knocked again, then leaned over the railing to peer in the window. Through the sheer white curtain I saw a tall figure standing in a nearly empty living room. Her back to me, she rested one hand on a fireplace mantel and the other on her chest. Her shoulders rose and immediately fell, like she was trying to catch her breath.

'Please,' I tried again, my voice cracking as I tapped on the window. 'I need your help.'

She lifted her head but didn't move towards the door. I thought she was going to stay like that, listening but ignoring me, and I looked around to see if anyone was near enough to overhear what I was about to say. She didn't have to invite me in, but I wasn't leaving until I'd said what I'd come here to say.

'Hello, Vanessa.'

I turned back. While I'd checked for eavesdroppers, she'd opened the door.

'Willa?' I asked, not sure it was really her. I'd only

seen her in the coffee shop, when she'd worn baggy pants and an oversize shirt, her hair pinned up under a baseball cap and her face partially hidden by the hat's brim. Now she wore dark jeans, a soft silk blouse, and an ivory cashmere housecoat that hung down to her ankles. Her long white hair was pulled back in a loose braid. Her blue eyes popped against the soft, creamy folds of her skin. 'You're so pretty,' I said.

She smiled quickly, hesitantly. 'Would you like to come in?'

She held the door open. As I walked past her, I thought she looked familiar – and not just because we'd already met. Before I could figure out where else I might've seen her, she motioned for me to sit down.

'Are you moving?' I asked. Besides the soft chenille sofa I sat on, the only items in the room were a matching armchair, a coffee table, and a vase of white lilies. The walls were bare, the built-in bookshelves empty.

'I like to keep things simple,' she said, sitting across from me.

'Is that why you never wanted to see me?' The question came out automatically. She pulled back like I'd slapped her. 'I'm sorry, that came out wrong. I just meant –'

'Don't apologise.' She shook her head, relaxed. 'You're entitled to every emotion you're experiencing right now

– confusion, disappointment, anger. You haven't been told much, and I'm very sorry for that.'

I nodded, looked down at my hands in my lap. Now that I was here and we were actually talking, I was having trouble remembering everything I'd wanted to say. 'But you were told about me, right?' I asked quietly. 'My dad sent you regular updates?'

'He did. At my request.'

'You said you'd tell me whatever I wanted to know about my mother.'

'I did.' She leaned towards me. 'What would you like to know, Vanessa?'

Who Charlotte had been, why she'd done what she'd done. Why Dad wasn't able to resist her despite loving Mom. Why she'd left so suddenly after a year, leaving me with a family who would never understand me the way she would have. The questions spiralled and spun, making me dizzy.

'How did they meet?' I finally asked.

The folds in her skin deepened as she offered me a small smile. I could see the resemblance between her and the only photo of Charlotte I'd seen, but she appeared to be much older than Charlotte would have been now; I guessed she was in her early sixties.

'At Charlotte's bookstore. Your father came in to browse and was very impressed by her collection of first editions. They got to talking, and he came in every few weeks after that.'

'Did she know he was married?'

'Yes.'

'And she encouraged him anyway?'

'I wouldn't say that. She enjoyed his company, but she respected his situation.'

'Then how did they go from casual conversation to ... more than that?' I asked.

She paused. 'It was complicated.'

I opened my mouth to protest but then remembered Caleb's heated comments about quantum physics and Captain Monty's moods. 'Okay,' I said.

'Vanessa,' she said softly, her eyes meeting mine, 'I want to tell you the truth. At the very least, you deserve that from me. But to do so, I must also tell you about a siren's physical limitations and requirements. That might be difficult to hear, and I don't want to over-whelm you.'

'You won't.' My veins ached as blood shot through them. 'I can handle it.'

The corners of her mouth turned down in doubt – or sadness – but she continued anyway. 'In his e-mails, your father told me about what happened last summer. He told me about Justine's accident, and about what

319

happened at the end of the summer, when you jumped off the cliff and ended up in the hospital.'

My face burned; I clasped my hands together to keep from fanning my skin.

'You unintentionally transformed that night, didn't you?'

I swallowed. 'I think so.'

'Then you already know how a siren's body depends on salt water, how she grows weaker and increasingly fatigued the more that time passes without a fresh infusion.' She hesitated. 'How have you been coping with that?'

'As well as can be expected, I guess. Sometimes I feel okay. Other times, I feel like I'm constantly seconds away from passing out. I take salt-water baths, I drink salt water by the gallon, but how my body reacts seems to change day to day.'

'You use table salt?'

I nodded.

'Natural salt water is a million times more effective. That's why most sirens settle by an ocean. It makes life easier when you don't have to travel far for a fix.'

A fix. Like salt water was to sirens what sugar, caffeine, and nicotine were to other, normal addicts.

'Unfortunately,' she continued, her voice softening, 'salt water alone isn't enough. It is for a while, especially immediately following the transformation, but its efficacy fades over time.'

'What happens then?'

She looked towards the open windows, her gaze locking on the water in the distance. 'When your father first met Charlotte, she wasn't well. Long ocean swims, which once satisfied her physical needs for days, began quelling them for mere hours. Her body was demanding that she move on to the next phase in her development, and she was resisting.'

'Why?' My chest tightened. Regardless of what she'd done, I didn't like the idea of my biological mother being sick beyond her control. 'If she wasn't well, and if there was something she could do to feel better, why didn't she want to do it?'

She turned her gaze towards me. 'There's a boy in your life, isn't there?'

I sat back.

'Forgive me if that's too personal a question, but the answer's important.' She waited a moment, letting me process. 'There is a boy, yes? Who was perhaps indifferent to you at first but is now coming around?'

She wasn't referring to Simon. Even before we were romantically involved, he was never indifferent.

She was referring to Parker.

'How do you know about him?' I asked. 'Did Dad tell you something?' And if so, how did he know?

'Of course not. Your father's too concerned about your relationship with *him* to pay attention to your feelings for anyone else of the opposite sex. I saw you and a handsome young man talking at the Beanery one day and put two and two together.'

'I don't know what exactly you saw,' I said quickly, the heat in my face shooting down my neck, into my chest, 'but I don't have feelings for Parker.'

'Emotionally, maybe not. At least not yet.'

I started to protest again but stopped when she reached forward and placed one hand on my knee.

'You feel better, don't you? When he's near you? When he says your name or touches you? No matter how thirsty or exhausted you are?'

I sank lower into the sofa, recalling Parker's fingers on my calf in the gazebo. Lying next to him on the yacht. Standing inches apart on the diving board. His arms around me on the bench outside the hospital. I hated to admit even to myself – *especially* to myself – but I was drawn to him. And just like Willa suggested, I felt better, stronger, even strangely excited every time we were close.

'That's your power at work, Vanessa,' she said gently. 'You may not realise when you're sending out signals, but you are. All the time. When he responds, your ability – and your body – strengthen. The more he responds, the stronger you'll become.'

I didn't want to become stronger. Not if it meant doing things with Parker I wanted to do only with Simon. 'What about my boyfriend?' I asked, intentionally leaving out the 'ex'. 'I love him, and –'

'He loves you. And if he felt that way prior to your transformation, your powers have no effect on him.'

She paused, as if knowing this was the answer to a question I'd been asking myself ever since Simon and I had become more than friends. I appreciated the chance to let it sink in. Because if what she said was true, Simon loved me – he *really* loved me. He didn't just think he did because my abilities gave him no other choice.

Not that it mattered now.

'That's why being with Simon feels different from being with Parker,' she continued after a moment. 'He might fulfil you emotionally . . . but that's all he can do.'

I closed my eyes, tried to still my spinning head. 'And Charlotte? When she met my dad . . . ?'

'She was extremely weak. She needed to do something before her body failed her completely. But she resisted because she didn't want to do what was required. She didn't agree with it.' Willa sighed. 'Your mother, Vanessa, would have rather let her own life go than interfere with someone else's.'

'But she went through with it,' I said.

'Yes. Unfortunately, hers wasn't the only life at stake. There are thousands of sirens living in small coastal communities all over the world. For better or worse, the Winter Harbor settlement is quite powerful, and its members take their standing extremely seriously. When it became known that Charlotte was throwing away the power she'd been given, there were threats. To her family, friends . . . everyone she knew. These communities are small enough that losing even one member severely alters the future population, and the other sirens took her refusal as a personal affront. Eventually, it was either use her abilities and affect one life, or die quietly while potentially hurting dozens.'

'So Dad just happened to walk in on the wrong day at the wrong time?'

'It's hard to believe that that was all there was to it, but yes. He did.'

Hard to believe was putting it mildly. 'But how did that work? He loved my mom – Jacqueline. I know he did. Isn't being in love the one way a man can resist a siren?'

'For most men. But your mother . . . and you . . . come

from extraordinary lineage.' Willa's voice hitched on 'extraordinary'.

'What do you mean?'

She stood, walked to the open windows, and breathed deeply. 'You're descendants of a small group of sirens based in northern Canada called the Nenuphars.'

Nenuphars. I remembered the name from the entry about Charlotte's death in Raina's scrapbook.

'And these . . . Nenuphars,' I said carefully, 'what makes them so special?'

She turned towards me and leaned against the wall. 'There are two ways a group builds collective power. The first is for its sirens to do what we've been talking about – use their abilities to make men love them. The second is to harness those feelings in the form of children.'

'The more men a group hypnotises, and the more babies they have, the stronger they are as a whole?'

'Exactly. For hundreds of years, the Nenuphars have overcome a challenging geographical landscape and limited resources to succeed at both. As far as we know, no other group facing similar conditions has survived. The next oldest community after the Nenuphars is a tiny group in Scandinavia, and they're younger by two hundred and fifty years.'

I struggled to make sense of this. 'So I'm the result of some sort of weird natural selection?'

'In a way,' Willa said. 'The Nenuphars' increasing strength has been passed on over time, making each generation stronger than the one before.'

'And this relates to Charlotte and Dad how?'

She crossed the room and joined me on the couch. 'When a man is targeted by a Nenuphar, he has no defence. Love might make him indifferent at first, but it doesn't take much to win him over. The force is too powerful.'

My head filled suddenly with an image from last summer. 'The Winter Harbor sirens . . . they killed a lot of people. A few months ago, the night the harbour froze, they gathered on the ocean floor and lured dozens of men underwater with the intention of killing them.' Willa's face was blank as I spoke. If I had a specific question, I would have to ask it. 'When you said the Nenuphars succeeded with men . . . does that mean they simply made the men fall in love with them? Or did they kill them, too?'

'To date,' she said, her face remaining expressionless, 'the Nenuphars have taken the lives of thirteen thousand four hundred and twelve men. At their largest, the group had eleven members.'

'Sorry,' I gasped. 'May I have – Do you have –'

Willa jumped up and left the room. Seconds later, she reappeared with a pitcher of blue-green liquid and a glass. It took three glasses for me to catch my breath. That didn't make the words come any easier.

'Do you . . . ?' I started. 'Have you . . . ?'

'Taken lives?' she finished. She waited for my nod, then took another minute to consider her response. 'No. I've done everything I can to avoid it.'

I filled another glass. My hands trembled so much, water sloshed out of the pitcher and onto the table.

'It's a lot to process, I know. And I'm so sorry you've gone so long without the truth.' Willa held out one hand, like she was going to brush my hair back from my forehead, but then seemed to think better of it and rested her hand in her lap. 'But that's why Charlotte did what she did. That's why your father did what he did. Neither had a choice.'

I gulped down the glass of water before speaking again. 'Why did she let him live? Why did she leave Winter Harbor a year later – and then give me away when he found her?'

'Despite her reasons for initiating a relationship with him, Charlotte cared about your father. She couldn't do what was expected of her. So she let him go, and she let the other Winter Harbor sirens believe otherwise. Eventually, worried that they were growing suspicious and fearing they'd do something to you as punishment, she fled. When your father came all that way, she realised how much he cared about you – and how much safer you'd be with him and away from her. They didn't know who he was, after all. They grew suspicious because her health started to fail again. That wouldn't have happened – at least not so soon – if she'd taken his life.'

'And the bookstore? The fire?'

Willa paused. 'It wasn't an accident. Your mother thought having no connection to her was the best way to protect you.'

I raised my eyes to hers. 'Is that why you never wanted to see me? Because you were a connection to her?'

'Yes. It's also why I vowed a long time ago never to listen to your thoughts, the way all sirens can to some degree. Even though there were times, like last summer, that I so desperately wanted to check in and make sure you were all right. If I'd done that, in time you would've been opened up to mine . . . and that would've made everything even more complicated.'

I looked away, at the spotless coffee table, the empty bookshelves, the fireplace that looked like it had never seen a match. After everything she'd just said, knowing the truth she'd been keeping to herself all these years, I couldn't blame her for wanting to keep things simple.

'They're back,' I said a moment later, my eyes landing

on a piece of seaweed stuck to the side of the empty pitcher. 'The Winter Harbor sirens. The ice has thawed . . . and now they're back.'

'I know.' Her voice was quiet, steady.

'My friends and I . . . we're the ones who stopped them last summer.' I looked at her, tears filling my eyes. 'I think they're coming for us.'

This time, she didn't resist the urge. She reached forward, gathered me in both arms, and pulled me close. As my tears soaked her shoulder, she stroked my hair.

'You're not alone any more, Vanessa. They're not going to hurt you – or anyone else – ever again.'

'How do you know?' I whispered.

'Because we're going to do it right this time.' She hugged me tighter, rocked me gently back and forth. 'We're going to drown them.'

CHAPTER 25

'How are you feeling?'

Paige looked up from the magazine she was reading. I started towards her, encouraged by the fact that she was awake and sitting up. She'd been home for two days after a week-long stay in the hospital, and though she was improving physically, emotionally, it was hard to tell.

'Okay,' she said with a small smile. 'Tired, but okay.'

'That's progress.' I returned her smile and lowered myself to the edge of the bed. I hated what I was about to do but knew I had no choice. 'Paige . . . I have to talk to you about something.'

'Me, too,' she said.

'Can I go first? Please?' We still hadn't discussed what she'd tried to do, and I knew that's what she wanted to explain. But I thought her explanation might change once she heard what I had to say. When she nodded, I continued. 'You were right.'

'About what?'

My fingers grew moist around the rolled-up newspaper I held. 'Do you remember a few weeks ago, when you thought you saw Raina and Zara? In the park during class?'

What little pink coloured her face faded to white. 'I remember imagining they were there, yes.'

'You weren't imagining it.'

She looked down at the newspaper when I placed it on the blanket between us. Matthew Harrison's stiff, smiling face had made the front page. 'Is that . . . ? Is he . . . ?'

'The Bates recruiter from the café. Parker and I found him floating in the school pool the same afternoon you tried to transform.'

Her head snapped up. 'What were you doing with Parker?' she asked sharply.

The question and tone were so unexpected it took me a second to respond. 'Talking, taking a break from the whole college scene. We're friends, sort of.'

'Parker doesn't have friends who are girls. He has girls he hooks up with.'

The picture of us by the river. She must've seen it with the added caption. 'Paige, Parker and I . . . it's not what you're thinking. I promise.'

She frowned but didn't press. Instead, her gaze fell back to the paper. 'This doesn't mean anything,' she said. 'He's one guy. It could be a coincidence.'

'Except it's not just one guy. They caused the BU bus crash, made Colin Cooper jump off a bridge, and killed the two divers who'd discovered them in the ice. Matthew was the only one who was found smiling because the siren who claimed him was finally strong enough to have that effect. The deaths leading up to his were practice, rehab.'

'That doesn't make any sense.'

I tried to explain it the way Willa had explained it to me. 'The sirens lost most of their power during the three months they were frozen. In order to grow stronger, they had to pursue again, which was a much more challenging task in their weakened states. To tip the odds in their favour, they started with men who had limited or no defence – those who couldn't refuse them if they'd wanted to. That's why Zara stepped in front of the bus and caused the accident, so they could prey upon the hurt and injured.'

'So these guys, lying in hospital beds, professed their love to a bunch of strange women?'

'The ones who made it to the hospital were lucky. The ones who ended up in the water, who weren't found until their bodies washed up by the airport, they're the ones the sirens went after. They were so close to death it didn't take much to finish the job.'

Her face twisted. 'And Colin Cooper?'

'His situation was more complicated.' I took a thin stack of print-outs from beneath the newspaper. 'But I think they found him on an online dating site and began corresponding with him once they learned of his association with Hawthorne. They wanted to make sure we heard about it. According to these e-mail exchanges, he had a history of depression and nearly overdosed once. For weeks the e-mails led up to a single meeting, which he thought went well, and in the next, the young siren ended the relationship, guessing he'd do something drastic in response. She was waiting for him in the river when he jumped.'

'How do you know –?'

'I found the e-mails in Betty's house.'

She stared at me, mouth open, eyes wide.

'I went there after you . . . after I found you in the bathtub. When Betty didn't visit you in the hospital or even return my calls, I got worried. I thought something might have happened to her, and if it hadn't, I wanted to talk to her about what you'd done.' I took her hand; it was limp, but she didn't pull away. 'I was worried about you, too.'

She shook her head. When she spoke, her voice wavered. 'She said that they were dead, that she couldn't hear them. She said she just wanted me to protect myself from others by becoming more like them, so that I could defend myself if ever I needed to again.'

'Paige,' I said quietly, squeezing her hand. 'When I

was up there, Oliver attacked me. He knocked me unconscious.'

'Oliver's, like, a hundred years old. He couldn't swat a mosquito without breaking a bone.'

'Then he's somehow stronger under Betty's spell.'

'Her *spell*?'

Willa and I weren't sure about this part, but it was the best we could come up with without more evidence. 'We think the sirens are somehow controlling Betty to act on their behalf. To get Oliver to care for them . . . to get you to become one of them.'

She held my eyes for a second before yanking her hand away, pushing aside the newspaper and e-mails, and picking up her magazine. 'I appreciate your concern, Vanessa, I do. But the summer's over. All of that? It's *over*. You should move on.'

How I wished that were possible.

'I saw them,' I said. 'I saw Zara, and at least a dozen others. They were in Betty's basement, sleeping in wooden bins filled with ocean water . . . just like I was.'

In her hands, the magazine trembled. I focused on the cover as I spoke; if I looked at her, I wouldn't get through it.

'You don't want to transform, Paige,' I continued softly. 'Believe me. You'll be tired, and weak, and thirsty. All the time. You'll have to drink constantly and bathe in salt water. Eventually, you'll have to make guys like you just so you have enough energy to get through the day without passing out. Your life will change completely. For ever.'

There was a long pause. Outside, the brisk autumn wind whined, sending dead leaves flicking against the bedroom windows. I raised my eyes to Paige's, but she still stared, not blinking, at the magazine.

'How do you know this?' she finally whispered.

Here it came. The truth I'd been hiding for three excruciatingly long months. Once I admitted it out loud, it would be real in a way it hadn't been before now.

But there was no use denying what could never be changed.

'Because I'm one of them,' I said.

She jumped just as the bedroom door flew open. Mom came in carrying a tray of sandwiches and iced water.

'I figured you might be too tired to come downstairs for dinner.' She placed the tray on the nightstand and took a thermometer from her sweater pocket. Paige didn't seem to see it at first, but when Mom wagged it in front of her face, she opened her mouth obligingly. 'I brought enough for you, too, Vanessa.'

'Thanks,' I said, 'but I actually have plans.'

They both looked at me. 'Like a date?' Mom asked.

'Like a study session,' I said, avoiding Paige's questioning gaze.

I stood and waited at the foot of the bed as Mom straightened Paige's blankets and fluffed her pillows. Ever since the bathtub incident, she'd been in maternal overdrive, taking care of Paige and making sure she wanted for nothing. She handled the responsibility with the same energy and focus she'd once used at work, which was a promising change. It also meant Paige was rarely alone, and that allowed me to go to school, spend time with Willa, and do everything else I needed to without worrying about a second transformation attempt.

I wanted to talk with Paige more, but Mom was thorough. After the pillows, she checked the thermometer and sat on the bed while holding a cold compress to Paige's forehead. She seemed to be in no hurry to leave, and Paige wasn't protesting her presence, which made me think Paige welcomed the chance to process everything I'd just told her.

When ten minutes passed, I excused myself and told Paige I'd come see her when I got back.

I dashed to my room, where I'd laid out everything I needed for the night. I'd raided Mom's boxes of designer clothes earlier and found a tight, black satin miniskirt, a silky, red sleeveless blouse, and black pumps with four-inch heels. I kept the accessories simple, opting only for sheer black hose and a pair of ruby earrings. A fitted black satin trench completed the outfit.

Once dressed, I undid my ponytail and brushed my hair it until it fell straight down my back. I put on foundation, blush, lipstick, and mascara, all of which I'd bought at the pharmacy that afternoon, and sprayed vanilla-and-clove-scented perfume on my neck and wrists.

Not bad, I thought, examining my appearance in the full-length mirror. Not me either, but that was sort of the point. I grabbed my phone and clutch from the bed, listened by the closed door to make sure no one was in the hallway, and ran downstairs.

'Vanessa?' Dad called from his office as I breezed through the living room. 'Is that you? Can you come here, please, I want to –'

'Going out, be back later!'

Outside, I ran down the steps and up the street. My ankles wobbled in the heels, but any fear I felt about falling and breaking something was overwhelmed by nerves. After planning this night for days, I just wanted it to be over as soon as possible.

'Hey, beautiful.'

I stopped, but my heart kept racing. Parker stood beneath the awning of Il Cappuccino, an Italian restaurant that, according to its website, promised fine cuisine and the most romantic ambience Boston had to offer. He'd dressed for the occasion and wore black pants, a white button-down shirt, a fitted black suit vest, and a striped tie. He carried a black wool overcoat. His hair was brushed back from his face, like he'd run his fingers back after taking a shower and not touched it since.

This is no big deal . . . you're just two friends having dinner . . . it'd be no different if he were Caleb, or Paige, or –

He kissed my cheek. It was so soft I might not have believed it had actually happened if my knees hadn't buckled, leaving me no choice but to take his hand – for balance – when he offered it.

'This was a great idea,' he said. 'I'm so glad you suggested it.'

'Me, too.' I tried to smile, but looking at him only made my body sway again.

Inside the restaurant, I declined the hostess's invitation to check my coat, wanting to stay as covered up as possible. As I followed her across the main eating area filled with cosy booths and dim lighting, I struggled to remember everything Willa had told me about sending signals. I hadn't mentioned what I was doing with Parker, partly because I wasn't sure she'd approve and also because I was embarrassed, but she'd given me enough basic information about sirens to work with.

I knew I was supposed to be relaxed. The tenser I was, the less effective I'd be. I was supposed to strike a careful balance in conversation, letting him talk a lot so he knew I was interested, but also talking myself so that he could be lulled by my voice. Eventually, again when I was relaxed, I was supposed to touch him. It didn't have to be much – brushing his hand with mine or taking his arm when we left the restaurant would do – but the key was that it happen naturally.

Unfortunately, trying to remember everything I was supposed to do only stressed me out. So when Parker asked how my day had been, I told him it had been fine, reached for my water glass – and knocked it off the table. When he started to tell me about his, I rested my elbows on the table and leaned towards him, making the table tilt and the breadbasket fall into my lap. When our candle went out, I raised it to get the waiter's attention and ask for a new one, and sent a thin stream of hot wax sliding down my sleeve.

To me, this was sign after sign that what I was doing was wrong. Not just because I didn't know how to do it, but because I wasn't supposed to be doing it. I still loved Simon even if he no longer loved me, and this wasn't fair to him. And poor Parker actually thought we were on a real date. He'd probably made tons of girls cry over the

years, but that didn't mean he deserved what I was doing.

There was a reason I wanted to do this: to become as
strong as possible so that, when the time came, I could
take on Raina and Zara. But there had to be another
way.

'Listen,' I said, starting to wipe the wax from my
sleeve.

'Don't.' He reached across the table and tugged on the
cloth napkin. 'Once it's dry you can just pick it off. Wiping it now will ruin your jacket.'

'Oh.' I looked at the wax and lowered the napkin.
'Thanks.'

'So I have an idea.' He lowered his voice. 'Why don't
we take things down a notch? There's this place I like to
go not far from here. The food's not fancy, but it's good.
The atmosphere's unbelievable. We'd be a million times
overdressed, but I won't mind if you don't.'

'I don't,' I said, already standing. Once we were outside, I could break a heel and say I had to go. Or I could
come down with a sudden, fake illness. All that mattered
was that getting out of there was the start of the end of
the night.

'Blind date!' Parker called back to our waiter as we
slid out of the booth. 'Wrong girl!'

Realising he was talking about us, I stopped short.

He kept going until his chest pressed lightly against my back, and then he rested both hands on my waist and nudged me forward.

'Mistaken identity,' he whispered. 'Guaranteed to bring any romantic dinner to a grinding halt.'

Which, for some reason, cracked me up. I didn't know if it was my emotional state finally collapsing under the weight of the past few months, or if the idea of accidentally going on a date with the wrong person really was that funny, but I laughed all the way out the door and was still giggling as we started down the street. It had been a long time since anything had made me laugh like that – or even a little. The feeling was almost as refreshing as an impromptu swim in the ocean.

'Here we are,' Parker said a few blocks later.

I wiped my watering eyes and peered down the alley to the blinking TACO sign. It sat atop a skinny yellow hut covered in painted cacti, sombreros, and donkeys. On the pavement in front of the hut were dozens of plastic chairs – no tables – filled with couples and college kids wearing jeans and fleeces, eating the biggest tacos I'd ever seen and drinking beer. Strings of colourful lights crisscrossed overhead, and tinny mariachi music blared from an old cassette player on the ground by the order window.

'Actually,' I said, 'I think I'm a little underdressed.'

He laughed, which only made me start giggling again. I couldn't even catch my breath to protest when he laced his fingers through mine and led me down the alley.

But then, I wasn't sure if that was because I was laughing, or because his skin against mine sent a hot shock up my arm.

Either way, I went along with it. We got our food and found two empty chairs in the middle of the festivities. Sitting there with Parker, surrounded by strangers, eating messy tacos, yelling over the music and noise about TV, movies, and nothing important, I felt different. Happy.

Normal.

I didn't want it to end. And apparently, neither did Parker.

'Not to brag or anything,' he said, after we'd finished eating, 'but I have a pretty sweet entertainment centre at home.'

'Yeah?'

He nodded, grinned. 'Loews has nothing on King.'

Loews. The theatre. He wanted me to come over and watch movies. Most likely on a couch. Next to each other. In a dark room.

'It's pretty late.' I hated the words when they made his smile falter. 'I should probably get home.'

He raised both hands as if surrendering, then reached one towards me as he stood. I took it without hesitating.

I was going home instead of to his house. What was the harm in holding his hand along the way?

As we walked, Parker and I took turns singing – badly – our favourite cheesy movie songs of all time. (Mine: 'Danger Zone' from *Top Gun*. His: '(Everything I Do) I Do It for You' from *Robin Hood*.) Halfway home, I was laughing so hard I had to stop and ask him to be quiet until I calmed down enough to keep walking. The delay extended our time together by thirty seconds, which made me happy.

'Now I understand,' I said when we reached my block.

'What's that?'

'The Parker King phenomenon.'

'I'm sorry – I have a phenomenon?' He sounded pleased.

'You know you do.' I stopped walking in front of a brownstone a few down from ours and faced him. 'It's your magical ability to turn every single girl you meet into a puddle of sweet, messy goo.'

He made a face. 'Can't I, like, turn them into angels? Or rainbows? Or something prettier than goo?'

I smiled up at him as he stepped closer.

'If you understand this phenomenon,' he said, his voice softening, 'does that mean you've experienced it?'

Now my smile faltered. 'Maybe,' I said, knowing I shouldn't. Even though it was true. *Especially* because it was true.

My heart fought to break free of my chest as he lifted my hand, touched my sleeve, gently plucked off the dried wax.

'Good as new,' he said.

He was talking about the jacket. Logically, inside my head, I knew he was talking about the jacket. But every other part of me interpreted this statement another way.

'Parker,' I whispered, watching his lips come closer.

He kissed me in response. His lips were warm, and salty, and careful. They pressed gently against mine, like he was afraid I'd pull away.

Which is what I should've done. I should've pulled away and run down the block and inside my house. Instead, I kissed him back, softly at first, but then harder. When our lips parted and the tip of his tongue touched mine, I inhaled sharply, like I'd been punched.

Except it didn't hurt. It felt good. Amazing. My legs steadied, my arms grew firmer. My heart still thundered, but it sounded different in my ears – strong instead of weak, excited instead of scared.

And the *taste*. I knew the salt on his lips lingered from

344

dinner, but there was more to it than that. It was fresh, and invigorating, the way I'd imagined a glass of ocean water would taste after drinking tap water for weeks. Each kiss only made me want more.

'Get a room!' someone yelled from across the street.

Remembering we stood in full view in the middle of a public street, I took the lapels of Parker's coat and, still kissing him, gently pulled him onto the narrow strip of grass between two brownstones.

'Vanessa,' he breathed, leaning against me so that I leaned against the building.

I was aware of his fingers by my neck, unbuttoning my jacket.

'Come with me.'

'Where?' My eyelids slid closed as his lips trailed across my clavicle, my bare shoulder.

'Anywhere.' He brought his mouth back to mine. 'Away from here. Across oceans.'

'On your boat,' I said, vaguely recalling his post-high-school plan.

'Yes.' He smiled against my lips. 'You and me. On my boat.'

I could see it. The two of us. Nothing but blue sky and water for hundreds of miles. We could just disappear, together. No one would have to know. No one would get hurt.

'Okay,' I whispered.

For a brief second, he stilled. 'Really?'

I nodded, kissed him, pulled him closer.

In the distance, an engine growled, tyres squealed.

'And your boyfriend?' Parker asked. 'You guys are definitely done?'

My boyfriend. Simon.

My eyes snapped open. I squirmed out of Parker's grasp and dashed out onto the pavement.

Just in time to see a green Subaru with Maine licence plates reach the end of the street and fly around the corner.

CHAPTER 26

The next morning, I checked on Paige, who was still sleeping – just as she'd been when I got home the night before – made small talk with Mom and Dad over breakfast, and then, instead of walking to school, caught the bus to South Boston. Willa wasn't expecting me and I didn't have her phone number to call before coming over, but I had to go somewhere. Facing Parker today was impossible – especially because part of me ached to see him again, to pick up where we'd left off before I'd disappeared into the house without so much as saying goodbye – and I didn't think she'd mind my stopping by unannounced.

I didn't consider that she might not be home.

I stood on the front stoop, shivering in the cool morning mist and knocking on the door. I waited several seconds and tried again. When the door remained closed, I leaned over the iron railing and tapped on the window. Through the sheer curtain, I saw that the living room was empty.

Guessing she must be out for a swim, I sat on the top

step to wait. I took my phone from my backpack and, for the thousandth time since seeing Simon drive away the night before, checked for messages.

'Morning, sunshine.'

I glanced up. A middle-aged man smiled at me through the open window of a Department of Sanitation truck parked across the street.

'What's a pretty thing like you doing in this part of town?'

I looked down, held the phone to my ear, pretended to be listening to someone on the other end.

'Need a ride?' the man's co-worker asked. He tossed a fat garbage bag into the back of the truck and stepped into the street, towards me.

Afraid my voice would entice them further, I shook my head and hurried down the steps. A cracked wooden gate divided Willa's tiny front lawn from the back, and I pushed against it, relieved when it gave with little resistance. I closed the gate and lugged a heavy wrought-iron table in front of it, just in case.

Willa's back lawn was actually a patio. Like the house's interior, it was neat and simple, with an outdoor dining set and a few ceramic pots of wilting marigolds. A narrow wooden staircase led up to the back door.

As I sat in one of the chairs, my head throbbed once, then stopped. A few seconds later, it did it again. It didn't hurt, but there was definite pressure, like a bulging vein pushed against my forehead.

It's just stress . . . You're freaking out, and your body's reacting . . .

Trying to relax, I closed my eyes and took a deep breath. The throbbing came stronger, faster. I opened my eyes and dug through my backpack for a water bottle. I was taking a long swig when I noticed cream-coloured curtains floating out from three open windows on the second floor. The material lifted and dropped as if caught on a sharp, shifting wind – only there wasn't any wind. There wasn't even a breeze. The cool air was completely still.

Even stranger, each time the curtains rose, my head pulsated. When they drifted back towards the windowsill, the pressure faded.

I jumped out of the chair and dashed up the steps. The back door was locked, but the window next to it was cracked open. I hoisted myself onto the railing, shoved on the old window until it slid up another few inches, and reached in with one hand. I was too far away to grab the knob, but using the tips of my index and middle fingers, I managed to flick the lock. I hopped off the railing and threw open the door from the outside.

I'd only been in Willa's living room but I found the stairs easily, in the back of a tiny, immaculate kitchen.

349

I paused on the landing, afraid of what I'd find on the second floor, but then the throbbing intensified and I kept moving. If Willa was in some kind of trouble, if the sirens had come for her after discovering she was communicating with me, I had to do whatever I could to help.

Even if that meant confronting Raina and Zara.

By the time I cleared the last step, the pressure in my head was constant. It built as I ran down the hall and checked two empty rooms, until it felt like my head was gripped between the tightening prongs of a very large wrench. The feeling was uncomfortable but not painful – not even when I reached the last room at the end of the hall and another force swelled inside my head, pushing against the pressure outside.

Thin wisps of cold vapour streamed out from beneath the closed door. Leaning closer, I held my breath and listened . . . but all I could hear were the curtains snapping against the windows and walls. I raised my hand to knock, but then decided against it.

I took the knob – and my hand flew from the brass to my mouth to stop me from crying out. At first I thought the metal was scalding hot, but when I tried again, tapping it first to numb my skin to the temperature, I realised it was cold. Like ice.

I twisted the knob and pushed. The door didn't budge.

I tried again, pressing against it with my shoulder, and it inched open before closing again. Feeling stronger than I had in months, I shoved against it with all my weight. The door gave, and I fell into the room, landing hard on my knees.

My eyes closed automatically. I crouched there, waiting for Raina and Zara, bracing for pain.

But it didn't come. The pressure in my head remained, but that was all.

I opened my eyes tentatively, just in case they were simply waiting for me to see them before they attacked, and then scrambled to my feet when they weren't there. Besides me, there was only one other person in the room.

Willa. She sat in an ivory claw-footed bathtub, her back straight, shoulders squared. She faced the open windows opposite the door and didn't see me. I walked towards her slowly, through a cold, grey fog. As I neared the tub I saw that it was filled with blue-green water . . . and that the water was bubbling, bursting, as if an enormous fire roared beneath the floorboards. It splashed over the sides of the tub, and I jumped back when some hit my leg. But the water, like the swirling steam it created, was cold. A few degrees cooler and Willa would've been stuck in a block of ice.

As it was, she already seemed to be frozen. She didn't move once as I rounded the tub and stood before her.

Her long, white hair hung loose around her shoulders, which looked bony instead of soft, the way they usually did; they jutted out, stretching the thin material of her nightgown. Her arms seemed thinner, her skin greyer. Two days ago her face was lined with soft, shallow creases, but now it sagged. Her wrinkled forehead, eyelids, cheeks, and mouth drooped as if the tub was a vacuum trying to suck her down.

She looked old. Sick. Tired. The only signs of life came from her lips, which twitched erratically, as if silently mumbling an indecipherable chant . . . and from her eyes. They were largely hidden by the folds of her skin, but I could still tell that they were silver, and bright, and shifting back and forth without blinking.

I stood there, shaking from fear and cold, not knowing what to do. She didn't appear to be in pain, but that didn't mean she wasn't. What if this was some sort of hypnosis? What if the Winter Harbor sirens had figured out how to control her the way they were controlling Betty? What if it was a trap designed to lure me closer? Maybe she was a trigger that, once set off, would alert the sirens to my presence.

I stepped closer, opened my mouth. I was about to say her name again when the pressure in my head suddenly gave. I looked at Willa but saw Raina. Zara. Grey water. A red rowing boat. An oar lined with shiny stickers. A girl with empty eyes, a slack mouth, drifting on her back towards a blurred horizon.

'Is that me?' I whispered. 'Am I –'

'Vanessa.'

The images vanished.

'What are you doing here?' Willa demanded. Her frail body was visible through her wet nightgown, and she tried to shield herself with her arms and stand at the same time.

My eyes focused to see that hers were now bluish-green, not silver. The air was clear, the water in the tub still. The curtains hung, unmoving, before the windows.

'You shouldn't be here.' She reached for a robe on the floor by the tub. 'Wait for me downstairs. *Now*,' she added when I didn't move right away.

I went. Five minutes later, she joined me in the living room. She'd changed into jeans and a sweater and her hair was wrapped in a towel. She'd put on make-up, but her face still looked like it had aged ten years in two days.

'Why aren't you in school?' she asked, moving through the room slowly, like her joints ached. She sat down across from me.

'I made out with Parker last night.'

She looked at me. I could tell that wasn't the answer

she was expecting, and it definitely wasn't one I'd planned to give. But if I was honest with her, maybe she'd return the favour.

'The boy in my life,' I reminded her. 'The one who's not my boyfriend.'

'I see. And how did that happen?'

'I asked him out. On a date.'

She frowned. 'Because there was no one else to have dinner with?'

'Because I wanted him to like me. Even more than he already did.'

'Vanessa, this isn't a game. I thought you knew that.'

'I did. I do.' I leaned towards her. 'I want to be strong. I want to be able to help when the time comes.'

She held my gaze but didn't answer.

'It's coming, isn't it?' I asked. 'That's what you were doing. You were trying to listen, to find out what they're planning?'

'What I was doing doesn't concern you.'

I leaned forward. 'But I saw them. I saw Raina and Zara. I saw a red rowing boat – *my* red rowing boat.'

Her grey skin paled. 'What are you talking about?'

'Upstairs. I was about to say your name to make sure you were okay, but before I could, all of these pictures flashed through my head. Right after that, you woke up, or snapped out of it, or whatever.' I paused. 'Whatever that was, whatever I saw . . . it was part of their plan, wasn't it?'

Her lips turned in as she searched my face. 'Yes,' she said finally. 'But it's not going to get that far. They'll be stopped long before then.'

'How?'

'That's not for you to know.'

'But if I can help –'

'You can't,' she snapped, standing up. 'You're a target, but this isn't your fight, Vanessa. It's bigger than you. And they might be weak individually, but they still have strength in numbers.'

I stood, too. 'But what are you going to do? You're just one person, and no offence, but I think I might be able to swim a little further.' I felt guilty the second the words left my mouth, but that didn't make them untrue.

'You needn't worry about me being alone. I'm not as active in the community as I once was, but I still have connections. I just need some time.'

'What if we don't have time?' I asked. 'Do you know when they plan to act?'

'Not before I'm ready for them.'

I stepped towards her. 'Willa, please. My family, my friends, everyone I care about . . . they're a mess. Because of me. Because of who I am. My sister spent her whole life trying to stand apart from me, and it killed her. My mom raised someone else's child because my dad asked her to, and he's been living two lives ever since. Paige lost her family because we made the harbour freeze. Parker thinks that he's in love with me, that he wants to sail around the world with me, and I'm just using him.'

'Are you?'

The question burned. I shook my head to clear it. 'And Simon . . . all he's done is care about me, and all I've done is hurt him.' I blinked quickly when my eyes filled with tears. 'If there's any way I can help fix what I've broken, or at least stop things from getting worse, I want to. I need to. I think I'll be able handle the rest of it – the salt water and attention, the flirting and lying – if I can just help stop the sirens from hurting anyone else again.'

She was silent, and for a moment I thought she was seriously considering the request. But then she placed her thin, bony hands on my shoulders and looked me in the eye.

'I'm sorry you're hurting,' she said quietly. 'I'm sorry your family's hurting. But I promise you, Vanessa, the best thing you can do – the *only* thing you can do – is to go to school. Go home. Live your life the best you can, and eventually, this will all be behind you.'

She didn't get it. At this point she was the only person in the world who could actually understand what I was going through . . . and she didn't.

With tears rolling down my face, I brushed past her and headed for the front door.

'One last thing, Vanessa.'

I stopped, one hand on the door. *You were right. I was wrong. We can do this together.*

'Whatever you do, don't try to listen. To me or anyone else. If you do, it's over. Do you understand?'

I didn't. What was over? Our relationship? Wasn't that as good as over anyway? And how could knowing what the sirens planned do anything other than make us better prepared, and give us an advantage?

'Yes,' I said anyway, opening the door and letting it slam shut behind me.

I walked for hours after that. I walked along the water's edge, through South Boston, into the centre of the city, across the Longfellow Bridge, and into Cambridge. I walked until my feet were so tired I couldn't feel them, and until the sky turned from blue to pink as the sun began to set. Eventually, I grew thirsty and stopped into a deli for a bottle of water and a handful of salt packets. I sat on an empty bench in Harvard Square, surrounded by college kids talking, studying, and doing other things normal kids did, and drank.

I didn't try to listen. But sometime later, as I was staring at nothing across the square, a girl with long brown hair and blue eyes wandered into my view and stayed there, browsing magazines at the newsstand.

She wasn't Zara. But the longer I looked at her the fuzzier my vision grew, until her hair looked black instead of brown, her eyes silver instead of blue. My head swelled then cleared, and I saw Zara leaning against a green Subaru with Maine licence plates. Under a streetlight, before a boy whose face was hidden by shadows.

Not terribly loyal, but cute . . .

Which was what Zara had said about Simon last summer, the night she'd tried to mesmerise him and nearly succeeded.

The memory jolted me out of my thoughts. My vision cleared instantly, and I saw two things at once.

The first was my water bottle. It was in my lap, and the clear liquid inside bubbled . . . just like the water had in Willa's tub. As I watched, the bubbles grew bigger, popped faster, and spiralled up and down the bottle until the water turned to foam.

The second was my cell phone. I'd retrieved it from my bag somewhere in South Boston and had been holding it ever since. Now, its red light blinked with a new text message.

I LOVE YOU, V. WE CAN FIX THIS. COME TO WH? — S

CHAPTER 27

After everything I'd done, after breaking up with no explanation and kissing Parker, Simon still loved me. He
still wanted to be with me. No one else in the same
situation would . . . but Simon did. The closer I got to
Winter Harbor, the more certain I felt that, somehow,
we'd get through this. We'd fix things between us, and
then we'd deal with whatever came next together. The
way we should've been doing all along.

Because we were meant to be, just like Paige had said.

Once I'd texted him back and agreed to meet, Simon
had written again and asked me to come to his parents'
house, which was next door to my family's lake house.
I hadn't been back to the lake house since we'd packed
up and left for the season, and I was almost as nervous
about returning now because I was finally going to tell
Simon everything he needed to know. I hadn't been
there by myself since returning to Winter Harbor to
figure out what had really happened to Justine – and
learning the truth about myself. It'd been bearable the

rest of the summer with Mom and Dad there to keep me company, but I wasn't ready to go it alone again.

So when I finally reached the lake house six hours after leaving Boston, I drove past it and turned into the Carmichaels' instead.

The sun was setting, the house dark. The only other car in the driveway was Simon's, and I hoped that meant that the rest of the family was out. With so much to talk about, we could use some time to ourselves.

At the front door I rang the bell and stepped back to wait. A few seconds later, I rang again and then knocked. When no one answered, I stood at the edge of the porch and looked up; Simon's bedroom window, like the rest of the windows facing the front yard, was dark. I checked my phone, but there was only one message from Paige that she'd sent hours ago, asking where I was and saying we had to talk. Making a mental note to call her as soon as I could, I dialled Simon's number, dashed down the stairs, and headed around the side of the house. The family room faced the lake at the back of the house; maybe Simon was watching TV or sleeping in there and hadn't heard the bell.

His phone went right to voicemail.

'Hey, it's me. I'm here, outside. I rang and knocked, and now I'm heading for the back.' I paused. 'I love you, Simon. And I'm so sorry, for everything.'

Like the front, the back of the house was dark. I tried the door anyway, but there was no answer. Peeking into the family room, I saw that it was empty, the TV off. There were no dishes on the coffee table, no open books on the couch, no other signs that he'd been waiting for me there.

Had he changed his mind? Had his parents or Caleb convinced him that reconciling was a bad idea, that after everything we'd been through, we were better off apart? Maybe that's where they all were now – out to dinner somewhere, having a family intervention to keep Simon from getting hurt again.

I turned to run down the stairs when my phone buzzed.

'Hey,' I said, smiling in relief.

'Hey, beautiful. Missed you at school today.'

I grabbed the porch railing, looked around quickly to make sure I was still alone. I'd been so happy to hear the phone I'd answered without checking the number. 'Parker. Hi.'

'Everything okay?'

'Everything's fine.' I looked out at the water, tried to picture Simon swimming, sitting on the dock – anything to replace the image of Parker grinning, his lips nearing mine. I opened my mouth to ask if I could call him back, but nothing came out.

'So I was thinking today that summer's really far away.'

'Okay,' I managed.

'And it'd probably be a good idea to do a trial run.'

'A trial run?' I asked, my inner voice screaming at me to hang up.

'How about the Caribbean? You and me, Thanksgiving break?'

'That sounds . . .' My voice trailed off as I forgot what I was going to say.

Because there he was. Simon. Rowing on the lake.

'Vanessa?'

'I have to go,' I said, and hung up.

I sprinted across the backyard, aware that my legs felt stronger than they had even thirty seconds ago. Apparently, I didn't have to be right next to Parker to feel the effects of his admiration.

'Simon!' I yelled, reaching the end of the dock.

He didn't look up. He'd been rowing but drifted now, towards the centre of the lake. That was likely why he hadn't answered his phone – cell service was spotty throughout Winter Harbor and worsened the further you were from land. His head was lowered as he turned the pages of a book. Squinting, I could just make out small white buds in his ears.

He was reading and listening to music. A typical Simon activity, but I was surprised he wasn't doing it in

362

the house, especially since he knew how long the drive from Boston took and that I'd left right away.

I shouted his name again and waved, but his back was to me. I watched and waited to see if he'd turn the boat around, but he continued flipping pages, seemingly engrossed. I scanned the nearby shore, hoping to see Caleb's small motorboat back from the marina where he usually kept it, or a kayak left out by a summer resident. When there was nothing, I checked the Carmichaels' garage for a spare rowing boat, but it was empty except for yard equipment. I dashed back to the dock and tried yelling and waving for Simon's attention once more.

Nothing. And he was drifting further away.

I lowered myself to the edge of the dock. I ached to be with him now, this second, but it had already been several weeks, and I could wait a few minutes more. The sky was quickly fading from lavender to grey, and unless he'd brought a flashlight with him, it wouldn't be light enough to read much longer. He'd probably turn around and look for me before then anyway.

Talk about loyal . . .

The voice sliced through my skull. Crying out, I squeezed my eyes shut and gripped my head.

Three little words and you come running . . .

The pain intensified, rocked my body back and forth.

That might've made up for everything you've done . . . if Simon hadn't already moved on . . .

I stopped rocking. Stopped breathing. My eyes opened slowly, as if I were waking from a dream. A light gust of wind rustled dead leaves clinging to branches, rippled the water's surface . . . and turned the rowing boat until it drifted horizontal to the shore.

I didn't know if she'd been lying down or simply blocked by Simon, but I could see her perfectly now. She sat at the other end of the boat, wearing jeans and a maroon Bates fleece. She was thin, her skin white. Her long black hair had been cut into a sleek bob that framed her face and hid the newly sharpened angles of her cheekbones.

Zara looked completely different – and more striking than ever.

I scrambled to my feet. 'Simon!'

Nothing. He turned another page, like he was completely alone on the lake.

'Simon! It's Vanessa! Please, turn around!'

I stared as he lifted his iPod and turned up the volume. Whenever he'd been mesmerised by Zara before, hearing my voice had snapped him out of it. The fact that he was calmly sitting two feet away from her meant that he was under some kind of hypnosis, but was he using music to drown *her* out now . . . or me?

Stop. The word burned in my head. *Please, he's done nothing to you. Leave him alone.*

I didn't know how to silently communicate with another siren, how to invade her thoughts the way Zara just had. Willa hadn't wanted me to listen, and she hadn't wanted me to talk either. But Zara seemed to hear my silent pleading; she didn't say anything in response, but she turned towards me, a slow smile creeping across her face, a low light brightening in her eyes until they shone. Then, when she was certain she had my attention, she leaned forward and rested one hand on Simon's knee.

He didn't flinch, the way he should. The way I wished he would. Instead, he lifted his head. Returned her smile. She slid down the boat until they were separated by inches, gently tugged on the iPod cord until the earphones gave, and said something that made him laugh.

'Simon!'

I screamed loud enough to make nearby loons cry in response, but he didn't hear me. That, or he ignored me. He tucked Zara's hair behind one ear, letting his fingers caress her cheek the way they'd caressed mine thousands of times. Her face tilted into his palm, and her eyes shifted up to his.

'No,' I whispered as the distance between them grew even smaller. 'Please . . . don't do it.'

But they did. Right there, with me unable to look away, like they were two cars careening towards, then crashing into each other, Simon and Zara kissed. A real kiss, with touching and embracing and no coming up for air.

I sank to my knees. How was this happening? If Zara was weaker than she'd been before, how had she transfixed Simon at all, let alone enough to make him climb into a boat, drift to the middle of the lake, and kiss her? Had she gotten to him before or after he'd asked me to come here?

The second I wondered, I knew. She'd gotten to him before. Because if Simon still loved me, her powers wouldn't work. Or if they started to, they'd stop when I called out to him.

Before this realisation could paralyse me completely, they pulled apart. Zara stood, making the boat wobble slightly, and, not taking her eyes from his, unzipped the fleece. It slid down her arms and fell to the bottom of the boat. She leaned to the right, then to the left, and I knew she was removing her shoes. It was probably fifty degrees out now, but she wore only a tight white tank top and jeans as easily as if it were late summer instead of fall. The effect wasn't lost on Simon, who watched her without moving.

Until she dived into the water. Then he jumped to his feet, making his book hit the floor with a thwack and the boat drop sharply from side to side. He lost his balance and fell back to the small bench twice before standing still enough to pull off his jacket and sweater.

'Simon!' I tried again, desperate. 'Stop! You don't know what –'

It was too late. Apparently unable to bear to be apart from her a second longer than necessary, he jumped into the water still wearing his pants, T-shirt, and shoes.

I didn't have a plan. I didn't know what I'd do once I reached them, or if Simon would even know who I was. But I didn't care. Ignoring my pounding head and throbbing heart, I tore off my jacket, kicked off my sneakers, and tossed my cell phone onto the dock. I flew into the water, which was so cold my muscles stiffened instantly, and paddled and kicked until my arms and legs regained full range of motion. I must have been in shock, though, because, despite my efforts, I couldn't seem to swim as fast as I had the last time I'd been in the ocean, and it took me minutes instead of seconds to reach the boat.

By the time I did, Zara and Simon were several feet away, treading water and kissing over the deepest part of the lake . . . and directly in front of my family's house.

'Let him go, Zara!' I yelled, hanging on to the side of the boat.

'Oh, Vanessa,' she called out casually, like this was totally normal, like we were old acquaintances who'd just run into each other on the street. 'So nice of you to join us.'

'You don't need him,' I said. 'You can have any guy you want.'

'True. Thank you for noticing.' She tightened her arms around his neck. 'But he's the one I want. And I'm happy to say, the feeling's mutual. Isn't that right, Simon?'

He tried to kiss her again, but she pulled back slightly. When it became clear she was waiting for a response, his lips lifted in a slow, lazy smile. He said something so quietly I couldn't hear, and Zara urged him to repeat himself, louder.

'I love you,' he said.

I love you. My heart automatically lifted . . . but he was looking at her, not me. As his words entered the air, her face seemed to change – her skin glowed, her cheeks filled, her eyes brightened.

While she grew stronger, my body went numb. I started to sink, using the boat to pull myself up when the hot liquid burning my eyes mixed with cold lake water. I blinked quickly, and my vision cleared enough to see

Zara, still holding on to Simon, slowly disappear beneath the water's surface.

I lifted my feet to the side of the boat and shoved off, aiming for where they'd just been. When I got closer, I ducked my head, twisted so that I faced the bottom of the lake, and swam with long, even strokes. I couldn't be that far behind, but they were nowhere to be seen. Or if they were, it was too dark to tell. Unlike the night I'd jumped into the water at the base of Chione Cliffs, when the sirens' light had illuminated the ocean floor, the lake was black. I couldn't even see my hands as they cut through the water in front of me. When I tried listening for Zara, my head fell silent. The best I could do was to try not to think so that there was nothing to hear if someone listened for me.

After swimming for years as a normal person, I instinctively still held my breath whenever I went under and opened my mouth and filled my lungs only when my chest burned. When that happened a minute after kicking away from the lake's surface, I didn't hesitate to inhale.

Leaving so soon . . . ?

I barely heard Zara over the sounds of my choking and the gurgling water. I tried breathing in again, slower this time, thinking I must've gulped too much, too fast, but the same thing happened. The water should have soothed and strengthened my body, but it was suffocating it instead.

Had they poisoned the lake? Was that why Simon had asked to meet me here? Because they'd done something to it that made breathing impossible? It didn't smell or taste different, but –

The thoughts stopped when I held my breath and the water no longer swirled. A few feet away, Zara, her arms tight around a struggling Simon, smiled at me from behind a plastic diving mask. It was attached by a long tube to a clear sack clipped to the back of her waist.

We're going to do it right this time . . . We're going to drown them . . .

The memory of Willa's voice flew through my head so fast there was no way Zara could've heard it even if she'd been listening. But I did. And now I knew what she'd meant.

To sirens, the lake was poisonous.

Because it was made of fresh water, not salt water.

My lungs felt like they'd burst as my eyes met Simon's. Either Zara's power had a time limit, or the water had shocked him; either way, he was out of her spell and fighting to break free. I kicked hard, lunging towards them, but Zara swam easily down and away. I tried again, but she only went deeper. The pressure hit my

370

head and chest like a mallet, and soon I had no choice but to change direction.

I needed air. Or Simon and I were both going to die.

My head shot through the water's surface. Gasping for oxygen, I looked towards the houses lining the shore, hoping to see Caleb, Mr and Mrs Carmichael, straggling summer renters . . . but there was no one. The houses were dark.

I tried to focus on Willa for help, to send some kind of warning that would prompt her to contact the Winter Harbor connections she claimed to have. But before I could think of what to say, I saw white flashes. They started out small and dull but quickly grew bigger and brighter. At first I thought they were fleeting bolts of lightning, since the sirens had manipulated the weather to their advantage over the summer, but there were too many at once. And they shot up from the water instead of down from the sky.

They were eyes. Dozens of them. Silver, blinking, glittering, surrounding me like a wide fishing net.

Hello, Vanessa . . .

One set drew nearer. I recognised Raina's mouth beneath her mask, the small mole to the right of her nose.

It was so nice of you to take care of Paige in our absence . . .

Still treading water, I inched away from her. As I did, the eyes on that side moved closer.

I don't know what she would've done without you . . .
what she'll do *without you . . .*

'Please,' I whispered, blinking away water droplets as
they fell from my eyelashes. 'I'll leave you alone. I won't
tell anyone you're alive. Just let him go, and we can pretend like –'

'Like this never happened?'

I spun around. Zara and Simon had surfaced, just outside the circle of sirens.

'Vanessa!' Simon cried, spitting out water.

I shot towards them just as Zara clamped one hand
over his mouth. His eyes held mine, wide, worried – for
me more than him, I knew.

'I'm sorry,' Zara said, tilting her head like she was confused. 'Let's review the series of events, shall we? You
and your little brainiac here froze Winter Harbor, freed
our targets, deprived us of life for three months, stole my
boyfriend and my sister –'

'Caleb wasn't your boyfriend,' I shot back. 'And you
stole *my* sister. You took Justine away from me, and for
what? A clearer shot at a guy you were never going to get
anyway? No matter how hard you tried?'

Her hand tightened over Simon's mouth as her silver
eyes narrowed.

'As for Paige,' I continued, 'I've done nothing but be
her friend. And you were going to make her sick. As soon

as she had her baby, you were going to make her transform into an immoral, insatiable monster – just like you. Like all of you.'

There was a pause. For a second, everything – the water, wind, and trees – was still.

'Don't you mean,' Zara said, her voice as smooth as silk, 'like all of *us*?'

I looked at Simon, who stopped struggling and returned my gaze as Zara's words sank in. She let the shock settle, then took advantage of his weakness to drag him back underwater.

'No!' I lunged after them, but there was a hand on my left leg, another on my right thigh. Four more grabbed my arms, my shoulders. I writhed and kicked, sapping myself of any lingering strength. As my chin, then mouth, then nose sank below the lake's surface, it was all I could do to press my lips together and hold my breath.

They held on to me the entire way down to the floor of the lake. Raina swam ahead of the group, her silver eyes casting two long beams through the darkness. I searched for Zara and Simon, silently called for Willa, but outside of my abductors, I didn't see or hear anyone or anything.

At the bottom of the lake, the sirens lowered me to a cluster of rocks and bound my ankles and wrists with what felt like silk scarves. I struggled against them, but just as Willa had said, what they lacked in strength individually they made up for in numbers. Between my thirst and the lack of oxygen, my body felt like it had just passed through flames instead of water.

Which was why, when a young siren with long blonde hair fitted a mask over my mouth, I greedily gulped the salt water.

You're strong, Raina's voice sounded in my head. *Just like your sister. She put up a good fight, too.*

I stared at her as she lowered to the sand in front of me, her long white skirt billowing around her like a cloud. As I silently seethed, my head stayed clear. A moment later, Raina continued.

I must congratulate you. You and your friends did what no one in our long history has done before. You stopped us. Temporarily, but successfully all the same. That's an accomplishment in and of itself.

I focused on her eyes.

But what you must understand is that what you did – what you attempted to do – goes far beyond you or me, or Zara or Paige. Justine's death was unfortunate, and if circumstances had been different, it wouldn't have happened.

That doesn't sound like an apology, I shot back.

It isn't one. Her eyes flashed. *She was an accidental casualty. We always assumed you perished with your mother, and if your sister's death is what it took for you to reveal yourself – and for us to discover the one sleeping siren cap-able of silencing us all – then it was worth it.*

My thoughts started to veer towards what Willa had said about my ancestors in Canada, the powerful group of sirens that had killed thousands of men, but I stopped them before they potentially told Raina more than she already knew.

Now, some of our members feel that you're owed your due. That you should suffer the same fate you tried to be-stow upon us.

I scanned the sirens gathered around us without moving my head. They all breathed through their masks, studied me through skinny silver slits.

But because I strive to act only in the best long-term interest of the group, rather than simply killing you the way you might deserve . . . I'm giving you a choice.

I returned my gaze to Raina. Her face was blank as she prepared to issue me an ultimatum.

You can either give the ladies what they want, and endure what will likely be a long, painful death . . . we'll even be so kind as to escort your bloated, lifeless body back to the dock behind your family's house.

At this the white light surrounding me flickered and bounced as the sirens nodded their approval.

Or you can join us.

I glared at her, at the thought.

I wouldn't be so hasty, she warned. *Thanks to you, our prominent community has experienced a significant setback. However – and this could also be thanks to you – we will rebound. Healthier and stronger than ever. You have abilities sirens of your age and experience level shouldn't have. You could be an asset to us, and we, in turn, could be that to you.*

That, I thought, holding her eyes, *will never happen.*

No? She turned, peered over her shoulder. *Not even if it means saving the one person in the world you'd do anything for? Who you* should *do anything for, especially considering certain transgressions?*

A soft light glowed from the darkness behind her. Through it I could just make out Zara's smirk, Simon's chest rising and falling underneath her arms.

He was alive. As the water and light shifted, I saw a black nozzle lodged in his mouth. It was attached to a small oxygen tank lying in the sand next to him.

Hot tears stung my eyes before neutralising in the cold lake water. *You'll let him go? If I do what you want me to, you'll release him and leave him alone?*

Vanessa. Her red lips pouted. *Let's be realistic.*

Then what? I practically screamed the words in my head. *What exactly are you suggesting?*

In order to join us, you must take a life.

I breathed faster, the salt water pumping in and out of my mask.

If you take his, you'll be stronger than you ever imagined possible, and he'll die, looking at you, listening to you, and feeling happier in that one instant than he was in all of his days on earth. You hurt him greatly, which was why Zara was able to control him for a brief time, but he still loves you, Vanessa. More than ever.

I shook my head, squeezed my eyes shut. *How is that saving him?* I demanded.

I didn't say you could save him from death. What you can save him from is watching you slowly drown, which would kill him long before we actually stopped his heart. She paused. *Physically, he dies either way.*

He'll leave you alone, I said. *We'll both leave here and never come back. We'll move across the country, or even out of the country, if you want. He's too good . . . he doesn't deserve –*

Let's not forget, Raina said over my internal blubbering, *whose idea it was to freeze the harbour. This punishment isn't only about you.*

Zara, I implored, twisting in my restraints, *think of Caleb. I know you still love him. Think of how devastated he'll be if he loses his brother. If you think that his feeling totally alone will somehow increase your chances –*

There was a sudden rush of water and something

shoved against my back, hard. I collapsed, landing softly on the rocks. I clutched my head and tried to stand, but stopped when the water cleared and I registered the scene before me.

Raina's eyes flared as she faced a tall woman with long dark hair. The woman stood where I had seconds earlier; whoever she was, she hadn't wanted me to keep talking. The other sirens stood behind Raina, trying to appear threatening but clearly growing tired. Some trembled, others were hunched over, still too weak from their time in the frozen harbour to keep their backs straight. They stood between Simon and me, though I could still see his feet so knew he was there.

Of course, that didn't mean he was alive.

The Nenuphars wouldn't approve of this behaviour.

My head pulsated in protest. I knew that voice.

The Nenuphars have never known and will never know, Raina said. *They don't concern themselves with groups like ours.*

They will if I ask them to.

The woman with long, dark hair sounded exactly like Willa. But Willa had white hair, and her figure was rounder, softer. This woman's jeans and T-shirt hugged a thinner, firmer, younger body.

As if they'd welcome you back with open arms after a seventeen-year estrangement, Raina said. *For someone touting acceptable behaviour, you don't seem to appreciate that you've committed the greatest sin of all: abandoning your family.*

I left because I had to, the woman said. *Because of things you were going to force my child and me to do, to make us become.*

Which was precisely what your beloved Nenuphars would have expected under their command. Raina's lips turned up. *And strangely enough, here you are, not looking a day over, what? Forty-five? Forty-six?*

Let them go, Raina, the woman said. *If you do, I promise the Nenuphars will know nothing. I promise to do whatever you want.*

That's the funny thing about you and promises, Charlotte . . .

Inside the mask, my chin fell. I watched the Willa look-alike, waited for her to correct Raina and deny being Charlotte . . . but she simply stood there, still, strong, unwavering.

They never seem to stick.

Raina charged just as a scream seemed to shatter my skull. A blinding flurry of sand and water made it impossible to see its source. I was still trying when an arm latched around my waist and pulled me up and away from the lake floor. The further we swam, the clearer the view became.

Is that . . . That can't be . . . Please tell me it's not . . .

But it was. Paige was swimming away from Zara, carrying a salt-water mask and sack – and wearing one, too.

She just wanted to help, Charlotte answered. *Sound familiar?*

I couldn't respond. Paige had transformed. Somehow, she'd succeeded in becoming one of us. I felt so many things at once – shock, fear, disappointment, anger, love – that my head couldn't single out one to focus on and speak to.

Vanessa, Charlotte continued, lifting up a broken, sunken canoe and placing me underneath it, *I've tried to protect you from a distance for seventeen years. I know it's difficult to understand, and I promise to explain everything later . . . but please, let me do what I must to protect you now.*

She hurriedly untied my wrists and ankles. At one point her face was inches from mine, and I saw her smooth face, taut neck, silver eyes. She looked like two women at once: a younger version of the one I'd come to know over the past few weeks, Willa . . . and an older version of the one I'd first seen in a photograph in Betty's bedroom. She was both of them, somewhere in the middle.

Do you remember what you did with the water bottle on the bench in Harvard Square? she asked.

I nodded, picturing the water bubbling and foaming inside the plastic container.

Do you remember how you did it?

I think so.

When you hear me sing for you, I need you to do that again. Okay?

Here? With the –

I was going to ask if she meant with the whole lake, but she was gone before I could.

What about Simon? I yelled after her. *What about Paige?*

Nothing.

I lay there, breathing salt water, fighting to control my torpedoing thoughts. In the distance, there was the sound of rushing water. There were more screams, followed by gasping and weeping. Eventually, there was a single, high-pitched note. It started in the centre of my head and radiated outward until it seemed like the entire canoe vibrated.

My eyes settled on a smooth stone. I stared at it until it went out of focus, and until I pictured Zara. Raina. Paige. Charlotte. I concentrated so intently, seeing instead of thinking, watching instead of feeling, that I didn't notice when the water around me began to fill with tiny bubbles, as if on the brink of boiling. I saw Justine, focused on her smile, her dimples, her bright blue eyes. The bubbles swelled and burst, coming bigger, faster.

I saw Simon. Walking around the Bates quad, holding me on the hayride wagon. Watching me in a hospital room, checking on me as we hiked through the woods, offering me the popcorn bowl first as he, Caleb, Justine, and I watched a movie years ago.

I saw Parker. Leaning next to my locker. Bandaging my leg in the park bandstand. Diving off the side of a boat. Reaching for my hand.

And the water rushed and swirled, groaning like the ocean as it pummels the beach after a storm. The canoe lifted from the sand and spiralled away. I was next. The force was so strong it ripped the mask and case from my body. I tried to fight the pull, but I was too tired, my body wouldn't listen.

Until there was someone behind me. Pressing against me, wrapping arms protectively around my stomach, my shoulders. A face leaned into my neck, and I knew the familiar profile immediately.

He'd come for me. Somehow, perhaps with Charlotte or Paige's help, he'd found me in this twenty-acre whirl-pool.

My body came back to life. I placed both hands on his arms so he knew to hold on, and then I twisted and turned, feeling the currents, listening to them, riding them towards the shore, the wailing sirens, the red and blue lights flashing across the water's surface.

When my head finally broke the surface, I saw that the police were in our backyard. So were Betty, Oliver, and Caleb.

I made it as far as the diving raft thirty feet from shore. I lifted Simon's limp body onto the bobbing metal ladder and held it there with my own. My lips, pressed against his neck, were warmed by a faint, fading pulse.

I stayed there as help came, counting the seconds between beats like I once did the seconds between lightning bolts, and whispering the same four words over and over.

'We're meant to be . . . we're meant to be . . . we're meant to be . . .'

CHAPTER 28

'The University of Hawaii's sounding pretty good right about now.'

I lowered the *Globe* and looked up as Paige sat in the Adirondack chair next to mine. She rubbed her hands together, then cupped and blew into them. In her lap was a nearly empty orange plastic pumpkin.

'What do you think?' she asked. 'Palm trees? Warm turquoise water?'

'I thought you wanted to be as far from water as possible?'

Her smile faltered. She zipped up the down coat she wore, crossed her arms, and shifted her gaze to the lake. 'We're down to sugar-free gum. Maybe I should run to the store and get more candy. Trick-or-treaters talk, and I wouldn't want you to get a reputation as the house without chocolate.'

Somewhere behind us, there was a long, loud clattering, like the sound of dishes falling to a tile floor. A second later, Mom called for Dad.

'I don't think that matters,' I said.

She frowned. 'They're really selling it?'

I looked out at the lake. Its flat, still surface reflected barren treetops, a cloudy grey sky. 'They're really going to try.'

'But haven't they had this house –'

'For ever?' I finished. 'Yes.'

She leaned towards me, lowered her voice like we weren't the only two people sitting outside in the freezing cold. 'But she knows, right? Your mom? You explained that they're definitely gone this time, and that what happened last week will never happen again?'

'I did. But after being lied to for twenty years, I don't think she knows what to believe any more.'

'Your dad didn't know that part, though, right? About who Charlotte really was – who she really is?'

'No. Because she never took lives; by the time he saw her again, she looked decades older than she really was. And just to be on the safe side, she dyed her hair and wore coloured contact lenses.' My eyes fell to the newspaper. On the front page was a photo of a man in a Red Sox jersey and hat, cheering in the stands of Fenway Park. Beneath the photo was the headline I'd read a hundred times in twenty-four hours:

Body of Missing City Sanitation Worker
Gerald O'Malley, 43, Found in South Boston

Despite seeing him only once, I'd recognised him immediately. Gerald O'Malley was one of the city sanitation workers who'd spoken to me outside of Willa's – outside of *Charlotte's* – house. According to Charlotte, after I'd left that day, they'd come back around to collect the trash on the opposite side of the street. She'd followed them as they continued on their route down to the water, and then, in her words, she'd done what needed doing.

She claimed it was the first time she'd taken a man's life. And that she'd done it only to gain the strength she needed to help save me from the Winter Harbor sirens. She said she'd changed her name when she moved to Boston in hopes of keeping her true identity from Dad and everyone else, and that not giving in to her body's demands had aged her drastically. When the life left the men's bodies and entered hers, it turned back the clock by years.

Like Mom, who'd locked herself in her bedroom for two days after being told the truth about my biological mother, and about Dad, and about me, I was no longer sure what to believe. That was why, after I thanked her for helping Paige rescue Simon and me from the swirling, suffocating sirens, I told Charlotte that I needed not to see her for a while. I needed time to think – preferably without anyone listening.

'Why'd you do it, Paige?' I asked quietly.

'Vanessa . . . I already told you.'

'Tell me again.' I looked at her. 'Please.'

She sat back, hugged the plastic orange pumpkin. 'After last summer, after losing . . . everything . . . I wanted something that was just mine again. You and your parents were wonderful to take me in, but they were still *your* parents. I was living in your house, going to your school. And then, in the middle of all the college frenzy, I realised I was trying to figure out a future that belonged to someone else. Because if last summer hadn't happened, if I'd finished high school here, I probably wouldn't have gone to college. I would've worked at the restaurant, eventually married some local fisherman when Jonathan inevitably left me for some pretty, Ivy League genius who his parents would've approved of, and had a million babies.'

I reached for her hand. She let me take it.

'And then . . . I don't know. Betty had been trying to convince me to transform because that's what Raina and Zara wanted, but even if they'd had nothing to do with it, I think I still would've been tempted.' She paused. 'At least the powers will be all mine, you know? To use the way I want to – to help people instead of hurt them.'

'But –'

'Vanessa.' She gave me a small smile, squeezed my

hand. 'I know. It's hard, and complicated. But it's also too late.'

I struggled to return her smile, picturing her in the ocean and choking on salt water before her body finally relented. Unfortunately, my telling her about me had only convinced her all the more to go through with it – especially since she thought that together the two of us had a better of shot of defeating the sirens for good. Shortly after I'd left for school and gone to Charlotte's instead, Paige had asked Mom if she could borrow her car to get out of the house, and then she'd driven to Maine. She'd found Betty in her room, standing transfixed before the open window, and managed to break the trance by calling out to her, hugging her.

Apparently, when it came to sirens, love's power worked on women the same way it did on men. That was actually how Raina and the others had managed to control Betty this time.

Despite what Simon had sworn time and again, that the sirens couldn't last two months packed in ice, they'd survived. They were unconscious until the ice began to thaw, but once it did and their bodies absorbed the salt water, they slowly came to. The only ones who didn't were the sirens the deep-sea divers had found still frozen; they'd been brought up too soon, and the divers paid dearly for their discovery.

The sirens who survived started with Oliver and used their weakened powers to convince him that if he really loved Betty the way he claimed, then he should do whatever he could to bring Paige home – even though Betty had insisted that being in Boston was best for her granddaughter. Because Oliver's feelings for Betty were greater than his fear of the sirens, it worked, and he did what they told him to, including building their tubs, helping them heal, tracking their targets – and manipulating Betty to manipulate Paige. Their ultimate plan was to transform Paige so they would have another member in their ranks, and to either convince me to join them . . . or to kill me.

Fortunately, once Betty was herself again, Oliver was, too. Reluctant but too weak to refuse, they'd helped Paige transform in the ocean behind their house. Paige had recovered quickly, and she and Betty had listened for the other sirens. After they heard them, they'd alerted the authorities to possible drownings and reached the lake seconds after Charlotte. Caleb, returning home from the marina, saw the lake frothing and lights flashing beneath the surface, and joined the others in our backyard.

'But look on the bright side,' Paige said a moment later, jarring me from my thoughts. 'Now we're more like sisters than ever before.'

Before I could decide how to respond, the doorbell rang in the distance. Paige jumped up and hurried towards the house.

'Hope the little monsters don't mind minty-fresh breath!' she called over her shoulder.

Little monsters. She referred to trick-or-treaters, but I still found the reference strange. Just like other things we hadn't wanted to talk about a few weeks ago, we hadn't really talked about her transformation or what it meant; this last conversation was the most time we'd devoted to the subject. When we finally did discuss it, though, one of my many questions would be how she was able to treat it so lightly. Was it merely a coping mechanism, the way I hoped . . . or was she really that happy to be one of us?

'Peppermint?'

My head snapped towards the voice. Simon stood behind the empty Adirondack chair, fiddling with a pack of gum.

'I hope you're saving the good stuff for the kids in costumes,' he added. 'You don't want to be known as the only house in Winter Harbor that cares about cavities on Halloween.'

I stood, stepped towards him, my heart straining against my ribs. 'Simon –'

He held up one hand, then lowered it, palm side up.

I took it carefully, afraid he'd pull away. My eyes welled when he didn't. We walked silently down the lawn, putting more distance between us and the house.

After inhaling enough lake water to fill a small pool, Simon had been hospitalised for four days. I'd visited him at least a dozen times, but whenever I did, other people – Caleb, his parents, even old high-school teachers – had been there, making it impossible for us to talk. Now I didn't know where to start.

'Your glasses are back,' I attempted after several minutes.

He smiled, absently pushed the black bridge up his nose. 'They didn't make a difference.'

We stopped at the edge of the dock. 'What didn't?' I asked.

'Contacts. They were Riley's suggestion. He thought they'd help.'

'Your vision?'

'In a way.' He released my hand, slid both of his in his coat pockets. 'I saw the way those guys looked at you, Vanessa. At school, in the coffee shop. Of course, then I assumed it was just because you were amazingly beautiful and that any guy who *didn't* notice you was blind. I couldn't blame them – but I could work on my own appearance to keep you from looking back.'

'You didn't have to do that. You didn't have to do anything.'

'Right. You would've broken up with me anyway.'

I started to reach for him but stopped when he tensed. 'I was trying to protect you,' I said, my voice wavering. 'I didn't know how to tell you, and I knew as soon as I did we couldn't be together.'

'You assumed,' he said quickly. 'You didn't know. You couldn't have without talking to me first.'

'I get thirsty,' I said, my throat automatically drying. 'When I'm happy, excited, stressed, angry – all the time. I have to drink gallons of salt water every day. I have to take salt-water baths and swim in the ocean whenever I can. You don't want to deal with that. I don't *want* you to deal with that.'

'Vanessa,' he said sadly, 'when you love someone, you don't just deal with her problems. You don't tolerate them and simply hope they pass. You work through them together – not because you hate being inconvenienced, but because your lives are connected, intertwined. When you're happy I'm happy, and when you're not . . . nothing else matters.'

I looked down, brushed at my watering eyes. 'I didn't think you loved me.'

'You didn't – How could you –'

'I believed you only *thought* you did. Because of who

392

– what – I am. And I wanted to believe, so much, that that feeling was real . . . but I didn't know if it was.'

He didn't say anything. When I looked up again, he was staring out at the lake, his jaw clenching and releasing.

'What I did know,' I continued, my voice barely a whisper, 'was that I loved you.'

His jaw tensed, then froze. His eyelids fluttered closed as his Adam's apple sank and rose.

'And that as much as I couldn't stand the thought of not being with you, I hated the idea of your not having a full, genuine life more. So when you said you were thinking about leaving Bates for BU and changing your entire life for something that might not even be real . . . I couldn't let you do it.'

He opened his eyes. I followed his gaze to the square diving raft, where, days before, I'd clung to him as if our hearts, like our problems, were connected. Intertwined.

'It was real.' He looked at me, waited for our eyes to meet. 'Want to know how I know?'

I hesitated, nodded.

'Because when I saw you with that guy, I broke. I totally fell apart.'

That guy. Parker. 'Simon, I can explain –'

'All three times?' The sadness in his voice sharpened. 'You can explain what you were doing on his boat, in that picture online, and on the street in Boston? Not to mention whatever I didn't witness first hand?'

'Nothing happened,' I said, my chest burning. 'We kissed a little, but –'

'Vanessa.' He shook his head. 'I saw you. That wasn't just kissing. That wasn't an accident.'

I tore my gaze away. Should I tell him? About how the attention made me stronger? And why I'd wanted to be stronger? Or should I just let him believe the worst so that he could finally move on?

'I'm sorry.'

My head snapped back towards him. He looked at me, tears filling his warm brown eyes.

'I'm so sorry', he said quietly, 'for letting Zara get to me. I'm sorry I kissed her. I'm sorry I told her that I . . . felt something I've only ever felt for you.'

'Stop.' I stepped towards him, gently placing my hands on his face and wiping away his tears with my thumbs. 'It doesn't matter. You did nothing wrong.'

He took my hands in his, pulled them away from his face. 'It does matter. Because I wouldn't have done it if my feelings for you were as strong as they'd always been.'

'But I hurt you,' I insisted. 'Whatever I did or didn't do, I hurt you. Of course you felt differently.'

'Feel.'

I watched fresh tears slip from his eyes and slide down his cheeks. 'What?' I whispered.

'I *feel* differently.' His hands, still holding mine, trembled. 'That's how I know it was real. Because if it wasn't, your powers would've fixed everything already. I would've forgotten what you did even before I'd forgiven you.' He paused, took a shallow, shaky breath. 'I'd love you now as much as I did before.'

As our hands slowly lowered, then released, I was vaguely aware of the feeling drifting from my legs, my arms.

'I do love you, Vanessa,' he said, his voice cracking. 'For better or worse, I don't think anything will ever change that. It's just, right now, there are other feelings, too. Strong ones. Painful ones.'

I searched his face, tried to imagine not being able to see it whenever I wanted to, whenever I needed to. 'What are you saying?' I asked.

'I'm saying . . . that I think I need some time to figure them out.'

I had no right to ask, but I had to know. 'How much time?'

'I'm not sure. I hope less rather than more.' He looked at me, his eyes full. 'But you have Paige. And your family. Things are okay with them, right?'

Okay, yes. Enough? That was another thing entirely.

'I'll be there if you need me,' he said softly, backing away. 'But if you could try not to need me for just a little while . . . I'd really appreciate it.'

I watched him go. He continued walking backward for several feet before finally turning around and jogging. Instead of going back inside our house, the way he'd come, he cut across the side yard and headed for his own.

I didn't move for several minutes. I stood there, barely feeling the cold breeze or hearing the loons crying on the lake, the music playing inside the house, and the trick-or-treaters laughing down the street. I waited for Simon to come sprinting back across the yard, to sweep me up in his arms and tell me he'd made a terrible, awful mistake. That we both had, but that we could work through those mistakes together, since together was what we were supposed to be no matter what.

But he didn't. And eventually, as the season's first snowflakes began floating down from the sky, sprinkling the lake and stinging my hot skin, I stopped expecting him to.

I started slowly up the lawn. Reaching the house, I went inside and walked through the living room and past the kitchen, waving to Dad, who was wrapping dishes in bubble wrap and stacking them in cardboard boxes. I continued down the hall and up to the second floor, peering through the stairwell windows at Paige tossing packages of gum into the plastic pumpkins of a trio of young witches. Upstairs, I passed my parents' room and the spare bedroom without glancing inside. At the end of the hall, I turned and stopped in the open doorway.

Mom was in the room Justine and I had shared, sorting through the summer clothes she'd been unable even to look at when we'd left Winter Harbor at the end of the summer.

'Hi,' I said.

She spun around, gave me a quick smile. 'Hi, sweetie. How are you feeling?'

'Okay.' I came into the room, my eyes travelling over the old lobster bake posters and vintage Lake Kantaka postcards taped to the walls. 'You?'

'A little crazed, but fine.' She lifted a stack of folded T-shirts from Justine's dresser and put them in an open suitcase on the bed. 'Did your father tell you that we've already received an offer? It's not official yet, but the buyer said he's ready to move when we are.' She stopped, rested her hands on her hips. 'We just have so much stuff to sort through, there's no telling when that'll be.'

'I still can't believe you guys are really selling the house.'

'Well,' she said with a sigh, moving on to a chest of

spare blankets, 'when the tides change, you have two choices. You can either stand there, letting the water wash over you and your feet sink deeper into the wet sand . . . or you can get out of the way. You can move up the beach – or off the beach, if you want. The point is not to get stuck.'

'I don't want to be stuck.'

She turned to me, her mouth set in a straight line. 'Me neither.'

After a moment she continued packing, and I leaned against the dresser. I looked across the room, towards the window and the snow falling heavier, faster, outside – and then to the antique hand mirror hanging next to it. The mirror was tarnished silver, but for a brief second, it glinted like new.

'Do you still have all of that college stuff you bought last year?' I asked, joining Mom by the wooden chest.

Her hands stilled only briefly before resuming folding. 'What stuff?'

'The mugs and keyrings? The umbrellas and sweat-shirts?'

'I might've saved a few things,' she said.

'Good.' I paused. 'I think I'm going to need them.'

She stopped folding and looked at me. 'Why?'

And then, thinking of Justine, Mom and Dad, Charlotte and Paige, Simon and Parker, of facing your fears and confronting ghosts you'd rather pretend weren't there, I revealed something I'd only just realised I'd been contemplating for months.

'Because I'm applying,' I said, 'to Dartmouth.'

ff

Faber and Faber is one of the great independent publishing houses. We were established in 1929 by Geoffrey Faber with T. S. Eliot as one of our first editors. We are proud to publish award-winning fiction and non-fiction, as well as an unrivalled list of poets and playwrights. Among our list of writers we have five Booker Prize winners and twelve Nobel Laureates, and we continue to seek out the most exciting and innovative writers at work today.

Find out more about our authors and books
faber.co.uk

Read our blog for insight and opinion on books and the arts
thethoughtfox.co.uk

Follow news and conversation
twitter.com/faberbooks

Watch readings and interviews
youtube.com/faberandfaber

Connect with other readers
facebook.com/faberandfaber

Explore our archive
flickr.com/faberandfaber